Praise for
What Happens at Night

"In his characteristically precise and lucid prose, Peter Cameron invents a virtuosic tale that is by turns terrifying, comic, and heartbreaking. We do not always know whether we are in the realm of the real or the hallucinatory in this thrillingly mysterious and gorgeously written novel. What is never in doubt is that we are in the hands of a ravishing stylist and a supremely gifted storyteller."

—SIGRID NUNEZ, author of *The Friend*

"The prose in *What Happens at Night* is faultlessly elegant and quietly menacing, like a tuxedo lined with knives. I can't think of another book at once so beautiful and so unnerving, so poised between miracle and disaster. Peter Cameron is one of America's greatest writers, the living stylist I most revere." —GARTH GREENWELL, author of *What Belongs to You* and *Cleanness*

"This book is a masterpiece—reading it reminds me of the first time I read Kafka. A whole new vision is suddenly revealed: unique, unexpected, unforgettable. Get ready for a new adjective: *Cameronesque*."

—EDMUND WHITE, author of *A Boy's Own Story*

"Peter Cameron is a compassionate and unsparing surveyor of all that comprises human character. *What Happens at Night* finds its home among the mid-twentieth-century classics of psychological realism, as brutal, in its way, as *The Sheltering Sky*, and just as memorable, just as peopled with the deep human mysteries. This new novel is a powerful and admirable addition to Cameron's estimable body of work."

—RICK MOODY, author of *The Ice Storm* and
The Long Accomplishment

"I don't think I've ever read a book by an American or by a living person that's as exquisitely rendered as *What Happens at Night*. Every word is exactly as it should be; there is not a single extra word out of place. The novel feels as though it traveled through time to arrive here. Cameron's prose creates an effect that is literally like a fugue (or cinematic fog): intense, beautiful, inescapable, and so much about grief that has been and grief that is to come, heartbreaking and tender. The story is so intense, such a fine reduction of the enormity of the dreams of marriage, the responsibilities of marriage, of life, of love, and the ways in which—unintentionally or not—we inevitably fail each other and ourselves."

—A. M. HOMES, author of *Days of Awe* and
May We Be Forgiven

"In the beautiful *What Happens at Night*, Peter Cameron sends a married couple to a mysterious northern country where only the schnapps is reliable. The world he creates is both recognizable and enchantingly strange. I never knew what was going to happen next, and I couldn't stop turning the pages. A profound pleasure for readers."

—MARGOT LIVESEY, author of *Mercury* and
The Flight of Gemma Hardy

"Peter Cameron's *What Happens at Night* is a surreal, funny, heartbreaking story about love and mortality. Cameron's sense of balance between the comic and the catastrophic, between cynicism and sincerity, is astonishing. This book reminds me of nothing else I've ever read, which is high praise indeed." —MICHAEL CUNNINGHAM, author of
The Hours and *The Snow Queen*

Praise for Peter Cameron

"[Cameron's] chief literary virtues are wit, charm, and lightness of touch, qualities infrequently found in contemporary American fiction . . . Cameron is above all a novelist of manners, building his effects from the drama and comedy of human relationships, working always on a small scale . . . [He] specializes in emotional subtlety and unspoken desires—all the while hinting at an almost overwhelming disorder swirling beneath the placid surface . . . We may be so slow to recognize Cameron as a twenty-first-century American master because he has the sensibility of a twentieth-century British one."

—CHRISTOPHER BEHA, *Bookforum*

"Pull up a chair by the fire and settle in, but don't get too lulled by the domestic setting, because Cameron's writing is full of sharp angles and unanticipated swerves into the droll and the downright weird . . . I mean it as the highest compliment when I say that *Coral Glynn* is not 'about' anything so much as it is about the pleasures of storytelling . . . [Cameron] artfully compresses so many beloved English stories and tropes into one smashing novel."

—MAUREEN CORRIGAN, NPR

"Peter Cameron [is] an elegantly acute and mysteriously beguiling writer . . . The plots, the ventures, the encounters of his characters, instead of taking them from point A to point B, abduct them into unintended and more expansive itineraries."

—RICHARD EDER, *The Boston Globe*

"Mr. Cameron announces his talent in the way that matters: by telling a riveting tale with an often heartbreakingly pure prose style . . . [Cameron's] writing . . . is bracingly

unvarnished and unsentimental, stripped of pity or con-
descension. It is as though he has set an X-ray machine
before the traditional English drawing room, leaving its de-
mure occupants exposed in their loneliness and well-meant
follies—and revealing them as movingly human."

—SAM SACKS, *The Wall Street Journal*

WHAT

✦

HAPPENS

✦

AT

✦

NIGHT

PETER CAMERON

✦

WHAT HAPPENS
AT NIGHT

✦

A Novel

CATAPULT  NEW YORK

ISBN: 978-1-948226-96-7

Jacket design by Nicole Caputo
Book design by Wah-Ming Chang

Library of Congress Control Number: 2019955150

Printed in the United States of America
1 3 5 7 9 10 8 6 4 2

for
Eric Ashworth and Irene Skolnick
in loving memory

Miss Goering looked up at the sky; she was looking for the stars and hoping very hard to see some. She stood still for a long time, but she could not decide whether it was a starlit night or not because even though she fixed her attention on the sky without once lowering her eyes, the stars seemed to appear and disappear so quickly that they were like visions of stars rather than like actual stars.

✦

JANE BOWLES
Two Serious Ladies

WHAT

✦

HAPPENS

✦

AT

✦

NIGHT

ONE

Evening descended with unnerving abruptness, like a curtain hurriedly lowered on an amateur theatrical gone horribly awry. And then the man noticed that the darkness was not the result of the sun setting but of the train entering a dense forest, leaving behind the open fields of snow it had traversed all afternoon. The fir trees, tall and thick, crowded closely along the tracks, like children pressing themselves up against a classroom window to get a better view of some gruesome accident in the street.

His wife sat on the seat across from him; they were the only two people in the small, wood-paneled carriage of the old-fashioned train. For a long time she had been staring absently out the window, mesmerized, it seemed, by the endless expanse of tundra, but she suddenly recoiled when the train entered the dark woods as if the trees brushing the sides of the carriage might reach in and scratch her. She touched the tender place on her cheek where the skin had been nastily scraped the night before.

They had visited the market of the city where they were staying, for although they were not tourists, they were strangers, and eager to feel a part of some place, any place, if only for a night. And so the woman had been trying to find some charm in the market, for she was at a place in her life where it was necessary to discern and appreciate any charm or beauty she encountered, but this market was singularly without charm, for it contained nothing but fish and meat and root vegetables, and the fish did not look fresh and the meat was not muscle but organs and brains and feet and lips and hearts, and the vegetables were all winter vegetables, roots and tubers and other colorless things that had been savagely yanked from their cold earthen beds. No bright pyramids of tomatoes and peaches, no bouquets of basil and nasturtium, no glistening jeweled eyes of fish, no marbled slabs of beef. And then she had seen, in the distance, one stall that sold spectacular hothouse flowers, and had run toward it, desperate to find something that did not entirely turn one away from life. Her husband had noticed their artifice before she did, and had tried to steer her down another aisle, but she pulled free of him and ran toward the colored brightness of the flowers, wanting to bury her face in their fragrant petal softness, buy an armful of them and carry it around with her, like a bride, like a diva in the footlights, but in front of a fishmonger's stall she had slipped in a puddle of frigid water and fell to the floor, scraping her cheek and palms on the wet, fishy concrete.

It was not until her husband had caught up with her and helped her to her feet that she realized that the flowers were plastic. Not even silk! She could have at least touched them if they were silk.

After a moment the woman returned her attention to the book that lay open upon her lap. She had found this old book, *The Dark Forest* by Hugh Walpole, in the waiting room of a train station that they had passed through, obviously abandoned by a fellow traveler. For some time after the darkness fell—or was entered—she continued to read, but suddenly she looked up from her book at the dark rushing windows of the carriage and asked, Is there a light?

There was just enough light remaining in the carriage to see that there was no light.

I don't see one, her husband said.

You'd think there'd be a light, she said.

Yes, he said, you'd think.

She sighed disappointedly, whether at the lack of a light or at his response to such a lack, he knew not. Probably both, and more.

They had been traveling for days, first by plane, and then by train and ferry, and now once again by train, for their destination was a place at the edge of the world, in the far north of a northern country, and not easily gained. Their journey was like a journey from a prior century, a matter of days rather than hours, the earth serious and real beneath them, constantly insisting on its vastness.

An authentic evening was now occurring, the darkness a product of the sun's absence rather than its obscurity. They both watched it through the window. The woman touched her reflection, which the darkness outside had just revealed. Look at me, she said, so gaunt. My God, *gaunt*: how I hate that word. *Gaunt* and *jackal* and *hubris*. *Seepage* and—what are the other words I hate?

She had begun to do this recently: familiarly allude to odd, supposedly long-held predilections or positions that had never previously been mentioned. Or existed, as far as the man knew. So he ignored her nonsensical question by asking her what the book was about.

For a moment she said nothing, just watched her reflection hurtling along the dark scrim of pines. About? she finally said. In what sense do you mean?

He did not answer, because he did not like to indulge her contrariness.

After a moment she said, It's about the war.

Which war?

One of the World Wars, she said. The first, I think. They're in trenches.

And?

And? War is awful. It's bad enough I'm stuck reading it; don't make me talk about it too.

Okay, he said. I'm sorry.

She looked at him, her audacity suddenly collapsed. No, she said. Don't be ridiculous. I'm sorry. I'm just on edge, you know—about everything.

I understand, he said. I'm on edge too.

About everything?

No, he said. Not everything. Just, you know—how this all will go.

Or not go, she said.

◆

They had both fallen asleep and were simultaneously awoken by a peculiar sensation: stillness. The train had stopped. Outside the carriage window they could see, through the veil of fog that their breaths had condensed upon the glass, a platform and a building. There was no one about and no sound but the tickling sifts of snow gusting against the window. The man thought of the warm molecules of their breath, trapped against the cold glass of the windows, a union outside of, independent of, them.

This must be it, she said. Wasn't it the first stop?

Yes, he said.

Then this is it, she said.

I don't see any sign, he said.

No. She rubbed a messy circle on the window, but nothing helpful was revealed, just more of the wooden plat-form, on which a single lamp separated a conical swath of snow from the huge surrounding darkness.

This must be it, he said. He stood up and opened the carriage door.

Don't go, she said.

But this must be it, he said.

It can't be, she said. It's not a real station. There's no town, nothing. It must be a way station.

A way station?

Yes, she said. A pause, not a stop.

He stepped out onto the platform, disturbing the perfect blanket of snow. He felt like a barbarian. But once its perfection had been defiled he knew he must continue, for a hairline crack on a beautiful piece of china is more upsetting than the same piece of china shattered on the floor. So he ran about in ever-widening circles, kicking up the snow about him as messily as he could, and drew near enough to the building at the platform's edge to see, in a sort of echo of faded paint, the name of the town that was their destination.

He suddenly felt foolish and stopped his cavorting, and in the ensuing stillness he became aware of some frightening engagement in the darkness behind him. The train. He turned to see it slowly moving, so slowly that for a moment he thought it must be the darkness moving behind it, but then he knew it was the train, for he could see his wife leaning forward, looking out of the still-opened door, her white face silently surprised, and for a second it felt like death to him, like how one must let one's beloved depart this world, gliding silently slack-faced into the snow-dark.

But then a sense of emergency successfully obliterated

that vision, and he called out to the woman and ran toward and then alongside the hastening train, and she was up and throwing their bags out the open door as if it were all part of a well-rehearsed drill, and just before the place where the platform ended she leaped into his arms.

The train clacked into the darkness, the door of their carriage still flung open, like a dislocated wing.

For a moment he held her closer and tighter than he had held her in a long time. Then they unclasped and went to fetch their bags, which appeared artfully arranged, dark rocks on the snowy Zen expanse of the platform. Then they stood for a moment and looked about them at the darkness.

This can't be it, she said.

He pointed to the letters on the station wall.

I know, she said, but this can't be it. There's nothing—

Let me look around front, he said. Perhaps there's something there.

What?

I don't know. A telephone, or a taxi.

Yes, she said. And perhaps there's a McDonalds and a Holiday Inn as well. She laughed bitterly and he realized that she had finally turned against him, forsaken him as he had watched her forsake everyone else she had once loved, slowly but surely drifting toward a place where anger and impatience and scorn usurped love. She stepped away from him, toward the edge of the platform, and for a moment they silently regarded each other. He waited to see whether her fury was rising or falling; he suspected she was too exhausted to sustain such glaring fierceness, and he was right—after a moment she staggered and reached out to steady herself against the metal railing.

With his outstretched arm, shrouded in his Arctic parka, he swept a cushion of snow off a bench that stood against the station wall. Sit down, he said.

No. I'm coming with you.

No, sit. Are you cold? Do you want my coat?

There's nothing around the front, she said. There's nothing anywhere.

Don't be ridiculous, he said. Sit.

I'm not a dog, she said. But she sat on the bench.

I'll be right back, he said. He waited for her to object but she did not. He bent down and kissed her cold scraped cheek. Then he walked along the platform and around to the front of the building, where no one was, and even though their encounter had been conducted quietly, he had the disturbing feeling one gets upon leaving a pulsating discotheque late at night—the sudden absence of sound more jarring than its presence.

A few dark cars and trucks stoically amassed garments of snow in the small parking lot. A single road disappeared into the forest that surrounded everything. There was no sign of life anywhere, just trees and snow and silence and the shrouded slumbering vehicles.

And then a light shone from one of the cars in the parking lot, and its engine started. The silence and stillness had been so deep that witnessing the car come to life was as eerie as watching an ambered insect unfurl its frozen wings and fly away. A bubble of white at the center of the car's snow-covered roof glowed from within, suggesting that the car was—might be—a taxi. The door opened, and the man watched the driver light a cigarette and throw the still-flaming match into the air, where it somersaulted into the snow, and died.

The man assumed that it was his appearance that had roused this vehicle from its slumber, yet the driver gave no indication that this was the case; he smoked his cigarette and regarded the parking lot and the train station with disinterest.

So the man walked down the wooden steps and crunched across the hard-packed snow of the parking lot. The driver made no response whatsoever to the man's approach, not even when he stood in the narrow alley of snow that separated the car from its neighbor.

After a moment the driver flicked his half-smoked cigarette into the snow at the man's feet.

The man realized that the burden of acknowledgment was his. Hello, he said. Do you speak English?

The driver looked at him with surprised curiosity, as if he had never heard a man speak before. He cocked his head.

Do you speak English? the man repeated.

The driver seemed to find this utterance amusing— he laughed a little and lit another cigarette, and dragged upon it contentedly. He scraped an arc in the snow with his dainty slipper-clad foot.

Confused by everything, the man looked into the warm

cavern of the car and saw two stuffed Disney Dalmatians hanging by their necks from the rearview mirror. The incongruity of this sight momentarily suspended the man's debilitating notions of foreignness and ineptitude. Emboldened, he pulled a slip of paper from his pocket and held it out toward the driver and pointed to the words, as if they were not the only words written on the paper.

Borgarfjaroasysla Grand Imperial Hotel
Furuhjalli 62

For a moment the driver did not respond. Perhaps he wasn't looking at the words, or perhaps he couldn't read; it was impossible to tell. But then, in an oddly unaccented voice, he spoke the words aloud: Borgarfjaroasysla Grand Imperial Hotel. And he pointed toward the road, the only road that left the parking lot, narrowing into the dark forest, like an illustration of perspective.

Yes, I know, the man said. But we cannot walk. He marched in place for a second and then wagged his finger in the air: Walk. No.

The driver continued to observe him with silent amusement. He made a little shrug and pointed to the man's feet, indicating that apparently he could walk.

My wife, said the man. His hands outlined an hourglass in the air between them, and as he did this he thought of his wife's emaciated angular body. He pointed toward the station house. My wife, he said. My wife no walk.

The driver nodded, indicating that he understood. He shrugged a little and toked on his cigarette, as if there were many worse fates than having a lame wife.

You drive us? The man held an imaginary steering wheel with his hands and turned it back and forth. Then he pointed at the driver. You?

The driver did not respond.

I'll pay you very good, the man said. He removed his wallet from his coat pocket and showed it to the driver.

The driver smiled and reached out his hand.

You'll drive us to hotel? the man asked.

The driver nodded and tapped his open palm with the fingers of his other hand.

The man opened his wallet and, holding it so that the driver could not see how much cash it contained, took out two bills. He handed one to the driver.

The driver pointed to the second bill.

I get my wife, the man said. Once again he caressed an hourglass and pointed toward the station house. Then he shook the second bill in the air. I give you this at hotel, he said.

The driver nodded.

The man ran across the parking lot. He slipped and fell on the snow-covered steps and cut his chin on the edge of the deck: he saw the red bloom on the snow. He removed his glove and gingerly touched the abrasion. His teeth hurt, and he could feel the warm saline seep of blood in his mouth. He stood up but felt dizzy, so he steadied himself for a moment against the wall. When he felt a bit better he walked carefully around to the back of the station house.

The woman was still sitting on the bench. She was being slowly covered by the snow. It was falling so quickly and thickly that it had already obscured the disruption he had made by dancing on the platform; there was just a ghostly trace of it remaining.

The woman was so still that for a moment the man thought she was dead, but then he saw the fog of her breath tumble from her half-opened mouth. She was sleeping.

He stood for a moment, watching the snow settle upon her, watching her breaths condense and unfurl in the cold air. For a moment he forgot about the taxi waiting in the parking lot, and he forgot about the Borgarfjaroasysla Grand Imperial Hotel. He forgot their miserable endless journey, and the illness that had left her gaunt and mean. She had rested her head against the wall of the station house, and the lamplight reflected softly off the snow, and like a gentle hand it caressed her face and restored to it a beauty her illness had completely eroded. He forgot everything and for a moment remembered only his love for her, and, by remembering it so keenly, he felt it once again, it flooded him, and he could not contain it, this sudden overwhelming feeling of love, it rose out of him in tears, and he dropped to his knees before her.

✦

The lobby of the Borgarfjaroasysla Grand Imperial Hotel was dark and seemed cavernous, because its walls could not be discerned in the gloom. They had to cross a vast field of intricately and endlessly patterned carpet in order to arrive at the reception desk, which stood like an altar at the far side of the huge room, opposite the revolving entrance doors. A young woman, wearing an official-looking uniform, stood behind the high wooden counter, on which perched two huge bronze gryphons, each holding a stained-glass iron lantern in its beak. The woman stood rigidly between the two lamps, staring placidly in front of her. She seemed as eerily inanimate as the creatures that flanked her.

It was the final leg of their journey, this trip across the oceanic expanse of lobby. The man and the woman waded through little islands of furniture—club chairs reefed around low circular wooden tables.

It was only when they were standing directly in front of the reception counter that the woman behind it lowered her gaze from the dimness above them all and seemed at last to see the two weary travelers who stood before her.

Welcome to the Borgarfjaroasysla Grand Imperial Hotel, she said. She did not smile.

Thank you, the man said. We have a reservation.

Your name?

He told the woman his name.

Ah yes, she said. We've been expecting you. Did you have a pleasant journey?

It's been a difficult journey, the man said.

It often is, the woman behind the desk allowed. Your passports?

The man handed these over and they were duly scrutinized and returned. Then the woman turned around and contemplated a huge warren of cubbyholes, each containing an enormous key. She reached her arm up and plucked a key from one of the highest cells. She turned back to them and laid the large iron key, which was affixed to a heavy tasseled medallion, on the counter.

Five nineteen, she said. Your room may be chilly, but if you open the radiators it should warm up quickly. The bellboy is away at the moment, but if you leave your bags, he will bring them up to you later.

I think I can manage them, said the man.

The woman behind the counter said, The bar is open all night. She pointed toward the far end of the vast lobby, where a faint red light shone through a curtain of glass beads. But I am afraid the kitchen is closed.

There's no food? the man asked.

I'm afraid not. Well, perhaps something inconsequential in the bar.

I just want to go to bed, the woman said. Let's go.

You're not hungry? he asked.

I just want to go to bed, she repeated, enunciating each word emphatically, as if it were she who was communicating in a second language, not the woman behind the counter.

The man sighed and lifted the heavy key off the counter

and picked up their bags. In an apse behind the reception desk a grand staircase wound up through the dark heart of the building, and a small wire-caged elevator hung from cables in its center. The man opened the outer and inner gates. There was just enough room for the man, the woman, and their bags in the tiny cage, and the limited space forced them to stand so close to each other they almost touched. Their room was on the top floor—the fifth—and each landing they passed flung a skein of pale golden light through the intricately wrought bars of the elevator, so that a delicate pattern of shadow bloomed and faded, again and again and again and again, across their faces.

Surprisingly, the dark gloomy grandeur of the hotel did not extend into their room, which was large and sparsely furnished. The walls were paneled with sheets of fake plastic brick and the floor was covered with a gold shag rug that crunched disconcertingly beneath their feet. The room was, as the receptionist had predicted, very cold.

The woman dropped the bags she was carrying and sat upon the bed. She sat rather stiffly, staring intently at the faux-brick wall.

The man watched her for a moment, and said, How are you feeling?

She turned away from the wall and lay back upon the bed, gazing now at the ceiling. Fine, she said, given that I'm dying.

But we're here, he said. Doesn't that count for something?

After a moment she said, Do you want me to live?

What? he asked. Of course I do.

Do you?

Yes, he said.

I think if I were you I wouldn't, she said.

Of course I do, he repeated.

I think I'd want me to die, she said. If I were you.

I want you to get better, he said. To live.

Perhaps you really do, she said. But it seems odd to me. I know what I've become. How I am. What I am.

He sat beside her on the bed and tried to hold her, bend her close to him, but her body remained stiffly upright. He stroked her arm, which felt as thin as a bone beneath her layers of clothing.

Of course you're the way you are, he said. Anyone would be that way, under the circumstances. But if you recover, you won't be.

But what if I don't?

Don't what?

Don't recover. Or what if I recover my health, but don't recover my—I don't know. You know: myself. My joie de vivre. She gave a hollow laugh.

Of course you will, he said. How could you not?

I think it might be gone, she said. I'm sorry. I didn't want to be like this.

You're exhausted, he said. But we've made it. We're here.

I don't feel it yet, she said. Do you feel it?

Yes.

Perhaps if I take a bath. That always changes things, doesn't it? At least for me it does.

The woman got up from the bed and opened the bathroom door. She turned on the light. The bathroom was very large and very pink. The ceramic toilet and sink were pink, as was the large bathtub, and all the floor and all the walls were tiled with pink tiles. Even the ceiling was tiled pink.

What a lovely pink bathroom, she said. And look at that enormous tub.

You can have a nice bath in that, said the man. A nice hot long bath.

Yes, the woman said. A nice hot long pink bath. She smiled at him, a real smile. She entered the bathroom and closed the door behind her.

✦

The man crossed the large crunching field of carpet and knelt beside the radiator. Praying, he turned the knob. It stuck for a moment and then released itself, and a spire of steam gushed out of the ancient Bakelite valve, like the smoke from a train engine in a silent movie. The coiled intestines of the radiator liquidly rumbled like the bowels of a person about to be sick. He placed his hand against the roughened rusty skin and felt it slowly warm to his touch. He kept his hand there until it burned.

He stood up and moved around the perimeter of the

room, closing the curtains across the dark freezing windows, and then he turned on both bedside lamps, which wore little pink silk bonnets. He walked back over to the door and shut off the calcifying overhead light, and the room looked almost warm, almost cozy. He sat back upon the bed, which was covered by a quilted spread of slippery golden fabric, and listened for his wife in the bathroom, hoping to intuit from whatever he heard some clue as to how she was, but he heard nothing. After what seemed like a very long time the door open and she emerged, wearing only the long silk underwear they had both layered beneath their clothes ever since arriving in this cold country. She had pulled her damp hair back and gathered it into a ponytail. Her hair had grown in much thicker than it had ever been before the chemotherapy—the only good the poison did, she claimed. She looked very clean and fresh, flushed and almost healthy.

She stood near the bed and looked at him oddly, almost shyly.

I've turned on the heat, he said. He pointed toward the hissing radiator. So it should warm up.

Good, she said. Thank you.

He drew back the golden bedspread, revealing the white pillows and sheets it had covered. It was like layers of skin, he thought, one lying atop the other, and somewhere far beneath them all the bones, the blood. He patted the blank space he had revealed. Get in, he said.

No, she said.

It's cold, he said. He could see the blunt points of her nipples interrupting the smooth silk outline of her underwear. You're cold. Get in.

No. Wait.

What's wrong?

Nothing is wrong, she said.

She reached out and touched his face. Don't you see? We're here. We made it. So nothing is wrong. Everything is good. This thing we've wanted, and planned for, suffered for, this thing we thought we would never have, never share, will soon be ours. I'm amazed. Aren't you?

Things could still go wrong, the man said. I don't want to jinx it.

No, she said. Don't think like that. Believe it now.

I do, he said. I didn't before, but now I do.

I love you, the woman said. And I'm grateful. I know I forget that sometimes, but I am. Grateful for everything you've done for me. Not just now, not just this, but everything. From the beginning.

I love you, he said.

I love you, too, she said. Will you get into bed with me, now? Will you get into bed and hold me?

Yes, he said.

She slid into the bed and moved toward its center. He began to get in beside her but she said, No. Get undressed. Please.

Oh, he said. He undressed beside the bed, aware of her watching him. He let his clothes drop onto the floor, onto the horrible shag carpet. He stood for a moment in his long silk underwear and then began again to enter the bed, but once again she stopped him.

No, she said. Take those off. I want to feel your skin. Please, she said. It's warm in the bed.

Is it?

Yes. It's deliciously warm.

He took off his underwear and slid quickly into the bed beside her. He pulled the sheets and coverlet over him. It was freezing in the bed.

It's freezing, he said. You tricked me.

Wait, she said. Be patient. It will get warm. She pulled him close to her and he held her body tenderly against his own.

When he was sure she was sleeping he carefully slid out of bed. He stood and watched her for a moment. Sleep was a refuge for her, it returned her to a former, undamaged self, and so he liked to watch her sleep.

The room was warm now and so he knelt again beside the radiator and twisted the knob, and it sputtered fiercely at his interference, as if he were throttling it. He persisted and twisted it into silence.

✦

The lobby was deserted; the woman behind the reception desk was gone and the lanterns the gryphons held no longer glowed.

Because it was now darker in the lobby, the light in

the bar that lit up the red glass beads of the curtain seemed brighter than before. The man crossed the lobby and paused for a moment just outside the entrance, and then pushed his hands through the hanging beads and lifted away a space through which he entered.

The bar was as small and intimate as the lobby was cavernous and grand. It was a long, low-ceilinged wood-paneled room, and for a moment the man felt himself back on the train, for in shape it was exactly proportional to the carriage. The bar itself, which stretched across the length of the room, was inhabited by two people, one at each end, as if carefully placed there to maintain balance. At the end of the bar nearest the door the bartender stood, leaning back against the dimly illuminated shelves of liquor, staring far ahead of himself, although the room was very shallow and there was no distance to regard unless it was inside himself. At the far end of the bar, at the point where it curved to meet the wall, at that last and final seat, a woman sat gazing down into her drink in the same rapt way the bartender looked ahead.

The placement of these two people at either end of the bar made clear the position the man should take, and so he sat on a stool midway between them. For a moment neither of them moved, or responded in any way to his presence, and he felt that by positioning himself so correctly he had not upset the equilibrium of the room, and they would all three continue to maintain the quiet stasis he had feared to interrupt, as if he had assumed his given place in a painting, or a diorama. This notion affected him with a debilitating stillness, as if one's goal in life was simply to find and occupy a particular ordinate in space, as if the whole world were an image in the process of being perfectly arranged, and those who had found their places must not move until the picture was complete.

He gazed through the regiments of bottles that lined the mirrored shelves behind the bar at his reflection, which peered back at him with an intentness that seemed greater than his own, and for a second he lost the corporeal sense of himself, and wondered on which side of the mirror he really sat. In an effort to reinhabit himself he reached out his hand and patted the copper-topped bar, and the touch of the cool metal against his fingertips flipped the world back around the right way, but the bartender interpreted this gesture as a summons and unfurled his leaning body away from the wall, walked over, and placed a napkin on the bar in front of the man, in the exact spot he had patted, as if were applying a bandage to a wound.

The bartender was a young man, tall and dark, vaguely Asiatic and remarkably stiff, as if he had been born with fewer joints than normal; he seemed unable, or unwilling, to bend his neck, so he gazed out over the man's head and spoke to the alabaster sconce on the wall just behind them. The foreign words he uttered meant nothing to the man; in fact they did not even seem like words. He remembered how for a long time as a child he had thought there was a letter in the alphabet called *ellemeno*, a result of the alphabet song slurring *L M N O* together (at least in his mother's drunken rendition).

He assumed the bartender had asked him for his order, but what if he had not? Perhaps he had told him the bar was closed, or insulted him, or was merely inquiring as to his well-being. The idea that language worked at all, even when two people spoke the same one, seemed suddenly miraculous; it seemed like an impossible amount for two people to agree upon, to have in common.

It was the woman who saved them. She abruptly looked up from the depths of her drink and said, quite loudly: English, English! No one speaks your bloody language, you fool.

The bartender flinched, and waited a moment before speaking, as if he wanted to put a distance between the woman's admonition and his words, and then said, in perfect English: Good evening. What could I get you?

The man was unsure of what to order. The constellation of bottles was arranged on the glass shelves of the bar in a pattern that seemed to him as intricately undecipherable as the periodic table, and to choose a liquor seemed as daunting as picking one element out of the many that comprised the world. The man shifted his head a bit so he could look around the bartender at the bottles behind him, hoping one bottle would call out to him—he wanted scotch, a large glass of scotch, neat, that he could warm between his palms and sip, he wanted the liquid gold of scotch, the warmth of it, but he had lost some fundamental confidence in himself over the course of the journey that made it impossible for him to ask for what he wanted—but once again, the woman at the end of the bar, apparently displeased with his indecision and the bartender's inertia, apparently wanting to make something, anything, happen, said, Have you tried the local schnapps? It's made from lichen, which sounds horrible, but it's not, I promise you, it's one of the loveliest schnapps I know. Lárus, give him some schnapps, let him see if he likes it. I think he will like it.

The bartender turned around and selected a large, squared, unlabeled bottle half full of clear liquid. He pulled the silver stopper, which resembled a stag's antlered head, from its mouth and poured a dram into a large snifter, which he set before the man, who realized the liquid was not clear, but tinged with the silvery blue glow that snow reflects at twilight. He picked up the snifter and swirled the liquid up and around its glass walls, aware of both the bartender and the woman watching him, waiting, and then lifted it to his mouth and smelled the clean bracing smell of institutionally laundered linen and poured a little into his mouth, and let it pool there for a moment, cool and aromatic, tasting faintly of bleach and watercress and spearmint and rice.

He slowly lowered the glass to the bar and said, It's lovely.

I knew you'd like it, said the woman. Lárus, pour him more.

The bartender once again removed the stopper from the bottle's throat and held its open mouth above the man's glass and, when the man nodded, he poured another dram of schnapps into the snifter. He then walked to the far end of the bar and poured more into the woman's glass. She raised her glass to the man and looked into his eyes. She was old, the man realized, probably in her seventies, but there was something overtly and disconcertingly sexual about her. She wore a tight-fitting black gown adorned with iridescent sequins that reminded the man somewhat of fish scales—he thought of the prismatic bellies of fish lifted out of the water, how their flexing struggle made them gleam—and her long silvery-gray hair was swept back from her face and coiled atop her head in an intricate, antique sort of way. Her face was lean and strong, her eyes dark, her nose sleekly formidable, and her lips polished a deep wine red that separated them irrevocably from her pale skin. Her eyes were large and seemed to be set a fraction too far apart, as if some constant eagerness to see both what was in front of her but also beside her had caused them to become unfixed and migrate to either side of her face.

One shouldn't shout in bars, she said, especially this late at night. I'm an actress, my voice is trained to project, but allow me to come sit next you, for I know you won't come sit next to me, and it's really too ridiculous to have this distance between us.

Without waiting for his reply, she stepped down off her barstool and picked up her drink and walked around the corner of the bar and reseated herself on the stool next to the man. She carefully placed her glass on the bar at the same latitude as his and then looked not at him but at their reflection in the mirror, through the interruption of bottles. Their eyes met and held there in the mirror, and the man felt the strength of the schnapps like electricity coursing through his body.

Are you here for the healer? the woman asked him. Or the orphanage?

The orphanage, said the man. There's a healer?

Yes. Brother Emmanuel. Surely you've heard of him.

I haven't, said the man. A healer? How do you mean?

How do I mean? What do you mean? He's a healer. He heals people.

For real?

They say he does. I, myself, have not been healed by him—at least not yet—so I can give you no definitive answer. But why do you ask? Are you looking to be healed?

No, said the man. But my wife is ill. Very ill.

Incurably ill?

Well, said the man, I suppose it remains to be seen.

Of course, said the woman. Everything that's coming remains to be seen.

The man realized that the bartender had somehow floated back to his original position at the end of the bar and was pretending he could not hear them, or see them, was pretending that he was alone onstage in some different play, a one-man show. The woman sighed and touched her hair, first one side of her head and then on the other, and the man realized she wore it as intricately coiffed as she did so that it could occupy her at moments like these; it could always be attended to, adjusted, primped.

It *can* work, she said. I've seen people arrive here at death's front door—in the vestibule, even—and a few days later skip merrily away.

The man did not reply.

But I think for it to work you have to *believe*. Do you believe in that kind of thing?

I don't know, the man said.

Then you don't, said the woman. If you did, you'd know. What about your wife? Does she believe in it?

I don't know, said the man. I doubt it.

Well, I don't suppose it can hurt her to see him, so you might give it a go, since you got yourselves here. People come from all over the world to see Brother Emmanuel. Fortunately, I've never been ill a day in my life. My eyes are fine, my teeth—everything works fine. Knock wood. She rapped the underside of the bar with her knuckles. I don't know why. I drink. I smoke.

You're very fortunate, said the man.

Yes, she said. About that. My body has never failed me. Everything else, yes—but my body, no. I wonder how I'll die. I am Livia Pinheiro-Rima. Do you mind if I smoke a cigarette? It makes me nervous to talk and a cigarette calms me.

The man shook his head, indicating that he had no objection to the woman smoking, and she fished a silver cigarette case out of her bag and sprung it open and slid one

29

out from beneath the clasp. She held it between two of her fingers, and with her thumb she flicked it cartwheeling up into the air and caught it neatly by the filtered end in her mouth.

That's a trick from my circus days, she said. She bent her face down and stuck the tip of her cigarette into a candle, sucked at the flame, and then raised her head, exhaling smoke through her nostrils.

I really was in the circus, you know, she said.

What did you do? the man asked.

I swung from the trapeze and rode atop an elephant. This was centuries ago, of course. But some things last.

It's a good trick, the man said.

I know, she said. That's why I've kept it. There are certain things I do every day, and that's one. If you do something every day, you'll never not be able to do it. People give up too easily in this regard. You, for instance.

What? the man said.

I can tell. You've given up, let go of certain things. I've had this dress since I was twenty-seven. And do you know, I was one of the original Isadorables.

You mean the children who danced with Isadora Duncan?

Yes. Although she didn't think we were children. She thought anyone over the age of three was autonomous.

I don't see how that's possible, said the man. You'd be one hundred years old.

Perhaps I am. But don't you know it's rude to talk about a woman's age?

I'm sorry, said the man. You're remarkable.

Yes, but a lot of good it does me. It's like a tree in the forest falling: if there's no one there, who cares if it's remarkable or not? I used to spend a lot of time in forests, waiting for trees to fall. It happens, you know—they suddenly just let go and crash. It's the most intimate thing I've ever witnessed. And I've witnessed an awful lot of intimacy, believe me. Oh dear God the intimacies I've witnessed! By rights I ought to be blind. Do you believe in that?

What?

Hysterical blindness. The optic nerve ceasing to function as a result of a shock to the psyche.

I don't know, the man said. I suppose—

I don't want you to get the wrong impression, the woman hurriedly continued. I wasn't in the circus for long. You see, I wanted to act, I wanted to be in the theater, and you've got to start out however you can. Wherever you can. So I started out dangling upside down from a rope and doing the splits atop an elephant. I don't know if it still happens, but once upon a time there were people who were born to be on the stage. I was. They say I got down from my mother's lap and crawled up the aisle towards the stage of the New Harmonium Theater when I was one year old. Who'd want to sit in the dark when they could be up there in that gorgeous light?

I would, said the man. Lots of people.

Yes, and God bless them! It's the beauty of the world, isn't it, that there are both kinds. The ones who will sit in the dark watching the ones on the stage. The ones who like to feel pain and the ones who like to give it. I've never believed in God because I think men's and women's anatomy is all wrong. The invariability of sexual intercourse, of men penetrating women, is amateurish; it wasn't created by a God. I think homosexuality is proof of this. And my God, in the insect world, the horrible things that happen! Traumatic insemination! Postcoital chomping! I was once married to an entomologist.

It doesn't sound very pleasant, said the man.

Being married to an entomologist?

No, said the man, the trauma and chomping.

Oh. No. Well, neither was being married to an entomologist for that matter. Have you heard of Kristof Noomeul?

No, said the man.

I was married to him too. He was a theater director. The last really great theater director. I'm talking about real theater, pure theater, of course. It's how I ended up here, at the end of the world. Of course, it being round, it doesn't really have an end, but you got yourself here, so you know what I mean.

The woman looked down into her drink.

The bartender once again lifted himself away from the wall. He selected the schnapps bottle, uncorked it, and stood before them. Another? he asked.

The woman looked up from her drink, turned, and looked at the man. She saw that he was crying, silently, the tears on his cheeks. She nodded at the bartender and he poured some schnapps into both their glasses. He corked the bottle and left it on the bar in front of them and resumed his post at the far end of the bar.

You're thinking about your wife, aren't you?

Yes, said the man.

That you may lose her.

Yes, said the man.

After a moment the woman said, It's startling for me, to encounter such depth of feeling. Of love, I suppose. Perhaps it's not love, but to be moved to tears . . . When one stops feeling, one forgets that feelings exist, that other people actually do *feel* them. Like love. Perhaps it's simply a result of aging—perhaps feelings, like muscles, atrophy. I'm sure it's so, at least for me—it's why I keep performing, even though hardly anyone comes to hear me—I play the piano and sing for my supper in yonder lobby five nights a week and Sunday afternoons. I do it, you see, because it's the only way I can feel anything these days, even if they're not real feelings, only facsimiles of facsimiles of facsimiles. And here you are feeling something real, right beside me. I'm ashamed. And privileged.

The man crossed his arms on the bar and then leaned forward, so his forehead rested on his arms. I'm so tired, he said. The schnapps has made me tired.

No, said the woman. It isn't the schnapps. She placed her hand gently on the center of his back.

The man felt the pressure and warmth of her large hand and was afraid she would take it away.

Your hand is so warm, he said.

It isn't either, said the woman.

It feels warm, said the man.

That's something else entirely, said the woman.

No one comes? asked the man.

Occasionally there's someone. She carefully did not move her hand, carefully did not increase or decrease the pressure of it against the man's back.

But most nights the lobby is empty, she continued. Or there's a few businessmen chatting up whores. But I don't let that deter me. Anyone can perform for an audience, can't they, for that warm welcoming murmur out beyond the footlights that's so often mistaken for love? Other people go on doing other things, so why shouldn't I? It doesn't hurt anyone, as my mother would say. Five nights a week, as I told you. Do you know, I've never understood why there are seven days in a week, it seems such an odd number, why not ten or five? It's another reason to doubt the existence of God, for wouldn't he have divided up time more neatly? It's all rather a mess, it seems to me.

She gently removed her hand from the man's back and said, Are you still weeping?

No, said the man. He sat up straight and wiped at his wet face with his hands. Then he lifted his glass of schnapps and drank it all down like a child swallowing nasty medicine as quickly and neatly as possible. He placed the glass back upon the copper surface of the bar and smiled wistfully at it. He reached out and touched its rim with his fingertip.

I'd like you to come hear me sing, the woman said. I think it might do you good. It might take you out of yourself.

Can that be done? asked the man.

What?

I'd like to be taken out of myself. And put away in a drawer somewhere. A drawer you open in a dream when you're packing in haste at the end of the world.

Oh, that dream! exclaimed the woman. That drawer! Well, I can only take you out of yourself. Where you go then is up to you.

Now I shall go to bed, said the man. He looked at the bartender. What do I owe you?

Don't worry, said the woman. He'll charge it to your room. It's the beauty of hotel bars. It's time I left, too, but I'll let you go first. It would be unbearable to leave with you and say good night in the hallway.

Do you live in the hotel?

I do. I had a sweet little house but I didn't take good care of it, in fact I didn't take any care of it, and so it fell to pieces, it really did, you'd think houses would last, at least I did, but they don't. Especially here, with all the cold and the snow. Things expand and contract, and then collapse. So now I live in the hotel. Go, just go! I'm going to return to my original place over yonder and finish my drink.

The man stood up. Good night, he said.

Oh, don't say good night. Just go! I'm going back to my place. See.

Livia Pinheiro-Rima stood up and walked back to her seat at the end of the bar. She sat and placed her glass on the bar in front of her and gazed down into it. The bartender stood in his original place at the other end of the bar, gazing implacably in front of him.

The man dove back through the red beads, which trembled ecstatically behind him, but after a moment they hung straight and perfectly still.

The lobby, at this late hour, was surprisingly occupied. A large Nordic-looking man in a well-tailored business suit sat in one of the little leather club chairs surrounding one of the many low, circular tables in the lobby. He was furiously writing something in a small black leather journal and, by the looks of it, underlining much of what he wrote. As the man walked past him, the businessman violently shook his pen, stabbing the air with it and then returning it to the paper, where it apparently did not perform. He held it like a dart and threw it toward the shadowed corner of the lobby.

Cheap fucking pen, he cried, as the man walked past him. Don't you hate cheap fucking pens?

The man smiled and continued walking. He was tired and wanted to go to bed.

Yo! Yo! the businessman called after him. Come back here, *mon frère*. I asked you a question.

The man stopped walking and turned around. What?

You heard me! I asked you if you hated cheap pens.

Yes, said the man. Of course. Everyone hates cheap pens.

You look awfully familiar to me. Do I know you?

The man said, No. I don't think so.

I'm sure we've met. Do you work with the Turks?

The Turks? No.

Where do you live? The businessman took a cigarette case out of his jacket pocket, opened it, and offered the splayed case to the man.

The man shook his head. I live in New York, he said.

Ah, yes—that's it, said the man. I knew it! I'm never wrong. He took a cigarette out of the case and then clicked it shut. He tapped the cigarette on the case and then put it in his mouth. He felt in both his pockets and pulled a gold cigarette lighter out of one. I met you in New York, he said. I spent a lot of time over there a couple of years ago.

He lit his cigarette and returned the lighter to his pocket. He exhaled luxuriantly and nodded at the chair across from him. Now that the mystery's solved, why don't you sit down?

I've got to get back to my room, the man said.

Oh, just sit for a moment. Are you sure you won't have a smoke?

Yes. Very sure.

You wouldn't happen to have a pen on you, would you? And I don't mean some cheap plastic piece of shit.

I don't, said the man. Although he did. He always carried with him a Waterman fountain pen that had belonged to his grandfather. Every couple of years he took it to the fountain pen hospital in New York and had it cleaned and the bladder replaced. It was one of his most prized possessions.

It's all coming back to me, said the businessman. I think we met at that bar that's way up on top of that building with all the flags. What's it called?

I don't know, said the man. I don't believe we met. Something made him raise his hand and touch his chest, feeling for the pen inside his coat pocket. It was there.

The businessman laughed. How terribly humbling, he said. Apparently I didn't make much of an impression on you. Well, in any case, please sit down.

I've got to get back up to my room, the man said. My wife is ill.

I'm sure she's sleeping. Sit, please, for a just a moment. There's something I'd like to ask you.

I'm sorry. It's late. I really should get back to my wife.

Oh, let sleeping wives lie. Like dogs, you know. Or would you rather we went up to my room? Would you feel less jumpy there?

Listen, said the man. You've really mistaken me for someone else. This is ridiculous. Good night.

Excuse me, but I'm not ridiculous.

I didn't mean you. I meant this, this situation. This mis-understanding between us.

You think it's ridiculous?

Yes. I'm sorry, but it seems that way to me. I'm tired.

It's a shame you think that way. I was only trying to help. You looked as if you needed a friend.

I don't need a friend. I need to get back upstairs to my wife.

Oh, I get it, said the businessman. You're on the DL.

The what?

The down low. Don't worry. My middle name is discretion.

I don't know what you're talking about, said the man. Please excuse me.

Ha! said the businessman. I remember now. You were good. Very, very fine. We enjoyed each other, didn't we?

I'm sorry, but you've mistaken me for someone else.

Yes, said the businessman. I've mistaken you for your real self. A nice hot fuck. But I get it, baby. Go play house with wifey. We'll catch up later.

✦

The man entered the dark room quietly and carefully so as not to wake his wife. He intuited his way through the darkness into the bathroom, where he undressed, without turning on the light. He walked to the far side of the bed and slunk silently beneath the covers. He lay still for a moment, trying to forget everything that crowded and clung to him, wanting only to fall into the gorgeous annihilating embrace of sleep, but at the periphery of himself he felt a void, not a chill but a lack of warmth, and he reached out his hand across the sheet to touch his wife but touched nothing.

He turned on the little lamp beside the bed and saw that he was alone. The bedclothes on the side of the bed the woman had been sleeping on were neatly turned back, as if they had been carefully readied for a sleeper, rather than disgorged one. He looked about the room but she was not in it. Could she have been in the dark bathroom? He got out of bed and opened the door and felt the wall for the switch and once again found nothing, and then saw the string hanging from the neon tube coiled at the center of the ceiling, and pulled it. The suddenly bright and alarmingly pink bathroom did not contain his wife.

✦

The elevator did not respond to the call of the button no matter how often or determinedly the man pushed it. It hung sullenly at the bottom of the caged shaft five floors below, as if it, too, were exhausted and had had enough for the day. The man began to walk down the winding staircase. Perhaps the electricity had gone off, for the hotel seemed completely dark and silent. But as he approached the ground floor he saw the glow of lights reaching up the stairway and could hear someone crying. He knew it was his wife.

She was sitting in one of the club chairs, bent forward, her face cradled in her hands, weeping. Four identical chairs surrounded the little low table at their center, and in the chair directly across from his wife sat Livia Pinheiro-Rima. She was sunk back comfortably into the chair, a bare arm elegantly displayed on each armrest, her legs crossed so that one foot hung in the air, dangling a little velvet slipper. It was a discordant picture: his wife leaning forward, weeping, and Livia Pinheiro-Rima almost reclining, dangling her shoe.

Livia Pinheiro-Rima saw him first, as her chair was facing the stairway. She motioned for him to stop where he was, at the bottom of the stairs, and rose up from her chair and came toward him. The woman took no notice of either his arrival or her companion's departure, and continued weeping.

Livia Pinheiro-Rima gave him a tight smile as she approached and put her finger to her lips, although he had made no attempt to speak.

We're very upset, she said. Hysterical, perhaps. Certainly terribly overwrought. We woke up and couldn't find you. Ran out into the cold in nothing but our skivvies. Lost . . . I went out after her and brought her inside. She won't stop weeping.

Thank you, the man said.

Can she have a brandy or a schnapps or something? It might calm her. I've tried to give her some but she won't take it. I'd let her just cry it out but she seems very weak. I'm afraid she may injure herself.

She doesn't drink, the man said. She can't have alcohol.

Well, you must stop her crying somehow. I'd slap her if I thought she could stand it.

Oh no, said the man. I shouldn't have left her alone.

Apparently not, said Livia Pinheiro-Rima.

The man walked across the lobby and knelt beside his wife. He reached out and tried to hold her, but she shrugged his arms off her without even looking at him.

Darling, he said. It's me. Everything's okay. I'm here. You aren't alone. Please stop crying.

He touched her lightly on her shoulder. She was wearing a full-length fur coat over her silk underwear. He assumed it belonged to Livia Pinheiro-Rima. She did not shirk from his touch, but he wasn't sure she could feel it through the thick glossy pelt. He gently petted the fur. It felt marvelous. The coat seemed more vital and alive than its inhabitant. He placed his other hand on her forehead and stroked her messy damp hair off her face. Her ponytail had come lose and strands of her hair were pasted to her moist skin. She jerked her head, displacing his hand, but when he returned it and repeated the gesture she did not respond. She continued sobbing.

Ssssshhhhhhh, darling, he said. Please stop crying. Just stop. Everything is okay now.

He looked over to see that Livia Pinheiro-Rima had returned to her facing seat. She leaned forward and reached into her little sequined bag that lay on the table and pulled out her cigarette case. Might a cigarette calm her? she asked.

The man shook his head no.

How about you?

No, thank you, he said.

Livia Pinheiro-Rima shrugged and lit a cigarette for herself. She exhaled and then leaned back into her chair and watched the man try to comfort his wife. I still think a schnookerful of schnapps would do her a world of good.

The man was unnerved by the almost amused way that Livia Pinheiro-Rima observed them and saw an opportunity to send her away. Perhaps you're right, he said. Is the bar still open? Could you get her one?

The bar is always open, said Livia Pinheiro-Rima. She stood up and leaned over the table so that her face was level with the woman's, balancing herself on her arms. I'm going to get you a schnapps, she said, enunciating each word as if she were speaking to an imbecile. So stop your crying. As she stood she lost her balance and teetered a moment, and then steadied herself by leaning forward over the table again. She looked past the man, into the far distance, and softly belched. The man realized, for the first time, how very drunk she must be.

After a moment she stood up again, and when her tall body was unwaveringly perpendicular she patted her hair and set off toward the bar.

She's gone, the man whispered to his wife, as if it were the presence of Livia Pinheiro-Rima that had upset her. He leaned closer and kissed the tip of her ear, which a part in her hair revealed. I'm sorry, he whispered into it. Please stop crying. He gently pushed her back into the chair and removed her hands from her face. He looked around for something to wipe her tear-stained face with but found nothing, so used his own hands. The touch of his hands on her face seemed to calm her. She laid her own hands on top of his so that they were both holding her face, and she closed her eyes and rocked herself back and forth and trembled with hiccupping breaths. After a moment she was still and quiet. She removed her hands from his and he lowered his, in a way that seemed choreographed and ritualistic, like the unmasking of the blind.

She looked straight ahead, at the empty chair were Livia Pinheiro-Rima had sat.

I woke up, she said, and I didn't know where I was. You weren't there. I was all alone. I thought I was dead.

You're fine, he said. I'm here. I had just come down to the—

No, she said. Listen. For a moment she said nothing. She continued to stare straight ahead. I wasn't alone, she finally said. There was someone in the room with me. She came out of the closet and stood by the bed. I could see her. She just stood there, looking at me. And when I spoke to her, she disappeared.

You were dreaming, he said. It was only a bad dream.

You don't understand, she said. I saw her. And I saw her disappear.

We've had a terrible journey, he said. You're exhausted. Tomorrow we'll go to the orphanage and something new will begin. And you can forget all this.

I want to go now, she said.

Where?

To the orphanage! she said. I need to go now. I've got to see the baby now.

It's the middle of the night, he said. There's no way to get there. We'll go in the morning. Let's go back to bed.

She stood up and looked wildly around the lobby, as if a sign with directions to the orphanage might be posted somewhere. I'm going now, she said. I won't go back to that room. You're always—you never—you always abjure. You hesitate! You're never, never impetuous!

The beaded curtains made a shivering sound as Livia Pinheiro-Rima passed through them. With both hands she carried a small silver salver on which sat three little glasses of schnapps. She walked toward them very slowly, her head lowered, watching the silver coin of schnapps jiggle in each glass. There was something ceremonial about her approach, something that could be witnessed but not interrupted, and so both the man and the woman stood silently and watched her cross the lobby.

She set the tray down on the exact center of the table and one by one positioned the glasses at the hours of three, six, and twelve. There, she said. Not a single drop spilt. She sat down in the chair she had vacated and lifted one of the glasses off the table. Sit down, she said to them both.

We're very tired, said the man. We're going to bed.

No! said the woman.

The man realized that her energy, her fury, had reached its peak and was subsiding. He sensed that Livia Pinheiro-Rima realized this too and looked at her. She had once again leaned back into the chair and was dangling her slipper, but now she held the glass of schnapps in her hand about a foot

45

in front her, her naked arm curved, as if she were in an advertisement for that good, high life we all seek.

You've stopped crying, Livia Pinheiro-Rima said to the woman. Good for you.

I want to go to the orphanage, the woman said.

In the morning, said the man. Now we are going to bed.

I am going to the orphanage now, she said, but she just stood there, defeated, exhausted.

Livia Pinheiro-Rima sat with her little glass of schnapps still raised before her. She had not drunk from it, and her manner indicated she would not until the hysterical woman had resumed her seat. Sit down, she said again.

Sit, said the man, and gently pushed his wife down onto her chair. He sat in the one beside her and picked up the little glass before him. His wife sat but did not touch or acknowledge her glass of schnapps. She wore a vacant, defeated look. It was a look the man had seen on her face once before, many years ago, when they were first married and had invited some of her friends and some of his friends to a dinner party, their first dinner party in their new apartment, and it had not gone well, in fact it had gone horribly wrong: it was a miserably hot summer night and they had no air-conditioning, the food was badly cooked, and the guests—her friends and his friends—immediately assumed some weird hostility, and said unfortunate things to one another, and as the dinner progressed it became more and more palpably disagreeable, and the man had looked up from the table after the plates from the main course—a whole fish exotically baked in salt that was almost inedible—had been cleared to see his wife standing in the kitchen, gently tossing the salad, in a huge olive-wood bowl, a wedding present from her Italian grandmother, stoically lifting and turning the mess of leaves over and over again, and she had worn then a similarly stricken expression, as if she were tossing salad at the end of the world.

I think we should drink to miracles, said Livia Pinheiro-Rima. They happen. They have happened to me. She raised her glass a little higher in the air.

The man picked up his glass and held it out. The woman continued to stare vacantly in front of her. She was some-where else, he could tell. She was gone.

Yes, he said, to miracles. He touched his glass to Livia Pinheiro-Rima's and then swallowed the schnapps. Then he put his glass down on the silver tray and moved the woman's glass beside it. Livia Pinheiro-Rima still held her glass in the air.

We are going to bed now, said the man. You have been very kind to us both. Thank you.

He stood and helped his wife stand. He reached behind and lifted the fur coat off her shoulders, and she let herself be slid out of it. It was the heaviest coat he had ever encoun-tered, so heavy that it seemed to surpass the category of coat. This is yours, I assume, he said to Livia Pinheiro-Rima. He carefully laid it across the seat.

The woman held her arms across her chest and shivered.

As much as it is anyone's it is mine, said Livia

47

Pinheiro-Rima. She put her glass of schnapps down on the table and reclined back into the hollow of her chair. How sad everything is, finally.

Sad? asked the man.

Yes: sad. Everyone goes to bed eventually, don't they? It's what happens at night. People disappear. Or they're not even there in the first place. Life is so wicked. So cruel. And not only the weather. Not even the weather. She was looking not at them, but at some point past them, high above them, in the dim upper netherworld of the lobby.

The man did not know what to say. He was sure that the most necessary thing he had to do was to take his wife upstairs and put her in bed, and get in bed beside her, and hold her until they were both warm and asleep and continue holding her while they slept.

Livia Pinheiro-Rima sat forward, reached out, and stroked the fur coat.

This is bear, you know, she said. Russian bear. Oh God, how I love this coat! I bought it off a White Russian in Trieste in 1938. She wept when she was parted with it. It had been her mother's, and maybe her mother's mother's. God only knows how old it is. Fur lasts, if you take care of it. Your own skin doesn't, but fur does. I gave her twice what she asked for it, but it was still a crime. If I could find her, I'd give it back to her. The poor dear dead thing. Not the bear, the White Russian. The bear too, I suppose. But you can't give back to the dead, can you?

Good night, said the man.

Livia Pinheiro-Rima ignored him. She fell down out of her chair, onto her knees, and collapsed forward, weeping, on top of the coat.

He picked up his wife and carried her through the lobby, toward the elevator, but he could not see how he could open the gate and fit himself inside it, holding his wife, and operate it—all this assuming it worked—so he carried her up the five flights of stairs and into their room, which was once again freezing. He laid her gently in the bed and covered her with the sheets and blankets and the gold quilt and then went and crouched beside the radiator and twisted it open, allowing the heat to once again hiss into the room, and then he undressed and got in bed and turned out the lamp and held his wife close to him and eventually she stopped shivering and grew warm and fell asleep and still he held her, he did not let her go.

TWO

When the woman woke up in the morning she felt rested and calm, as if a storm had passed. She heard her husband gently snoring in the darkness. She turned on the bedside lamp and saw that he was sleeping, cocooned, the gold coverlet pulled up over his head. She watched him for a moment and then carefully slipped out of the bed.

In the bathroom she dressed in the clothes she had taken off the night before—because they needed to bring so many things for the baby, they had themselves packed lightly. When she emerged from the bathroom her husband was still sleeping. It was a few minutes before six o'clock and though she wanted to, she did not wake him. Now that they were here she wanted to get to the orphanage as soon as possible. How could they not? How could they wait? How could he sleep?

It was warm in the room. She lifted one of the heavy drapes away from a window but there was nothing to see: just her strange face peering back at her from the darkness. She dragged a chair across the awful carpet close to the bed so that the glow from the bedside light pooled on it, then sat in the chair and began reading *The Dark Forest*.

As a bookmark she had been using a photograph they had been sent of their child. In it he appeared to be quite beautiful, almost angelic, but the woman was skeptical, because it appeared to be a rather old photograph, like the ones found in photograph albums, the thick paper curling and a bit yellowed around the scalloped edges. Perhaps it was a photograph they sent to all adopting parents as a sort of lure, and their baby would look nothing like the one in the photograph. She had unwisely mentioned this possibility to her husband, who had told her she was crazy. You always expect the worst possible thing to happen, he had said. Yes, he was right about that, but how could she not? And that did not mean she was crazy. It meant she was wise.

✦

When the man woke up, he was alone in the bed. Assuming that his wife had once again bolted, he sat up quickly only to see her sitting in a chair beside her side of the bed, reading. She was dressed and looked unusually alert and alive.

What time is it? asked the man.

A little after seven, said the woman. She marked her place in the book and set it upon the table. Can we go now?

Go? Where?

To the orphanage!

I'm sure it's too early.

No. They will let us in now, she said, as if she knew.

Can I have something to eat? I'm starving. He stood up. Let me take a shower, and then we'll go downstairs and get something to eat. Quickly, I promise. And then we'll go the orphanage. Is that okay?

Yes, she said, it's fine. She smiled at him.

He walked across the room. The carpet felt unnervingly texturous beneath his bare feet. He leaned down over the chair and kissed his wife's forehead.

She reached up and touched his cheek, and then his lips. She looked at him, her fingers once again touching his cheek.

I love you, he said. Very much.

She said nothing but smiled at him once again.

✦

The dining room of the Borgarfjaroasysla Grand Imperial Hotel was at the opposite end of the lobby from the bar and was as large and cold as the bar was cozy and warm. Designed in the style of a ballroom, the vaulted ceiling was gilded and sprouted many crystal chandeliers, as if the huge one in the center of the ceiling had, like some invasive species of plant, sent out ineradicable shoots in all directions. The gleaming parquet floor was crowded with very large tables, all laid with white linen cloths and set with ten places of gleaming silver, porcelain, and crystal. Three of the walls were divided by marble columns into frescoed triptychs illustrating scenes from what appeared to be a belligerent mythology. The fourth wall was punctuated by French doors opening out onto a broad terrace on which stood many snow-covered iron tables. The chairs had apparently been taken away for the season—or seasons, more likely. It was very bright in this room, the light coming mostly from the chandeliers, not from the world outside the French doors, which despite the great white drifts of snow reflected no light from the sky, which was completely dark.

The man and the woman paused inside the doorway, immobilized by the room's size, glare, and silence. It was the kind of room that one feels reluctant to enter, as if in one of our former lives some great violence had been done to us in a room exactly like this. None of the tables were occupied or gave any indication of ever having been occupied, so complete was the stillness and silence that enveloped the room.

Can this be the restaurant? the man asked. It seems more a banquet hall. Perhaps breakfast is served in the bar.

The concierge did point this way, said the woman.

I suppose we should sit down and see what happens.

Or doesn't happen, said the woman.

But before they could execute this plan, one of the

frescoes on the far wall was bifurcated as half of the panel was swung outward into the room, revealing a large woman wearing a parka over her waitress uniform. She made a lot of noise as she crossed the room toward them, and this journey took some time, as she was forced to tack back and forth between the many tables, no path being cleared among them. As she came closer it became apparent that the noise was a result of the fur-covered mukluks she wore on her feet; some sort of metal contraption was affixed to the bottom of each boot to prevent slippage upon ice. She paused about three quarters of the way across the room and indicated one of the tables she stood amidst. Breakfast? she asked. Two?

Yes, said the man. Two for breakfast. He took his wife's arm and led her toward the table the waitress had selected for them.

Good morning, he said to her, as they sat at two neighboring seats.

She righted the cups that were overturned on the saucers at both their places and said, Coffee?

Yes, please, said the man.

Do you have any herbal tea? asked the woman.

Mint, chamomile, linden, anise.

Chamomile, please, said the woman.

Juice?

What kind? asked the man.

Orange, grapefruit, tomato, elderberry.

I'll try the elderberry, please.

Orange, said the woman.

The waitress disappeared back into the fresco and very soon returned with their beverages. She had removed both her parka and the cleats from her boots, so she seemed very different, almost unfamiliar. She had also brought them menus: thick leather-bound books that elucidated, in intricately italicized type, all the many dishes at the different meals served through the day and evening in the dining room. This vast menu was composed in the native language with its undecipherable alphabet so that no clues to the character of the dishes could even be guessed at by scrutinizing the many pages.

The waitress waited patiently while the man perused the menu, turning its pages, hoping to come across something that seemed familiarly breakfasty. His wife, apparently daunted by the menu's heft, had not even attempted to lift it.

Defeated, the man closed the menu and said, Eggs? *Oeufs*? What's *egg* in German? he asked his wife.

We aren't in Germany, said the woman.

Sie möchten Eiern? said the waitress, in German. You would like eggs?

Ja, said the man. Yes.

Scrambled, poached, fried, boiled, shirred? She apparently spoke excellent English.

What's shirred? the man asked his wife.

I don't know, she said. Like poached, I think.

En croûte, said the waitress. Baked in a casserole. With breadcrumbs and butter.

Sounds delicious, said the man, I'll have that.

Potato?

Yes, please, said the man. Bacon?

The waitress nodded. And for your lady?

Toast please, said the woman. Dry.

Jam or honey?

No, thank you. Dry.

The waitress collected their menus and once again disappeared through the door in the wall.

Well, said the man. That wasn't so difficult.

Why should ordering breakfast in a hotel be difficult?

Because everything else has been difficult, said the man. He tasted his elderberry juice. It's delicious, he said. Very tart. A bit like pomegranate. Would you like to try it? He offered the glass to his wife.

She shook her head no and poured tea into her cup.

It's funny, said the man, after a moment.

What?

The way things are difficult—or aren't. I mean when we arrived here, it seemed so impossible.

What do you mean, impossible?

Just everything. Starting in the market the other night. And then last night, at the station. And yet we're sitting here drinking elderberry juice, about to eat shirred eggs. At least I am. It amazes me, how things have a way of working themselves out, if you just persist.

The woman did not answer. She appeared to be studying the fresco nearest to them, which depicted a covey of young naked maidens chasing a somewhat obscenely tusked wild boar through a fairy-tale forest.

I'd like to remember that, he said. I think it would be good if we could both remember that.

Remember what? She did not like when he tried to interfere with, or direct, her thoughts.

That things don't always end badly.

Yes, said the woman. Things do work themselves out. She lifted the cup of tea to her lips but quickly replaced it in the saucer. It's too hot, she said. She looked down at the cup as if its inhospitable temperature were a personal affront.

He had gone too far, he realized. He always did. She would open up to him, and he would respond, only to shut her back up again. It was unfair of her, he thought.

They sat for a while in silence, until the waitress emerged from the kitchen, carrying a silver tray on her shoulder, on which sat two plates beneath silver domes. She placed one in front of each of them and then removed the domes, revealing on his plate a ramekin filled with eggs surrounded by fried potatoes and two slabs of very thick bacon, and on hers two slices of slightly scorched toast. A sprig of parsley had been added to her plate, perhaps to compensate for its meagerness, but it had the opposite effect, making the dry toast look even more desolate.

The man forked over his eggs, revealing a mattress of breadcrumbs beneath them. A fragrant steam rose up against his face. He looked over at his wife. She was staring despondently down at her plate of toast.

57

Is that not what you wanted? he asked.

She shook her head a little and smiled, sadly, at him.
No, she said. It's exactly what I want.

✦

They had been told to arrive at the orphanage for their ini-
tial visit anytime between ten o'clock and noon. The concierge was able to arrange a taxi to pick them up and it was
waiting for them outside the hotel when they emerged from
the ballroom after finishing their breakfast. The woman
had wanted to go up to their room to use the bathroom and
put some makeup on her pale face, but she was afraid the
taxi might not wait for them, and although the man said
of course it would, she insisted they get into it and leave
immediately.

✦

The hotel was at the very center of the old town, and the
streets around it were extremely narrow, made even nar-
rower by the towering piles of snow, so the taxi drove
slowly. The town seemed eerily underpopulated; many of
the stores were vacant, their glass windows empty or occupied by a desolate naked mannequin staring out at the cold
world.

The streets grew wider nearer the outskirts, and what
little charm the old city had was replaced by a modern

ugliness of concrete and glazed brick, but it wasn't long before they had left the town behind and were on a country road, bounded by snow-covered fields on one side and a forest on the other. They drove for quite a while through this unchanging landscape until a building appeared before them on the side with the fields, surrounded by a wall of very tall fir trees. It was set quite far back from the road, and the car turned off onto a narrow driveway and drove toward the building, passing through a gap between two trees that were spaced a bit farther apart than the others, but whose branches nevertheless entwined, forming a portal. Crows—or ravens; some dark large cawing bird—erupted from the trees as the car passed beneath them and flapped off, complainingly, over the empty fields.

The building they approached had the appearance of a manor house. It was three stories tall and made of stucco painted pale green. There was no sign or any other indication that the building was an orphanage and not a private home except for the sterility of its unadorned façade, whose starkness was vaguely institutional. Smoke rose from two chimneys that protruded from the slate-shingled roof.

The taxi drew up before the unassuming front door, which was raised above the level of the drive by a few stone steps, which had been carefully swept of the snow and sprinkled with dirt. The man, who was attempting to hew to his new philosophy of assuming the best in all situations, was heartened by these signs of hospitality and preparedness. They both got out of the car and the woman walked quickly to the edge of the gravel drive and leaned over, placing her hands on her knees. As her husband watched, she released a geyser of vomit onto the bank of snow. After a moment she straightened up, though she remained facing away from him, looking toward the wall of trees that surrounded the building. She raised one of her hands in the air with her fingers extended, as if she were taking an oath. It was a gesture the man knew well: it meant she wanted to be left alone. So, instead of going to her, he walked around the car to the driver's window, which unrolled as he approached. The concierge had informed him of what the trip should cost, and the man gave this amount to the driver, plus a little extra. He asked the driver if he would wait a moment, in case there was some problem gaining access to the building, and the driver nodded agreeably but drove away as soon as his window was shut. The man ran a few steps after the car, waving his arms and calling out, but the taxi took no notice of him and sped away through the arch in the trees.

What are you doing? asked the woman. She had turned away from the trees and was panting slightly: the effort of vomiting had exhausted her. Did you forget something?

No, said the man. I asked him to wait.

What for?

In case we can't get in. Or in case this isn't it.

Of course it's it, said the woman.

It doesn't look like an orphanage, said the man.

Have you ever seen an orphanage before?

No, the man admitted. Well, in movies.

Probably starring Shirley Temple, said the woman.

Are you all right? asked the man. You were sick.

Yes, I was sick, she said. You're very observant. She raised her hand and wiped the back of her leather glove across her lips.

The combination of the taxi driver's betrayal and his wife's recalcitrance momentarily defeated the man, and he knelt down on the hard-packed snow that covered the gravel drive. For the first time, he allowed himself to feel how exhausted he was. He wished he could lie on the ground and fall asleep.

After a moment the woman walked over to him. She reached down and laid her hand upon his head. His thick brown hair had recently begun to turn gray, and she noticed that it seemed suddenly much grayer than it had been. Was it because she was looking down at it? Or had the trials and tribulations of their journey hastened the process?

I'm sorry, she said. We just need to do this.

Yes, said the man.

Are you ready? asked the woman.

Yes, said the man.

Then come, she said. Let's do it. Let's find our child.

She reached out her hand. She had not replaced her glove. The man stood up and removed his own glove before grasping her hand, and she led him toward the stone steps, which were sheltered by a glass marquee that had obviously been added to the house after its origin and was now covered with at least a foot of snow. When they stood on the small landing outside the door she asked him again if he was ready. He told her that he was. She rang the bell beside the door, which was the old-fashioned kind that must be pulled and released. They heard nothing through the thick door and walls.

They waited what seemed like a long time, and the woman had reached out and was just about to pull on the bell again, when the door was flung open. A very tall black woman stood before them. She was wearing a dress similar to a caftan, but it hung closer than a caftan to her tall thin body. It was made from a boldly patterned fabric of giant mutant flowers in startling shades of orange, green, and purple and was the brightest and warmest thing that both the man and the woman had seen since arriving in this place.

Webegodden, she said. You are welcome here. She smiled brilliantly at them—her teeth were fascinatingly white, as white as the fields of snow that surrounded the house—and stood aside, holding the door open. They passed through, the woman first, the man after her. When they were both inside the foyer the woman quickly shut and bolted the door behind them. The foyer they stood in was small but had a very high ceiling; a staircase circled up above them to the third floor, where a pale snow-covered skylight dully shone. On either side of the foyer were large paneled doors; above each door was a transom of colored glass. The woman who greeted them opened one of these doors by pushing it into a pocket in the wall, revealing a large room full of Biedermeier furniture.

Please, she said, indicating with her pink-palmed hand

the room she had revealed. The man and the woman entered the room, which was large and bright, and it was, for both of them, like entering a sanctuary. The walls were painted pale pink and all the furniture was upholstered in yellow silk; the lamps were lit and a thriving fire burned exuberantly in the fireplace. On the mantel above it a large golden clock encased within a glass dome reassuringly marked the passage of time with whirring gears and a ticking heartbeat. A round table stood in the middle of the room; it was highly polished and inlaid with a garland of fruitwood. On it a small forest of narcissi rose out of a low gold bowl filled with gravel and leaked their peppery scent into the air. Two small golden carp swam in an apparent endless pursuit of each other in a round glass bowl. In one corner of the room, an ornate wire cage was suspended on a chain from the ceiling; in the cage a large scarlet, blue, and yellow parrot regarded them silently, sucking the inside out of a large purple grape it held in its claw.

Please, sit, the woman said, and indicated the largest of the sofas, which was placed before, but not too close to, the fireplace. The man and the woman sat and the woman stood before the fire, smiling at them once again.

You are very welcome here, she said.

Thank you, the man said.

It isn't what I expected, said the woman.

No? What did you expect?

I don't know, said the woman, looking around the room. But flowers—how beautiful everything is!

The woman smiled again and said, So, you have come to see Brother Emmanuel?

Brother Emmanuel? asked the woman.

Brother Emmanuel! the man exclaimed.

Yes, the woman said. Haven't you come to see Brother Emmanuel?

No—no, said the man. Oh!

We're here to see Tarja Uosukainen, said the woman. Isn't this the orphanage? She stood up from the sofa and looked wildly around the room as if this person, this Tarja Uosukainen, might suddenly appear from behind the drapes or beneath one of the other sofas. But no one appeared, and the woman fell back onto the sofa.

Their hostess remained standing in front of the fireplace. Her beaming smile had faded but she still wore a pleasant expression on her serene face. She regarded both the man and the woman calmly.

I think a mistake has been made, the man said, and laid his hand on his wife's arm. Brother Emmanuel is a faith healer. The woman at the hotel told me about him last night. The man felt for a moment that he wanted to put his hand on his wife's mouth, cover it, silence her, but stopped himself in time.

He is not a faith healer, said their hostess. He is an *angekok*.

The woman rose quickly from the sofa, so quickly that she lost her balance and fell forward. Their hostess caught her and gently reseated her upon the sofa, and then she

64

dropped to her knees before the woman. She took both of the woman's hands in her own and, looking intently and directly into her face, said, Please, don't despair. Take a deep breath. Now, please. A deep breath.

The woman took a breath but pulled her hands away. Where are we? she said.

You are at Brother Emmanuel's, said their hostess. You are safe here. Everyone is safe here. It is a good, safe place.

We wanted to go to the orphanage, said the man. I suppose the taxi driver made a mistake.

I don't think there has been a mistake, said their hostess. She rose to her feet but placed one of her hands on the woman's shoulder. We've been expecting you. Someone called us from the hotel and told us you would be here.

Who?

I don't know who it was. A woman. They often telephone us when someone from the hotel is coming here. It is not unusual. Will you please wait here? Just for a moment, I promise you. She left the room and slid the large wooden door shut behind her.

I think a mistake has been made, said the man. The taxi driver made a mistake and brought us here instead of to the orphanage.

But why? Why would the taxi take us here? Didn't you tell them—

Yes, said the man. It's the language, I suppose. The concierge misunderstood. Perhaps the words are similar— orphanage and . . . what did she say he was?

Some kind of kook, said the woman.

It's just a mistake, said the man. Don't worry. We'll call a taxi from here and go directly to the orphanage.

The woman nodded but said nothing. She sat with both feet planted firmly on the floor and her hands clutched in her lap. Her face was turned away from the man, toward the table in the center of the room. She watched the fish languidly revolve in the bowl. The man shifted closer to her along the settee and attempted to separate her clutched hands, but she said, Please don't touch me, in an odd voice, deep and choked with pain or tension.

Just wait a moment, he said. Just wait until that woman comes back. There's nothing we can do without her.

The woman keeled forward so her head was bowed above her lap. She put her hands on top of her head and seemed to want to pull her head closer to her body, roll herself up into something small and discardable.

The man tried to unwind her body but then remembered that she had told him not to touch her so he let her be.

Please, he said. Please try to collect yourself. Please, for my sake. I can't—

You can't what? the woman asked him. You can't bear this? You can't bear me?

No, said the man. Why do you always . . . no! Please, what do you want? Just tell me what you want.

Before the woman could answer they both suddenly became aware of another presence in the room, even though they had not heard the panel door slide open. They turned and saw a man standing midway between the door, which was closed, and their sofa. He looked rather young and was very tall and thin. Perhaps because his head was bald (or shaved), his skull and the bones and cartilage of his face seemed unnervingly apparent, as if his skin were one size too small and were being stretched to a preternatural smoothness by the bones beneath it. His eyes were dark and intense; his nose was aquiline verging on hawk-like, and his mouth was small, his lips very pale. He wore a black floor-length tunic that was tightly fitted above the waist, emphasizing the slenderness of his upper body. It buttoned diagonally across his chest, from the right shoulder to the left hip, with gold vermeil buttons.

Suddenly the parrot, which had been quietly sulking on one of its perches, fluttered its large wings and called out an ecstatic greeting. It leaped up and clutched itself against the bars of the cage and battered the air with its impotent wings.

Brother Emmanuel walked quickly toward the cage and touched the bird with a finger. *Requiescat in pace*, Artemis, he said, and the bird made another, deeper, less avian sound, almost like a sigh, and returned to its perch.

Brother Emmanuel then turned away from the cage and faced the two people on the sofa. He looked at them as if he was only now seeing them, and they both looked at him, and for a moment time suspended itself, and nothing moved, except for the fish circling the bowl and the tiny insistent flakes of snow falling gently outside every window. And the ticking gears in the gold clock.

The strange moment passed, and Brother Emmanuel said, I understand there has been a mistake.

Well, yes, said the man. Perhaps—

We are supposed to be at the orphanage, said the woman. This isn't the orphanage. She said this accusingly, as if Brother Emmanuel had somehow suggested it was, or was trying to duplicitously pass it off as an orphanage.

No, said Brother Emmanuel. You are correct. This is not an orphanage. And yet you are here. Something has brought you here. I am Brother Emmanuel.

The taxi driver, the man said. I suppose he misunderstood. Could you perhaps call a taxi for us?

Of course, said Brother Emmanuel. If that is what you wish. But does it not occur to you that perhaps you are meant to be here? That no mistake was made?

No, said the man. That had not occurred to me.

And you? Brother Emmanuel looked at the woman.

She was watching the snow fall outside the window and seemed not to hear him.

Brother Emmanuel waited. He stood very still and looked intently at the woman. Finally, she turned away from the window and looked directly at him. A log in the fireplace collapsed and sent a shower of chittering sparks up the chimney. The sudden commotion in the fire made the man flinch, but neither Brother Emmanuel nor the woman seemed to notice it.

Am I meant to be here? the woman asked.

Brother Emmanuel said nothing.

What is it you do here? Or pretend to do?

Brother Emmanuel smiled almost imperceptibly. You're very angry, aren't you?

Of course I'm angry, said the woman. We are not where we are supposed to be. We have been taken to the wrong place. Either mistakenly or maliciously, I don't know, and I don't care. We are in the wrong place!

This is my home, said Brother Emmanuel. It is never the wrong place. No one comes here by accident, or is misplaced here. Remember that. One moment, and I will have my helpmate call you a taxi. It is not terribly far to the orphanage. You will be there in no time at all.

◆

The man and the woman said nothing to each other in the taxi on their way to the orphanage. The sky was no longer night-dark, but it remained completely covered with low, densely opaque clouds. They sat close to the doors on either side of the car and left an expanse of seat empty between them, and both watched out their separate windows at the white fields passing by.

The taxi was driven by the same man who had brought them to Brother Emmanuel's, but no one alluded to this prior journey they had made together. The taxi retraced its original route back into the town, through the narrow streets, past the hotel, and then crossed over a bridge that spanned a frozen river into countryside that mirrored that on the city's opposite flank. They traveled about a mile in this direction and then the taxi pulled off the road and stopped in front of a two-story building that looked like a school. Its large windows were symmetrically arranged across its façade, which was covered in yellowish plaster that was, in several places, peeling away in large strips, revealing a wall of cinder blocks.

The driver turned around and said, Orphanage, and pointed at the building. The man leaned forward and gave money to the driver and then got out of the taxi, but the woman remained seated inside, so he walked around to the other side of the car and opened the door.

Let's go, he said. We're here.

The woman looked up at him and said, I'm a little afraid.

Afraid? he asked. Of what?

I don't know, she said.

We're finally here, the man said. It's not the time to be afraid. It's the time to be happy. Come, he said, and held out his hand.

She turned and looked at him. What if . . . she began, but then stopped.

What if what? the man asked.

She shook her head. Nothing, she said. She did not take his hand but lifted herself out of the car and stood beside him. The man shut the door of the car and the taxi drove away. They both stood and watched it disappear down the road, back toward the town, as if it were deserting them.

Well, said the man. Shall we go in? He held out his

hand and the woman paused for a moment, regarding it, as if she was not sure what his presentation of it meant.

Take my hand, he said. Please.

She reached out her hand and grasped his, and then they walked up to the front doors of the building, on which was spelled out in those cheap adhesive letters that are bought one by one in a hardware store:

ST. BARNABAS ORPHANAGE

There did not appear to be a bell or a buzzer so the man rapped on the frosted glass panel of the door.

They'll never hear that, the woman said, and knocked loudly on the wooden part of the door, which was almost immediately opened by a woman wearing a white nurse's uniform. She also wore white shoes, and a white paper cap was bobby-pinned to her obviously dyed red hair.

Hello, she said. She opened the door wider and stood aside and the man and the woman entered, finding themselves in a large foyer with a floor covered with linoleum tiles in a checkered pattern of red and beige. Two staircases, one on either side of the room, rose up to the second floor, where a gallery connected them.

You speak English? the nurse asked.

Yes, said the man. We do.

Welcome to St. Barnabas, said the nurse. May I help you?

We had an appointment, said the man. At ten o'clock this morning, and I'm afraid we're late.

We were taken to the wrong place, said the woman. It was the fault of the cabdriver. We got here as quickly as we could.

Of course, said the nurse. There is no need to worry. Perhaps you will sit here and I will see if Doctor Ludjekins can see you now. She indicated one of two pew-like wooden benches built into the wall on either side of the front door.

The man and the woman sat down on the bench and watched the nurse disappear through a door between the two staircases.

After about five minutes the nurse reappeared. She held her hands clasped in front of her breast and shook them a little, in a gesture of supplication. I am so sorry, she said. But Doctor Ludjekins is not here any longer. He will be back tomorrow, and I am sure he will be happy to see you then. You come back tomorrow?

Of course, said the man. He stood up. What time tomorrow?

Perhaps the time of your original appointment, said the nurse. I think that would be nice.

The woman had remained seated on the bench with her hands still tightly clasped in her lap.

Can we see the child? she asked. Our child?

The child? asked the nurse.

Yes, said the woman. The child. The baby we have come here to adopt.

Oh, said the nurse. Forgive me. I misunderstood. No, I

am afraid you cannot. It is only with Doctor Ludjekins that you can see her.

Him, said the woman.

Him?

Yes, him, said the woman. The child we are adopting is a boy. Not a girl.

Of course, said the nurse. I am sorry. I don't understand. Doctor Ludjekins, tomorrow, will help you, I am sure. I can be of no help today. I am sorry.

No, thank you, said the man. You've been very helpful. We will come back tomorrow.

Why can't we see our baby? asked the woman. She stood up. We have come so far—

Darling, it's all right, said the man. Tomorrow. We'll see him tomorrow. One more day. Would you call us a taxi? he asked the nurse.

Of course, said the nurse. Where do you go?

To the Borgarfjaroasysla Grand Imperial Hotel, said the man.

Of course, said the nurse. I will call now. A taxi will come in any minute. She turned away from them and hastened back through the doors.

For a moment neither the man nor the woman said anything. The man took a few steps across the foyer, carefully only stepping on red tiles. This made him remember his antic upon the snow-covered station platform the previous night, and he wondered why in moments of high stress he elected to move in these childish ways. He stopped his hopping journey across the foyer when he heard his wife speaking behind him. He turned back toward her but kept both feet on red tiles.

You didn't support me, she said. You never support me.

What? he asked.

When I asked to see him. You didn't support me. I'm sure if you had supported me, we could have seen him. She would have showed him to us.

I don't think so, said the man. She said only the doctor could show him to us—

I know that's what she said. But it doesn't mean anything. If you had supported me, if you had told her we had to see him, if you had given her some money—

Money?

Yes: money. You don't understand how anything works! If you had given her some money, a few kopecks or schillings or whatever it's called here, I'm sure she would have brought us to him.

We'll see him tomorrow, said the man.

The woman sighed. She pushed open the door and left the building, allowing the door to shut behind her.

The man stood there for a moment, regarding the closed door. He could see his wife's shadow figure, standing just beyond the smoky glass. He realized he still had his feet ridiculously splayed on separate red tiles and slid them back together.

When they returned to their hotel room the woman, exhausted from their travels and travails, once again stripped down to her silken underwear and got into bed.

Don't you want some lunch? the man asked.

No, the woman said. I just want to sleep.

I'm hungry, the man said. I'm going down to the restaurant. Should I bring you back something? You've got to eat.

I'm not hungry. Just go. She drew the gold coverlet up over her face. The man stood there for a moment, as if there was something else he could do, or say, but he could think of nothing, so he went down to the lobby.

The restaurant was closed. A chain hung across the open doorway from which depended a small sign that said CLOSE. The man looked into the vast, empty space. The lights were all turned off and the room was almost dark, although it was only the middle of the afternoon.

He walked back across the lobby to the reception desk, behind which there now stood an older man with a shiny bald head and a walrus mustache wearing the same sort of vaguely militaristic uniform as the young woman who had greeted them upon their arrival and striking the same sort of impassive, unseeing attitude. The man realized it was less than twenty-four hours since they had arrived, and yet it seemed they had spent days—months, years—in this place.

Good afternoon, the man said.

Good afternoon, said the concierge. May I help you?

I was hoping I might eat some lunch, said the man. But it appears the restaurant is closed.

Indeed it is. Lunch is never served in the restaurant on weekends. Only breakfast and dinner.

Perhaps the man had lost track of the days, but he was fairly sure it was not yet the weekend.

So there is nowhere I can get something to eat?

There are several excellent restaurants in the vicinity, said the concierge. Some may still be serving lunch, although it is late. Or if you don't wish to venture out, a limited menu of cold dishes is offered at all times in the bar.

Thank you, said the man. I will try my luck there.

✦

Lárus stood in his usual position behind the bar, and a young Japanese couple occupied the center of the bar, where the man had sat the night before. So he sat down at the far end, in Livia Pinheiro-Rima's place.

Lárus walked slowly toward him. Good afternoon, he said.

Good afternoon, the man said.

Would you like the schnapps, or something else?

The man had not intended to start drinking so early, but then he remembered it was already dark outside, and for all intents and purposes the day was over, since it had never really begun. He told Lárus that yes, he would like a schnapps. Please.

Lárus poured him a schnapps, set it before him.

Is it possible to get something to eat? asked the man. I'm very hungry.

Of course, said Lárus. He reached below the bar and placed a small red leatherette-bound volume in front of the man. The name of the hotel was stamped upon its cover in gold. Inside, a folded piece of paper was restrained with a gold tasseled cord. Four words appeared in a centered column on the first page:

Snacks

Закуски

Bocadillos

Grickalice

The man turned the page and the menu was repeated, once again in various languages. The options, at least in English, were:

Hard Eggs with Sauce

Cold Fish Croquette

Pickle Relish

Small Meat Sandwich

Salad of Potato and Ham

Lárus waited patiently while the man studied the menu.

The eggs, please, the man told him. And the meat sandwich, and the potato salad.

Would you like ham meat or potted meat in your sandwich?

What kind of meat is the potted meat? asked the man.

Potted, said Lárus.

Yes, I know. But what kind? What kind of animal?

Oh, said Lárus. Many, perhaps.

I'll have ham, said the man.

Ham meat?

Yes. Please.

Very well. Lárus held out his hand and the man returned the menu to him. Lárus replaced it beneath the bar and then unfurled a linen napkin in front of the man and set a place there with a pewter charger. He disappeared through a small door padded in a quilted pattern with green vinyl or leather. The man looked across the bar at the Japanese couple, who were staring at him. They were both very beautiful, with their small clean faces and dark shining hair. Could they be brother and sister? The man smiled at them, but they looked quickly away from him.

The man picked up his glass of schnapps and sipped from it. He loved this schnapps; it was like nothing he had ever tasted. He wondered if he could buy a bottle of it and take it home with him. Home seemed a long time ago, and far away. The comfort of thinking of home seemed almost illicit, like the comfort or pleasure that comes from picking at a scab, or the thrill of pornography. But nevertheless the man pictured their faraway home, their snug apartment, full of books and paintings and old rugs and quilts. And the tiny guest room that had been transformed into a nursery the first time the woman was pregnant, and had been empty, with the door closed, ever since.

Lárus reemerged and placed a white ceramic plate upon the pewter charger. He said, Egg, sandwich, salad, pointing at the three things in turn, although there could be no mistaking one for another. None of them looked particularly appetizing but nevertheless the sight of them, of something to eat so close at hand and readily available, delighted the man and he ate all of it hungrily and with great pleasure.

As soon as he was finished Lárus cleared everything away. He picked up the almost empty glass of schnapps and said, Another?

Yes, the man said. Please.

Lárus fetched the bottle and poured some into the man's glass and then returned to his post at the far end of the bar.

The Japanese couple was speaking very quietly and seriously, their heads bowed close together over the votive candle. They were both dressed elegantly and entirely in black. Suddenly the woman was crying, and the man reached out and grasped her arm, shook it gently, and said a word, again and again, that sounded like her name: *Mitsuko, Mitsuko*. She leaned back from him and wiped at her eyes with her hands and then stood up and left the bar. The man remained. He sighed and pushed forward his empty glass in a way that made it clear that he was not dismissing it, but asking for it to be filled. It was scotch he was drinking, and Lárus poured a finger or two into his glass.

What was wrong? the man wondered. What had happened? It is very difficult to witness the public and incomprehensible sadness of others. In New York, he often saw women crying in the streets, walking beside men in double-breasted suits with flamboyant hair. Of course there was nothing one could do.

✦

He lost track of time for a little while and when he returned he realized that the Japanese man had also left the bar. Had he fallen asleep? Lárus remained at his post, gazing implacably at the beaded curtain, which occasionally shuddered ever so slightly, as if a subway train were passing in a tunnel beneath the bar, but the man knew the beads were responding only to the tension of the world, the fraught energy that leaked from him, from the Japanese couple, even from the seemingly implacable Lárus, for who knew what drama, what passion, what sorrow, what joy his stoic countenance concealed?

It had always been a dream of the man's to be a regular at a bar, to be served by a bartender who knew him and liked him well, but since he rarely drank and hardly ever visited bars, this dream had forever eluded him. But perhaps, he thought, he would find it here, so far away from home, for he felt unusually warm and welcomed in the dark intimate bar of the Borgarfjaroasysla Grand Imperial Hotel. The feeling was probably an effect of the schnapps, but it was a lovely feeling nonetheless, and he wanted to acknowledge it in some way.

He stood up and walked around the bar so he was facing Lárus. Thank you, he said, and he offered his hand across the polished copper surface of the bar, for he wanted to connect with Lárus, even in so insignificant a way as shaking his hand. Touching him.

For a moment Lárus seemed puzzled by the man's hovering hand and looked at it questioningly, as if it were a curiosity. But then he reached out his own large warm hand and grasped the man's, and shook it, and said, You are welcome, and the man felt oddly victorious, and turned and stroked his way through the beaded curtain like a pearl diver who has been submerged too long and heaves himself up through the ceiling of water, gasping for breath.

✦

The room was dark and very warm when the man returned to it. He stumbled through the darkness and turned on one of the little bedside lamps. His wife was sleeping, but she had thrown back the covers and lay exposed on the bed, on her side, with one leg bent and raised as if she were running, or climbing a staircase. The man shut off the radiator and pulled the sheet and the blanket and the golden coverlet back over his wife.

He went into the bathroom and closed the door behind him and in the darkness groped for the string that hung from the round neon tube in the middle of the ceiling. He found it, and pulled, and the light crackled and blinked on.

The man opened the tap and filled the large porcelain tub with very hot water. It cascaded ferociously into the tub, and as it accumulated it took on a pale greenish cast, not unlike the pale wintry tint of the schnapps. When the tub was full the man reached up and turned out the light and then lowered himself, gingerly, into the water. When he could finally bear the heat, he extended his legs and leaned back against the tub's sloped wall. Even though it was completely dark in the bathroom, he closed his eyes.

When the water had cooled he stepped out of the bath and turned the light back on. He shaved very carefully, watching his reflection appear and disappear in the circle he cleared on the fogged mirror. No sooner had he wiped it clean than the fog returned, so humid was the microclimate of the bathroom.

He had not shaved for several days and when he was finally finished, and his face was smooth and clean, he looked down at the bowl of soapy water in the sink which was festooned with thousands of his black hairs, and it looked to him like a sea strewn with carnage, the flotsam and jetsam after a terrible naval battle.

He pulled the little rubber stopper out of the drain and watched it all wash away.

In the bedroom he found his wife sitting up in bed.

Both bedside lamps were turned on. He closed the golden drapes against the cold black windows.

How are you feeling? he asked.

Better, she said.

He was suddenly aware that he was naked, and he felt as if he was displaying, unfeelingly, the health and beauty of his body, so he quickly found a pair of underpants in his suitcase and put them on. Then he turned again toward his wife, who was watching him with a slight smile on her face, as if he had done something amusing.

You must be hungry, he said. Are you?

Yes, she said. A little.

Good, he said. Should we go down to dinner?

Oh, no, she said. I don't want to go down. I can't. I want to stay in bed.

Are you sure? It might be good for you to get up. You've slept all afternoon.

I'm sure, she said. Do you think they'd send something up?

I imagine they would, the man said. Although it seems that they're woefully understaffed.

I don't mind waiting, she said. Just some soup, or something.

Are you sure you won't come down?

I told you, she said. Please don't keep asking. You know I hate that.

He finished dressing in silence. She watched him, the same amused half smile on her face. He hated her a little.

All right, he said. I'll see what I can do. If they won't send something up, I'll bring it back myself.

Thank you, she said. Thank you for your love. And for your patience.

He walked over to the bed and kissed her cheek, which felt unusually warm. He resisted the urge to palm her forehead. He was sorry he had just felt hatred. But it was gone.

◆

The bald walrus-mustached concierge was gone, and the young woman who had welcomed him, so to speak, on the previous night had resumed her stoic vigil behind the reception counter. The man approached her. Good evening, he said.

Good evening, she said.

I wonder if . . . My wife is not feeling well, and is staying up in our room, but wonders if some food could be brought up to her. Is that possible?

Certainly it is possible, the young woman said. I believe that any dish on the restaurant's menu can be delivered to a guest's room.

Excellent, said the man. Thank you.

I hope you are enjoying your stay at the Borgarfja-roasysla Grand Imperial Hotel.

Yes, said the man. Everything has been fine.

Good, said the young woman. We strive hard to meet the needs of every traveler.

Do you? asked the man.

Yes, the young woman said. We do. Have we failed you in any way?

No, said the man. You have not failed me.

That is good to hear, said the young woman.

The man crossed the lobby and entered the restaurant. The huge, gleaming room was virtually empty. Only a few couples sat, ridiculously alone, at the large tables set for ten. A string quartet was playing what sounded to the man like a polka, and perhaps because they were seated just inside the large glass windows that overlooked the garden which must leak cold air, they all wore parkas over their formal attire.

There did not appear to be a hostess or a maître d' or any other person who might welcome and seat diners, so the man stood there, waiting. He looked at the menu, which was printed on a large piece of vellum and propped up on a gilt easel just inside the door.

Borgarfjaroasysla Grand Imperial Hotel
MENU
Table d'hôte

First Course
Hors d'Oeuvres Varies
Oysters

Second Course
Consommé Olga, Cream of Barley

Third Course
Salmon, Mousseline Sauce, Cucumbers

Fourth Course
Filet Mignons Lili
Sauté of Chicken, Lyonnaise
Vegetable Marrow Farci

Fifth Course
Lamb, Mint Sauce
Roast Duckling, Apple Sauce
Sirloin of Beef, Château Potatoes
Green Peas, Creamed Carrots
Boiled Rice
Parmentier & Boiled New Potatoes

Sixth Course
Punch Romaine

Seventh Course
Roast Squab & Cress

Eighth Course
Cold Asparagus Vinaigrette

Ninth Course
Pâté de Foie Gras
Celery

Tenth Course
Waldorf Pudding
Peaches in Chartreuse Jelly
Chocolate & Vanilla Éclairs
French Ice Cream

The man quickly realized he could not face the ordeal that this dinner promised to be and decided he would return to the bar and its menu of snacks. At that moment the hidden door in the mural on the far wall opened and a woman appeared, carrying a large tray laden with dishes hidden beneath silver plate covers. She was carrying this burden by resting the tray on her shoulder and supporting it with one hand, and consequently was slumped a little to one side beneath what appeared to be a great weight. She visited all of the occupied tables, placing a dish in front of each diner and removing the plate cover with a gesture that was obviously intended to be a flourish but which under the challenging circumstances better resembled a gesture of defeat. When she had completed her arduous journey around the room—for the three occupied tables were all as distant from one another as possible—the man raised his hand and called out to her. She looked at him wearily, as if she could cope only with the diners scattered among the tables but any other obligation or responsibility would cause her to collapse. And so the man felt guilty about summoning her, as if he had done something wrong, and stood sheepishly inside the door as she made her way toward him.

A table for one? she dispiritedly asked the man. He thought this was an odd question, since all the tables in the restaurant were set for ten people. And then he realized she was the same waitress who had served them that morning. She was wearing a more elegant costume and had put her hair up in a rather soigné fashion and applied a deathly red lipstick to her lips, but she was undoubtedly the same woman, and he suddenly understood her fatigue and impatience.

No, he said. I'm sorry to bother you, but my wife is upstairs in her room—she is not feeling well; she's sick—and I wonder if it's possible to bring her something small to eat? Some soup, perhaps. The consommé or cream of barley perhaps?

Oh, yes, she said. Of course. And perhaps some creamed carrots and rice?

Yes, said the man, that would be perfect. Thank you! Thank you so much.

Your poor wife! she said. I am sorry she is unwell. What is your room number?

Five nineteen, the man said.

Five nineteen, the waitress repeated. Yes. I will have the kitchen boy bring her up something nice very soon.

Thank you, said the man. You are very kind. Here. He took his wallet out of his pocket and opened it. He selected a bill of middling denomination and held it to the waitress.

Oh! she exclaimed. You are sure?

Yes, he said. Take it, please. And thank you very much.

The waitress took the bill and stuffed it into a pocket in her apron. God bless you, she said.

The man felt suddenly happy because he knew he had finally done something right and good: he had arranged for food to be brought up to his wife and had been blessed by the waitress. He smiled as he recrossed the lobby.

The businessman was sitting at the bar drinking beer from a ridiculously large glass stein and reading the *Financial Times*. In place of his suit he wore a velvet smoking jacket of deep bottle green and a white shirt opened at the throat to reveal a paisley-patterned silk cravat. He looked up as the man entered the bar, and chucked the newspaper to the floor.

My God, he said, I've been waiting for you. Where have you been?

Really? said the man. He knew that the businessman had probably not been waiting for him—why would he have been?—but nevertheless there was something very nice about the idea of being waited for.

Of course, said the businessman. I never lie. To lie is to betray yourself. Only cowards and faggots lie. I've been waiting here for you. We're going out to dinner.

Are we?

Yes, said the businessman. Unless you want that ancient régime pig trough they're serving in the dining room.

No, said the man. I've just fled from it.

I knew you were a compadre. We're venturing out. Have you got a coat?

Up in my room.

Then fetch it, man. Hurry. Time is a-wasting.

Where are we going?

Get your coat, baby. Bundle up. It's cold outside. We're going to a real place, with real food. For men. I'll wait here for you.

The man went up to his room. His wife was sleeping and did not awaken when he entered and turned on the light. His parka was on the chair where he had left it. He put it on. He stood for a moment and watched his wife sleep. There was so much he wished he could do for her, so much he wished he could give to her, but nothing he tried to do, or give, ever seemed to reach her. It was as if she wore a shield that deflected all of his love, an armor that protected her from anything he gave.

✦

The businessman was waiting just inside the revolving doors. He wore a somewhat ridiculous-looking woolen cape and a Tyrolean hat with a feather in its band. Without acknowledging the man, he pushed himself through the revolving door. The man followed behind him. The man always felt a strange intimacy with people with whom he shared a revolving door. They both ducked their heads because the wind, which was fierce, blew the falling snow directly into their faces. There were no cars or other people on the street; it was as if everything had been cleaned up and put away.

At the first intersection the businessman turned right onto a street that was almost as dark and narrow as an alley. The lashing wind subsided and the man realized he had been holding his breath. The alleyway was as deserted as the street and had not been plowed or shoveled, so the two men had to wade through tall drifts of snow. It was dark except for one light that faintly glowed about a hundred yards ahead of them. They passed several dark windows, and in the dim light in the center of each window, gold-stenciled words dully gleamed: HAMMASLÄÄKÄRI, MARKT. The man paused for a minute outside the market, but a drape was drawn across the window so he could see nothing inside. But it was good to know that there was a market nearby. They paused outside the lighted window and through the steamed-over plate glass the man could see a dining room that contained only ten tables. About half of them were occupied. The businessman pulled open the heavy door and they both entered. A velvet curtain hung just inside the door to impede the entrance of the cold outside air, and the businessman fumbled impatiently to find the parting, and then drew the two panels aside so they could step into the room. All of the diners were men eating alone except for one table, at which a husband and wife sat with their two young sons. The men all had the forlorn beaten look of workers forced by economic necessity to seek employment far from their homes and families; there was an oil refinery outside the town and the man assumed all the men must work there, or on one of the oil rigs out in the frozen sea.

Each man was at his own little table, and they seemed so alone, without even the benefit of camaraderie. He wondered what kept these men alive, how so much could be subtracted from a life—warmth, companionship, culture, even light—and yet the life itself endure. Was it the promise of some golden future, of returning to the bosom of a family in some sunlit paradise with pockets full of money that allowed them to toil so stoically in this cold dark place?

A middle-aged woman wearing a lumpy cardigan over a nylon dress with a leopard print appeared and showed them to a table. The menus were held upright between the salt and pepper shakers and the napkin dispenser, and the man and the businessman each extracted one and attempted to study it. Only three items were listed in the hieroglyphic native language. The businessman leaned forward and pointed at the man's menu and said, Each is a stew. Meat, fish, vegetable.

Their hostess, who was apparently also the waitress, approached their table and stood there, wearily, awaiting their order. The man nodded to the businessman and said, What are you going to have?

Fish stew, the businessman said, to both the man and the hostess.

She nodded and then looked at the man. Remembering the impressive linguistic capabilities of the waitress at the hotel, and hoping all those who worked in the service industry were fluent in English, he pointed to one of the choices on the menu and asked, What kind of meat?

The waitress's uncomprehending look confirmed that

she did not understand, so the man repeated his question, as if heard enough times, or at the right pitch, comprehension might occur. The waitress shook her head, indicating that her darkness was impenetrable, but a man with dreadlocks at a nearby table cleared his throat and lifted his finger in the air, and then pointed at his own dish. He made a bleating goatlike sound. Then he put both his fists atop his head with his pointer and middle fingers extended like floppy ears and hopped up and down in his seat. He smiled proudly at the man and returned his attention to his own meal.

Goat and rabbit? Or perhaps there was some sort of long-eared, hopping mountain goat native to the region? In either case his interpreter seemed to be enjoying his meal, which was composed of chunks of meat and potatoes and what appeared to be carrots in a gelatinous brown gravy. It looked tasty, so the man held up one finger and pointed to the dish at the neighboring table and said, Meat stew, please.

The waitress nodded and then pointed to the glass of beer on his friend's table and then turned and pointed to the carafe of red wine being shared by the married couple and then mimed throwing back a shot. The man knew what that meant: schnapps.

Shall we have beer or wine? he asked the businessman.

Beer, said the businessman. The wine here is piss. Two beers, he said to the waitress. *Grande.*

The hostess pushed through a swinging door into the kitchen. The businessman stood up and removed his cape.

He did not remove his hat. Take off that sissy jacket, he said to the man. I'll hang it up for you.

The man took off his parka and handed it to the businessman. Was it a sissy jacket? Maybe the halo of fur around the hood? But it was odd because if anyone looked like a sissy it was the businessman, with his velvet smoking jacket and silk cravat.

The businessman hung the man's parka on one of the many pegs that lined the walls of the restaurant and then slung his cape atop it so that the two outer garments appeared to be spooning. He returned to the table. The waitress arrived carrying a tray and placed two glasses on the table and then opened two green bottles of beer with no label and poured an inch or two into each glass. Then she hastened away.

The businessman emptied his bottle into the glass and waited while the man did the same. Then he lifted his glass and said, To the joys of fraternization!

The man lifted his glass against the businessman's glass and then they both drank.

It's nice to drink a beer with another man, isn't it? asked the businessman, when he had placed his glass back on the table.

Yes, said the man, it is.

There are some things I only do with men. Drinking beer. Playing polo. Smoking cigars. You wouldn't want a woman involved with any of that, would you?

No, said the man, despite his belief that gender roles

were obsolete. And he neither smoked cigars nor played polo.

The waitress reappeared. She placed the fish stew in front of the businessman and the meat stew in front of the man and a plastic basket with two small loaves of bread in the middle of the table. She hastened away.

For a few moments they both ate their stew. Then the businessman picked up the basket of bread and held it toward the man.

Would you like some bread with your stew?

Yes, said the man. Thank you. He felt ashamed that he had not thought to offer the bread to his dining companion before it was offered to him. He took the slightly smaller loaf of bread from the basket. The businessman took the remaining loaf and carefully replaced the basket at the center of the table. He turned away from the table and surveyed the room, and when he saw the waitress emerge from the kitchen, he raised his arm and summoned her. She came directly to their table and stood there uncooperatively, giving no indication she had any purpose there other than gazing disdainfully at them. But the businessman seemed not to notice, or to ignore, her attitude, for he said overemphatically, Two more beers, and a round of schnapps for us both!

The waitress departed without giving any indication she had heard or understood what the businessman had said.

I don't want another beer, said the man. Or schnapps. I can't get drunk!

Why can't you?

I'm not here to get drunk, said the man.

Then what are you here for? asked the businessman.

To get a baby, said the man. To get our baby.

What do you want with a baby? Don't tell me she's brainwashed you?

Who?

Wifey! Back at the hotel with her vapors. Is she the one who wants a kiddie?

We both do, said the man. That's why we've come here.

You poor sod. You might as well cut your balls off. Would you believe me if I told you that the moment you have a kiddie your primal life is over?

No, said the man. I think that is when your life begins. Your true life. He took another bite of his stew. He was enjoying it, but the meat had a strange flavor and texture. He tried not to remember that what is meat in one country is offal in another.

The waitress returned with their beer and schnapps and set them, unceremoniously, on the table.

Men like us were meant for finer things, the business-man said. He raised his little glass of schnapps. Let the plebs procreate and raise their litters, but let you and me enjoy the pleasures of fraternization. He reached out and petted the man's cheek.

The man pushed his hand away. Look, he said, I don't know what game you're playing but I wish you'd stop. It's become tiresome.

I'm not playing a game, said the businessman. I don't play games.

Well, whatever it is you're doing, please stop it. I don't like it.

The businessman leaned back in his chair and looked at the man appraisingly, as if he were seeing him for the first time. You've changed, haven't you? he asked.

No, said the man.

You have, said the businessman. You didn't use to be like this.

I've never met you before! said the man. You have no idea of how I was, or who I am.

Well, in that case I should introduce myself, shouldn't I? I'm Henk Bosma. He held out his large, fleshy hand. It stayed there a moment, hovering above the table, before the man reached out and shook it, and said his name.

Well, that's better, isn't it? said the businessman. Now we'll have no more of this useless prevarication.

They both returned their attention to their stews. After a moment the man, deciding to take the offensive, said, And you? What brings you here?

Business, said the businessman. Money. Nothing else could possibly get me above the sixtieth parallel.

What kind of business?

Oh, the crudest kind. Oil. The Russians want to buy the rig and refinery here from the Finns and I'm putting it all together. Or not. More likely not. Have you ever tried to do business with Russians and Finns?

No, said the man.

Well, count your blessings. They're both mad. But mad in extremely different ways. And now the Japs are up here too, trying to buy it out from under us.

And who do you work for? The Russians or the Finns?

Neither. I'm just the man in the middle. The punching bag.

The businessman laid down his fork and lifted both his fists. He took a few jabs at the man. Pow! Pow! he said.

Although the man knew that the businessman did not intend to punch him, he flinched. This amused the businessman. Relax, baby, he said. We're all friends here. He leaned forward and patted the man's cheek, then quickly withdrew his hand. Oh! he said. Pardon me. I forgot that touching was verboten. Nevertheless he touched the man's cheek again before picking up his utensils and attacking his stew.

The man felt ashamed that he had flinched at the businessman's playful sparring. He looked down at his own meat stew. The sauce was congealing, and the chunks of meat were looking oddly slick and somewhat purple. He realized he was beginning to feel sick. At first just a little sick and then, suddenly, very sick. He stood up and said, Do you know where the toilet is? I think I'm going to be sick.

It's downstairs, said the businessman, pointing to an open doorway beyond which a flight of stairs descended into the basement.

The man pushed himself away from the table and hurried down the steps into the basement, where he found himself in what was obviously a storeroom, with huge glass jars filled with what looked like pickled fruits and vegetables and perhaps, disquietingly, meat, stacked on the metal shelves. The man was almost sick on the floor because these glass jars filled with floating organic matter reminded him of a jar he had once seen that contained a human fetus with an abnormally large head similarly floating in dirty brine. There were two doors on the other side of the room, and the man raced toward the closest one and opened it. In the dark he could discern the toilet at the far end of the long narrow room, gleaming faintly, and he rushed toward it and arrived just in time to lean into it and allow his sickness to erupt. It came out of him in several almost crippling gushes, a violence he did not know his body was capable of manifesting. After the third great wave of sickness he was able to lay his head on the rim of the toilet and close his eyes.

He felt so much better, relieved to have such calamity behind him, and he thought, It isn't really so bad kneeling here with my head on the toilet. It's nice and peaceful. He kept his eyes closed and quietly allowed himself to sink into a place that was nearer to his true self.

And then he felt, suddenly, on his eyelids, the push of light, and he opened them see that the light in the bathroom had been turned on. He sat up and turned his head but before he could see anything the light was shut off. In his haste to reach the toilet he had left the door open. Now the door was closed and it was utterly dark. He could sense a presence just inside the door, hear someone breathing. He began to stand up but then thought better of it and tried to press himself back into the corner of the room alongside the toilet, but there wasn't enough room for him to fit between the toilet and the wall, so he thought he might be able to crawl past whoever had entered the bathroom if he kept low enough to the floor. He pressed himself against the nearest wall and began to slide forward on his belly, trying to keep his body parallel with the wall. Then he thought that if he kept perfectly still and flattened against the wall, the man would move past him and he could get up and run out the door. He stopped moving and pressed his body tightly against the wall. He felt the cold from the earth seeping through the concrete and he wished he had never come to this place.

It was very quiet in the dark room. He knew that the man was listening for him, so he kept perfectly still. And then he wondered if perhaps he had been wrong. Maybe there wasn't a man in the room. Could he have imagined it? But he remembered the light and the door being closed. And then he heard a sound he could not identify, but what-ever it was, it was coming closer to him, and he realized that there *was* a man and that he was kicking, kicking both feet in all directions trying to find the man. The first kick found the back of his head and smashed his face into the wall and the next kick landed on his spine just between his shoulder blades. He heard the other man saying something in his language and felt himself being pulled up, a hand beneath both of his arms dragging him up and pushing him hard against the wall, and then one hand held the back of his neck hard against the wall and other reached down and felt his ass, patting and squeezing it, and he thought he was going to be raped and tried to scream but his mouth was pushed hard against the wall, and then the other man found his wallet, stuck into his buttoned back pocket, and he pulled hard and ripped the pocket open—the man heard the button ping as it hit the floor—and grabbed the man's wallet. The hand let go of his neck and the man lost his balance and fell onto the floor and hit his head on something— the toilet, he thought—and he felt the mugger kicking him again, and then the mugger kicked the toilet and cried out in pain and kicked him once again very hard and then he was gone, a soft gleam of light as he opened the door and then darkness again.

The man lay quietly on the floor. He had covered his face with his hands and now he pressed them tenderly against his skin and this tender touching of himself calmed him. He rocked himself back and forth. He kept one hand on his face and with the other felt for his left ear, which he thought might have come off, but it was still attached to his head, and he pressed his hand tightly against it to keep it from falling off.

The next thing he knew was the light had been turned back on, and he curled himself more tightly into himself and waited to be kicked again.

Jesus, what's happened to you? He felt someone kneel beside him and a hand touched his upper arm, trying to pull him around, away from the toilet. But he managed to shirk off the hand and curl more tightly around the toilet.

It's me, the voice said. What's happened? Open your eyes. It's over.

The man opened his eyes and saw the businessman kneeling beside him. He gently patted the man's upper arm. Can you stand up?

The man nodded, although he wasn't sure if he could stand up.

Let me help you, the businessman said. With one of his hands under each of the man's arms he dragged the man up. The man stood for a moment but then dizzily sat on the toilet.

You've got a bloody nose, said the businessman. Here—he reached into a pocket of his smoking jacket but found nothing. And nothing in the other pocket. He reached up to his throat and removed his silk cravat and handed it to the man. You'd better do it, he said. I might hurt you.

Are you sure? the man asked. Your beautiful cravat?

Of course, said the businessman. Take it. I have thousands.

The man took the cravat and gingerly dabbed at his nose.

Just hold it there, said the businessman. Tilt your head back.

The man did this and the businessman stood beside him, moving his hand in a circle around the center of the man's back, but so lightly that the man felt the warmth of his hand more than the actual touch of it.

The woman was awoken by a knocking on the door. The utter darkness of the hotel room revealed nothing about who or where she was, and it took her a moment to remember her identity and circumstances. Then she heard the knocking again. Oh, she thought, it must be room service with my dinner. She reached out and turned on the nearest bedside lamp.

Come in, she called, but her voice sounded feeble, unused, so she repeated herself.

I would if I could but I can't, a voice called through the door. A woman's voice. The damn door's locked!

The woman drew back the covers and got out of the bed. She felt dizzy, so she stood for a moment, with one hand pressed tightly against the faux-brick wall. Then, when she felt able to, she walked across the room and opened the door. It was dark in the hallway—it seemed to be dark everywhere in this hotel—but in the gloom she could see Livia Pinheiro-Rima standing and holding a tray.

I've got your supper here, Livia Pinheiro-Rima said, and pushed past the woman into the room. Where should I put it? Without waiting for an answer, she lowered the tray onto the bed and then wrung her hands together, as if they were sore from carrying it. Your husband's gone out to dinner, she said, so I intercepted the swarthy youth they sent up because I thought you might like to see a friendly face, stuck up here all by yourself.

The woman remained standing by the open door. A friendly face? she asked.

Well, a familiar face, if nothing else. Or maybe not. Don't you remember me? I'm the woman who saved you from freezing to death last night when you ran out of the hotel in your skivvies. If that's not friendly, I don't know what is.

Yes, said the woman. Of course. I just didn't expect to see you again.

Really? Not ever again?

Well, not up here, said the woman. With the tray.

You've got to learn to take things at they come, said Livia Pinheiro-Rima. That's one thing I've learned. Now come, back into bed with you before you freeze to death. We'll pretend you're a little girl in the nursery and I'm your beloved old nanny. That should be a comfort to both of us, I imagine. Into bed, my poppet!

Although the woman had no desire to indulge this fantasy of Livia Pinheiro-Rima's, she was cold and tired and so dutifully returned to the bed, and in this way temporarily forfeited her rights to a rational existence.

There's a good girl, said Livia Pinheiro-Rima. Now let's see what Cook's sent up for our supper. She removed the two silver domes from the dishes on the tray and exclaimed, Lucky girl, it's your absolute favorites! Cock-a-leekie Soup and Toad-in-the-Hole! Let's get this soup in your tummy while it's still piping hot.

Livia Pinheiro-Rima replaced the dome on top of one

dish and carried the bowl of soup, a spoon, and a large white cloth napkin around the bed to where the woman lay. You'll have to sit up, my dear; you can't eat soup lying down like that. Let's prop you up and make you comfy cozy. She put the things she carried down on the bedside table and helped the woman sit up, placing the pillows behind her back, and drew the blankets tightly up and around her. There we are, she said. She sat down on the bed and tucked the napkin into the neck of the woman's underwear so that it fell down over the gold coverlet. Then she picked up the bowl of soup. She paddled the spoon through the soup and then lifted it out of the bowl and said, Open up.

I can feed myself, said the woman.

You keep your little mitts beneath the blankets where they belong, said Livia Pinheiro-Rima. *Ouvre la bouche, mon petit chat.*

The woman opened her mouth and was fed the soup. It's good, she said.

Of course it's good. Do you think I'd feed you bad soup? *Ouvre.* The woman opened her mouth and was fed more soup. She realized she quite liked being fed soup while snuggled up in bed in the dim pink-lighted room with the snow falling outside the curtained windows. It was the warmest and safest she had felt in days.

When the bowl of soup was finished, Livia Pinheiro-Rima pulled the napkin out and wiped the woman's lips. Then she re-tucked it beneath her chin. Ready for our Toad-in-the-Hole?

Yes, said the woman.

Yes, what?

Yes, please, said the woman.

There's a good girl.

Livia Pinheiro-Rima returned the empty soup bowl to the tray and lifted the dome from the other dish and returned to her place on the bed beside the woman. It isn't really Toad-in-the-Hole, she said. It looks like creamed chicken and mushrooms over rice. *Ouvre la bouche.*

As she fed the woman the creamed chicken, Livia Pinheiro-Rima suddenly said, in a voice quite unlike Nanny's, Now, listen, you've got tell me what you thought of him!

What I thought of who?

Who? Why, Brother Emmanuel, of course!

How did you—

How do you think? I set it all up. I told the taxi driver to take you there. The last thing you need is a child. It's obvious what you need is Brother Emmanuel. So I had to interfere.

How dare you! said the woman.

Yes, exactly, said Livia Pinheiro-Rima: How dare I! What is it they say—better to dare than to dream? Or perhaps it's the other way round, but in any case I got you there, didn't I? So the least you can do is tell me what you thought of him.

I think he's a fraud, said the woman. I mean, obviously.

But will you go back?

If he's a fraud, why go back?

Perhaps you aren't sure.

Oh, I'm sure, said the woman. It's really shameless, what he does. I think it's the worst deception that exists. To take advantage of vulnerable people—

He took advantage of you?

No. Of course not. I didn't allow him to. And I won't.

Then there's no harm in going back, is there?

Perhaps there's no harm, but there's also no purpose, said the woman. Besides, we're going to the orphanage to-morrow. Tomorrow we see our child.

And while we're on that subject, please tell me, what in the world do you need a child for? They're really nasty little creatures, babies.

Did you ever have a baby? asked the woman.

Yes. Several, in fact. I speak from experience.

And you didn't love them?

No, not when they were babies. What a nuisance they were!

But later you did?

Oh, yes. There are a few years—between five and ten, if I remember correctly—when they're lovely. But it doesn't last long.

Well, I'm sure we shall love our baby because we want it so badly and have gone through so much to adopt it.

If I may once again speak from my own experience—I suppose one always speaks from one's own experience so there's no need to qualify in this way—but my experience has taught me that things we badly want and strive desper-ately for are the things that most keenly disappoint us. For this reason alone I think you should forsake the orphanage and go back and see Brother Emmanuel. Of course one does not preclude the other. I understand why you might not listen to me—although you should, you really should—but my dear, don't you believe in fate?

Fate?

Yes, fate. Fate! Why else would you have come here, of all places, to adopt a baby, if it wasn't to meet Brother Emmanuel? I can't tell you how strongly I feel that you were meant to meet him.

Are you part of his scam? Does he give you a percentage of his blood money?

That's a vile, stupid thing to say, and if I've caused you to say something like that I'm truly sorry, because I know you are neither vile nor stupid. But let me tell you that Brother Emmanuel has never taken so much as a penny from anyone. And I have a lifetime sinecure at the National Theater, which I founded and ran for thirty-seven years, so I'm neither in need of nor in the habit of taking anyone's money, thank you very much.

I'm sorry, said the woman. It's just that I don't know what to think and so I don't know what to do.

All the more reason to listen to me, said Livia Pinheiro-Rima. Your husband told me how ill you are. Not that he needed to tell me—one look at you and I knew.

Knew what?

How ill you are. Let's not beat around the bush. I don't

have the time for that, and frankly, my dear, neither do you. You're far too ill to become a mother.

I know that, said the woman. Do you think I don't know that? But that's the whole point, the whole reason we're here, now. So we can be a family for however long it lasts. It may be as long as a year, and when it happens—when I die—they'll have each other. They'll be family. He won't be alone. You don't know how difficult it's been—finding someone who would let us adopt, at our age, and under these, under my conditions. That's why we've had to come so far, to this place. That's why we're here—to start something real. Not to see some charlatan.

But why not see him, now that you are here?

You don't understand! It's taken me so long, so unbelievably long, to resign myself to what's happening. But I am resigned. I can't allow any more possibilities, everything that can be done has been done, and I'm too tired, too—

Excuse me, but everything hasn't been done! exclaimed Livia Pinheiro-Rima. You haven't seen Brother Emmanuel! I mean you did today, but not properly, not the way you need to. Why would you not go back? Don't you owe it to yourself? Your husband? And yes, of course, if it gets there, your child?

I told you, I don't believe in that. I have this time—this short time—and I want to spend it living, not trying to stay alive, not even hoping to stay alive. I know my body. I know what it's doing.

Livia Pinheiro-Rima stood up and returned the emptied dish of not-Toad-in-the-Hole to the tray. She lowered the silver dome over it with a bit of a flourish, as if it were a magic trick. Without speaking she came around the bed and gently pulled the napkin from around the woman's throat. She shook it out and then folded it in half, quarters, eighths. After a moment she said, once again in her Nanny voice, You must have been a bad girl. Cook didn't send up a pudding. Now, hunker down. She pulled the pillows out from behind the woman and helped her to resume her recumbent position upon the bed and smoothed the golden coverlet over her. She pointed to the little bedside lamp and said, On or off?

On, the woman said.

Yes, said Livia Pinheiro-Rima, I should leave it on all night if I were you. It casts such a warm light. You're sure to have sweet dreams sleeping in such lovely light. She sat down on the bed beside the woman.

Close your eyes, she said. There's a good girl. She reached out and gently stroked the hair off the woman's forehead. That was quite a dramatic little speech you just gave. I think you've exhausted yourself. You need to go to sleep. It's only in English, you know, that people *go* to sleep. Everywhere else people sleep right where they are. You're ready to sleep now, aren't you?

Yes, said the woman. She was feeling full and warm and sleepy and a little narcotized, as if the meal she had just eaten had some magical restorative powers, and her body was full again, not hollow and brittle. It was the most she had eaten in quite some time.

Good, said Livia Pinheiro-Rima. She leaned forward and softly kissed the woman's forehead, which was slightly damp. She stood up and went into the bathroom and found a washcloth and doused it in cool water and then came back and gently touched it to the woman's face.

That feels good, said the woman. Thank you.

You're most certainly welcome. She paused for a moment, and then said, You're lost, aren't you?

Yes, said the woman. I am.

The thing to remember is that we're all lost, said Livia Pinheiro-Rima. We're living in a dark time. No one can find their way. Everyone's fumbling, blindly fumbling. Like those little underground animals who sightlessly push themselves through the cold damp earth, hoping to encounter the root of something edible. We're no better than that.

Is it that bad?

Yes, said Livia Pinheiro-Rima, it's that bad. But there are worse things than being blind, and stumbling in the dark. Much worse things.

What?

Being dead, said Livia Pinheiro-Rima.

I don't think that's worse, said the woman. It's just—nothing.

Perhaps. Who knows? But isn't nothing worse than this? Worse than this cozy warm bed and Nanny here beside you, to watch over you and protect you all night long, until the morning comes with the dew on the hyacinths and the roosters cock-a-doodle-dooing? Surely that's better than nothing?

Yes, said the woman.

Livia Pinheiro-Rima stood and picked the tray up off the bed. Can I get you a glass of water? Are you warm enough?

I'm fine, said the woman. Thank you, she said again. And then she said, Perhaps you're right.

Of course I'm right, said Livia Pinheiro-Rima. There'd be no point in telling you what to do if I were wrong. I'll come back and check on you later. Now you must sleep.

✦

The next thing the man knew was that he was sitting on the toilet in a bathroom and the businessman was dabbing at his head with a clean white handkerchief. The businessman had one hand at the center of the man's back, supporting him, while the other hand administered to his wounds.

It's stopped bleeding, he heard the businessman say. That's good—it means you won't need stitches.

Where am I? the man asked. How did I get here?

The businessman chuckled. Such existential questions, he said. We're back at the hotel. In my room. You were in need of a bit of patching up.

How did we get here?

I practically carried you. Not that you owe me your life or anything, but still. You're heavier than you look. Skinny blokes often are. I think you were in shock. How are you feeling now?

I don't remember much, said the man. What happened?

You were attacked down in the toilet at the restaurant. Do you remember that?

Yes, said the man. At least some of it.

Is there any reason why you might have been attacked?

What do you mean? the man asked.

I mean, might someone here want to attack especially you?

No, said the man. Of course not. I know no one here. I only arrived last night. I know no one.

You know me, the businessman said.

Did you attack me?

No, my friend. I saved you. Now I'm going to clean you up a bit and put you to bed.

The businessman put a washcloth in the basin of the sink. He turned on the hot-water tap. As the basin filled, he picked up a bar of soap and lathered it between his hands, allowing the suds to fall into the basin.

The man could smell the strong pine resin scent from across the room. When the basin was filled with suds the businessman turned the water off. He picked up a corner of the washcloth and swished it through the water, and then wrung it partially out. He walked back to the man and gently swabbed his bloody face with the cloth, and it felt good to the man, and smelled good, and he turned and lifted his face toward the businessman, like a sunflower following the sun.

The businessman wrung out the cloth in the basin several times. He cleaned the man's face, and his hands, and swabbed around his neck. A feeling of childhood overcame the man, of being tended to and cleaned.

Let's get you into bed, he heard the businessman say, and he forced himself to open his eyes and lift up his head, which felt clean but heavy, and said, What do you mean?

I'm putting you in my bed, said the businessman. You need some looking after. You're not completely out of the woods.

But my wife, the man said. My wife will be worried if I don't come back—

Your wife is fast asleep, the businessman said. Do you have any idea how late it is? And I honestly don't think it would be good for you to wake her up looking as you do now. Much better to sleep here and go up in the morning. How are you doing? Can you stand?

The man found that he could stand but immediately felt the entire world spinning around him, so he sat back down on the toilet.

Perhaps I have a concussion, he said. Everything spins around when I stand up.

All the more reason to get you in bed, said the businessman. Put your arm round my shoulder. Close your eyes. I'll heave you up and walk you to the bed. Just let me lead you. Can you do that?

Yes, the man said. He closed his eyes and felt the businessman hunker down beside him and throw his arm around his shoulder and grab him firmly around the waist.

One, two, three, the businessman said, and stood up, pulling the man up with him. Keep your eyes closed. Come along with me.

The man let the businessman half carry him into the bedroom, relaxing into the strength that supported him.

Sit, the businessman said, and the man sat.

You can open your eyes now, said the businessman.

Can I keep them closed? It's better that way, I think.

Of course you can. Whatever you like.

The man felt the businessman undressing him. He pulled his sweater off over his head and then unbuttoned his shirt and peeled that away, revealing the man's long-sleeved silk undershirt. The businessman quickly ran his hands down along both the man's arms, down the slippery slopes of silk, and said, We'll leave your silkies on.

Then he unbuckled the man's belt and unzipped his trousers. Lie back, he said, and the man, with his eyes still closed, lay back upon the bed. He felt the businessman lifting up his hips and sliding his pants down, but they would not come off over his boots.

Damn it, the businessman said. He knelt down and unlaced the man's boots and pried each one off.

Socks on or off? he asked.

On, said the man.

All right, said the businessman, I want you to stand up just for a second so I can turn back the covers. You don't really have to stand, just get your ass up off the bed. Can you do that?

Yes, said the man. He leaned up and off the bed.

The businessman steadied him with one arm while the other quickly snatched back the bedclothes. There we are, he said, and pushed the man back down on the bed. You can lie down now. Why don't you open your eyes now? It might make it easier.

Yes, said the man. He opened his eyes. The businessman's hotel room was similar to his own only all the colors were different. The coverlet, for example, was royal blue.

Lie down, said the businessman, and I'll tuck you up.

The man lay back upon the bed and let the businessman yank the bedclothes out from beneath him and then pull them to his chin and tuck them tightly under the mattress.

Don't move, he said. I'm going to get you something that will help you sleep.

The man watched him enter the bathroom. A moment later he returned with a glass of water in one hand and a pill in the other. He held out the hand with the pill but the man's arms had been tightly tucked beneath the coverlet and he did not want to extract them so he opened his mouth.

The businessman put his hand on the man's back and lifted him up a bit, and then he put the pill in the man's mouth. He held the glass of water to the man's lips and the man sucked in enough water to swallow the pill. The businessman put the glass, which was still almost full, on the night table. He turned off the bedside lamp. Now the only light came from the lamp on the other night table and from the open bathroom door. The businessman sat on the bed, stroking the hair off the man's forehead. I'll stay here till you fall asleep, the man heard him say.

Thank you, the man said. You've been very kind.

The businessman moved his hand from the man's forehead to his cheek, which he cupped with his large hand. The man felt the warmth and surprising softness of the businessman's hand on his cheek and pushed his face against it, like a cat making sure it gets petted the way it wants.

THREE

The lobby was empty and cold. It was the size of a skating rink. It was dark; there was no red glow from the bar. It looked like the photographs the man had seen of ballrooms in sunken ocean liners.

He had left the businessman sleeping in his bed and had gone down to retrieve his room key from the reception desk but there was no one there and his key was not in the appropriate cubbyhole. He could not remember if he had returned it to the reception desk before going out to dinner the night before. Or perhaps it was in the businessman's room, or perhaps he had lost it in the basement toilet of the restaurant. But in any case he did not have the key and if he wanted to get back into his room he would have to knock on the door and awaken his wife, assuming she was sleeping. Assuming she was in the room.

He took the elevator to the fifth floor and walked down the darkened hallway. Just as he was about to knock he noticed a mezuzah affixed to the door frame. He had not noticed it before. Was it the wrong floor? Or the wrong room? But no, there was the number, 519, affixed in faux-gold plastic numbers at the center of the door.

He knocked, quite loudly, because he wanted to only knock once. He waited a moment, but nothing happened, so he knocked again.

He was about to knock a third time when he heard his wife say, Who is it?

It's me, he said.

The door opened and his wife stood there, but for a moment, in the dimness, he did not recognize her. She was wearing a long velvet dress that was too big for her and was cinched around her tiny waist with a thick tasseled cord. She looked at him and said, Oh, it's you.

My God, he said. What are you wearing?

A dress, the woman said.

Where did you get it?

That woman—the one we met here the other night—gave it to me.

Livia Pinheiro-Rima? When did you see her? You didn't run outside again, did you?

No, of course not. She brought up my supper. She was so kind, so lovely. We had an interesting talk and she let me sleep for a while and then came back and told me I'd feel better if I got out of that long underwear and into something pretty. And she was right. We went to her room and she showed me all her clothes. She gave me this dress. It doesn't fit now, but it will when I regain the weight. We're the same size. Or were. It's a Balenciaga. And this cord is from the old Metropolitan Opera House. It held back the curtains or something. Can you imagine! She's got the most amazing collection of things—not just clothes, although, my God! the clothes she's got—a Balenciaga!

I think she's a bit mad, the man said. But I don't understand. She brought up your dinner?

Yes. I told you. She saw the boy bringing it up and commandeered it. She thought I might be lonely, up here without you. She saw you go out . . .

The man said nothing but moved past her into the darkened room. Even though it was obviously their room, and his wife was his wife, it seemed all wrong. Changed, somehow. He couldn't remember the last time she had worn a dress or spoken with such ardor.

The woman closed the door and turned on the overhead light. Oh my God, she said. What happened to you?

I was mugged. Last night at the restaurant. He stole my wallet. And my watch. He held up his left hand and shot the cuff back, revealing his naked wrist. My beautiful watch. My father's watch.

She came close to him and touched the bruised and discolored flesh beneath his eye and on his cheek.

He winced. This is a horrible place, he said. A horrible country.

We've just had bad luck, she said. It was bound to happen sometime. In a way it's a relief.

What's happened to you?

I told you. What's happened to you? Where have you been all night?

The businessman took me to his room. He cleaned my wound and put me to bed. I slept there.

The businessman? What businessman?

That giant Nordic businessman who's always sitting in the lobby.

Why did he bring you to his room? the woman asked. Why didn't he bring you here?

I don't know, said the man. An excellent question.

You didn't ask him to bring you here?

I was in shock! the man said.

Are you still in shock?

I don't know. Perhaps. Or maybe a bit drugged—he gave me something to help me sleep.

And then what happened?

What do you mean, what happened?

A strange man takes you to his hotel room, drugs you, and puts you in his bed. What do you suppose happens next?

Nothing, said the man. They sleep. What's come over you?

I don't know, said the woman. But it's remarkable. Something has—something's changed. I feel different. I feel changed.

The man sat down on the bed. He felt suddenly as if

the world was too big and complicated for him to manage. He lay back upon the coverlet and looked up at the ceiling, which was tiled with what looked like white linoleum floor tiles. Looking up at what appeared to be the floor thoroughly disoriented him, so he closed his eyes. What a relief it was to see nothing.

He felt his wife sit down near him on the bed. For a moment she said nothing, and then she said, Actually, I do know.

Know what?

I know what's changed. I think I have been cured.

The man opened his eyes. He sat up. What do you mean, cured?

Cured, she said. I feel well. All that was happening inside of me, the damage, the disturbance—I don't feel it anymore. I know it's impossible but it's what I feel. I think he's cured me.

Who?

Who! Brother Emmanuel of course. Who else? I've got to go back and see him. I've got be near him again, so that it doesn't reverse itself. We've got to go as quickly as possible.

What's happened to you? the man asked. I think you've gone mad. Will you get out of that ridiculous dress!

No, she said. The dress may be part of it. As soon as I put it on, I felt it. It's a combination perhaps, of the dress and Brother Emmanuel. So I'm not taking it off and I've got to see him again. We should go now, shouldn't we? What's the point in waiting?

What time is it? the man asked.

It's about six, she said. Twenty past six. By the time we get there it will be seven, or maybe even eight. He must be used to people arriving at odd times.

Take off that ridiculous dress, the man said. Take off that dress and come to bed. It is time to sleep.

No, she said. It isn't time to sleep. Don't you believe me?

The man shook his head. No, he said. I don't—can't believe that. We've got to go and get our child this morning. That is where we have to go.

The child can wait. We've all waited this long. A little longer won't matter. I've got to see Brother Emmanuel first.

Then go see him. Go! Wear that ridiculous dress. Put on a hat and gloves while you're at it. I'll go get our child.

Why are you being mean? Why are you being mean about something so wonderful? Don't I matter? Don't I matter more than the child?

The man lay back upon the bed and said, I just want to go to sleep. I don't feel well. I'm exhausted. I was mugged. He kicked me in the balls. Hard.

I was hurt too, said his wife. In the market. Maybe I had a concussion. But did I curl up into a little ball and cry boo-hoo? No.

I'm not crying, said the man. Nor am I curled.

Don't pretend you don't know what I mean.

The man said nothing. He closed his eyes.

Don't go to sleep, said the woman. You've got to come with me, now, to see Brother Emmanuel.

The man turned on his side and curled himself into a fetal position. Now I'm curled up, he said.

He felt his wife get off the bed but she could not have moved far, because the carpet made no sound. After a moment he opened his eyes and saw that she was facing the wall, bracing herself against it with both hands. Her head was bowed and she appeared to be looking down at the floor. Was she doing yoga?

Are you doing yoga? he asked.

She did not answer. It took him a moment to realize she was crying. He got up from the bed and stood just behind her but did not touch her. She had told him, several months ago, that his touch was painful. That any amount of pressure applied to any place on her body hurt. She would wince when he forgot and tried to embrace her. Once, when he went along with her to an appointment at her oncologist, he mentioned to the doctor that his touch seemed to hurt her. When you touch her where? the doctor asked. Anywhere, said the man. Everywhere. Right? he asked his wife. Yes, she told the doctor. Sometimes I feel very sore—very tender all over, and it hurts when he touches me. Is this usually after you've had a chemotherapy? asked the doctor. No, said the woman. Not necessarily. Well, said the doctor, as I've said before, communication is very important. You've got to let him know how and when he should touch you.

In the taxi going home she had said, Did you think I was making it up?

What?

That it hurts when you touch me. You didn't believe me?

No, he said. Of course I did—

Then why did you ask him that?

Because I thought he might be able to do something—

What? What could he possibly do? There's nothing he can do.

Fine, he said. I won't touch you anymore.

Now, in the hotel room, close to her but not touching, he said, What do you need? What can I do?

I need you to believe me! she said. Can you do that? Even if you don't, just say you do. I can't be alone in this.

Of course I can, the man said. Of course I do. He reached out and very tenderly, very tentatively, put his hand on her shoulder, not resting it upon her but keeping it poised in the slightest and most gentle contact he could sustain. She neither flinched, as he had feared she would, nor acknowledged his touch, and so he rounded his hand the slightest bit so that it touched more of her shoulder, assumed the shape of it, and it seemed to him she had the bones of a bird, so delicate, so breakable, and his fear of breaking them caused him to take his hand away.

◆

This time, when Brother Emmanuel's helpmate opened the door of his house, she did not greet the man and the woman with warmth and welcome. She stood there before them, holding the door open, regarding them with a troubled, puzzled look. Oh, she finally said, after a moment. Good morning. But she made no motion to welcome them into the house.

The man could sense that his wife had expected to be welcomed with open arms and was taken aback by the lack of greeting they received. So the man stepped forward a little and put his hand on the opened door, as if he were helping the woman to hold it open, or preventing her from closing it, and said, Good morning. We have come back, as you see.

Yes, said the helpmate. I see.

My wife would like to see Brother Emmanuel again. May she?

I'm afraid not. Brother Emmanuel is in sequestration today.

But I've got to see him! exclaimed the woman.

Why is that? asked the helpmate.

He's changed something inside me. I think he's cured me. Or is curing me. So I must see him again, now, before it . . . before it changes. Or stops.

The helpmate looked at the woman for a moment, calmly, as if she were trying to discern something by gazing at her. Then she stepped back and opened the door wider, causing the man to lose his balance and fall forward, but he caught himself before he fell.

Come in, the helpmate said. It's cold outside. She stepped aside and the man and the woman crossed the threshold and stood in the large front hall. The skylight was no longer occluded with snow; someone must have gone out onto the roof and shoveled it, the man thought. Or perhaps it had blown off during the night.

They all stood there silently for a moment, as if the atmospheric pressure were different inside of the house and needed adjusting to. Then, suddenly, the woman said, Oh, please, can't I see him? I feel it so strongly: this urge—this need—to see him! To be in his presence, if only for a moment. I won't even speak to—

The helpmate reached out and grabbed the woman's arm and shook it slightly. The man noticed that his wife did not recoil or even react to this ungentle touch and realized that something had changed.

Listen, the helpmate said. Listen to me! Brother Emmanuel can't have cured you. It doesn't work like that. He can't have changed you in any way—he only spoke with you for a few moments. To help you he must spend more time with you. A lot of time. It's real, what he does; it isn't magic. What you're experiencing is false. We call it a therapeutic delusion; you feel you're cured because you want to be cured. It happens often. But it is good, I assure you. You cannot be cured unless you want to be cured. And you want that so badly that you have fooled yourself. So do not despair.

But nevertheless it is a kind of a cure, said the woman. It's not delusional; it can't be.

You may think whatever you like, said the helpmate. But I have told you the truth of your situation. That, too, is a kind of cure.

Would you tell him I was here? I think he might see me if he knew I was here.

As I told you, he is in sequestration. He talks with no one on these days. Not even me.

Perhaps you could give him a note?

That's impossible. He does not interact with anyone in any way on these days. If you want to see him, you will have to come back another time.

Tomorrow? the woman asked.

No. His schedule for tomorrow is complete. It will probably not be until next week that he can see you.

That's impossible! I've got to see him tomorrow; it's a matter of life and death.

The man stepped forward slightly, so that he was standing in front of his wife. My wife is very ill, he said. Gravely ill. Can't you find time for her to see Brother Emmanuel tomorrow? It would mean so much to us both. I beg you.

Do not insult me by begging, the helpmate said. This is not that kind of place.

I implore you, then, the man said.

It is not for me to decide in any case, said the helpmate. I will talk to Brother Emmanuel when he emerges from his sequestration later tonight. If you call tomorrow morning I will give you his answer. Call the number on this card—and she picked a card off a small wooden table and handed it to the man. And now I must ask you to leave. We try to keep the house inviolate on days of sequestration.

They waited outside, on the dirt-covered steps, for the taxi to arrive.

Thank you for speaking like that, the woman said. Thank you for supporting me.

Of course, the man said. I think he will see you tomorrow.

The woman said nothing. Her face was trembling, perhaps because her jaw was tightly clenched.

The man looked down at the card he had been given. It was pale gray and slightly larger than a normal business card. On one side was printed an address and telephone number and on the other side a single Bible verse:

The Hermitage
Ulitsa Zarechnaya 36
Borgarfjaroasysla 9

☎ 6 - 238 - 994

★

Trust in the Lord with all your heart;
do not depend on your own understanding.
Proverbs 3:4

As soon as they got into the taxi the woman told the driver to take them to the hotel. Then she leaned back against the seat and closed her eyes. Her face had relaxed itself.

They drove out onto the road through the gap in the pine trees and headed toward town. They had gone quite far, perhaps half the distance from Brother Emmanuel's house to the hotel, when the man said, You don't want to go to the orphanage?

The woman opened her eyes and shook her head slightly, as if she had been asleep.

Oh, she said. The orphanage. I forgot.

You forgot? How could you forget? It's the whole reason why we're here.

I don't think it's the whole reason. It's *a* reason. And really, who knows why we're here?

I know why I'm here, the man said. I'm here to get our child.

The woman turned away and looked out the window.

Do you really want to go back to the hotel?

The woman did not answer him but continued to gaze out the window.

Sometimes you amaze me, she said.

How?

You're so unempathetic. Do you have any idea what it's like? To feel that I'm cured, or being cured? To think that perhaps I won't die?

I suppose I don't, he said. How can I? How could anyone?

She turned to face him, and her face was flushed with rage.

But you could try! Couldn't you stop for a single moment and try?

I do try, he said. I try all the time. But it's never enough for you. You want me to be something I'm not, to give you something I can't. I'm tired of feeling that I'm failing you. I know how difficult, how impossible, this has been for you but that doesn't make you exempt. It doesn't mean . . .

Mean what?

You could be a little kinder, the man said. A little more patient.

She once again turned away from him and regarded the implacably white landscape they drove past. They traveled for a while in silence, and then she sat forward and reached out and touched the taxi driver gently on his shoulder.

I'm sorry, she said. There's been a mistake. It was my mistake. We don't want to go to the hotel. We want to go to the orphanage. Do you know where it is?

✦

They climbed up the steps of the orphanage but before the man could open the door the woman touched his arm and said, Wait. Please. Just a moment. Aren't you scared?

Scared? he said. Scared of what?

Of seeing—of meeting—the child. Of it finally . . . happening.

No, he said. Why should I be scared?

I'm scared, she said.

Why?

Because what if it's a terrible mistake? What if it's all wrong?

It isn't a mistake and so it can't be wrong.

How do you know?

The man shrugged. I don't know, he said. I just feel it.

I don't, the woman said. I don't feel whatever it is you feel. It's different for me. I mean different from how it was.

How? asked the man

If I'm cured, the woman said. That makes everything different, doesn't it?

How?

How! Really, you ask how?

Yes, said the man. I do. I really ask how. Can we go in? It's freezing out here. He reached out to open the door but the woman grabbed his arm and held it.

No, she said. Be a man. It isn't so cold.

Be a man? The man laughed. What is this? Who are you?

The woman said nothing.

Let go, the man said.

The woman let go of his arm with an abrupt, dismissive gesture as if it had been he who was holding her.

I'm having a hard time keeping up with you, the man said. I'm feeling a little overwhelmed by all this . . .

Overwhelmed? the woman asked.

For lack of a better word, the man said. Yes: over-whelmed. Can we go in now?

You really did think I was going to die, didn't you?

What? asked the man.

You heard me. You thought I was going to die. You had no hope. No faith. For lack of a better word. You resigned yourself to the idea that I was going to die. Didn't you? Tell me. Be honest.

Well, the man said. Given what the doctors told us, given what you yourself told me, given what I know about stage-four cancer, yes, to be honest, yes, I thought you were going to die. Think you are going to die.

So you don't believe in anything outside your scope of knowledge or experience?

I suppose not, said the man. I'm sorry. You asked me to be honest.

So you don't think I could possibly be cured? That I might live?

You might be cured, the man said. Of course, it's possible. But not by that man. Not in that way.

Why? asked the woman. Why not?

How could he possibly cure you? He didn't even know that you are ill.

Of course he knew. Why else would he have come in to see me? There was no other reason for him to come in.

Then why didn't he see you today?

Perhaps because he didn't need to. Perhaps I don't need to see him again. You're being rational, asking these questions. Trying to make sense of it. But it isn't rational. It doesn't make sense.

So it's some kind of miracle? asked the man.

That's all there is for you? Reason or miracles?

I suppose so, said the man. I'm very literal. I have no imagination, or so you have often told me. Remember when we tried to role-play? What a disaster that was?

Yes, the woman said. I remember. You couldn't even pretend to be a chef.

A chef? I thought it was a cowboy.

First it was a cowboy and then it was a chef. You failed at both.

And I fail at this too. Whatever it is that this is.

It's quite clear what this is. It isn't role-playing. It doesn't require imagination. It's very simple. It's my thinking I've been cured. Or rather, my *feeling* that I'm *being* cured.

Yes, the man said. We've established that, so can we please go in now?

Yes, the woman said. We can go in now.

✦

It became clear that the building that now housed the orphanage was once a school—or perhaps still was, for several of the rooms the man and the woman passed as they followed the nurse down a long hallway on the first floor were furnished with rows of desks, and chalkboards hung on the walls. At the end of the hallway the nurse opened a door that revealed a stairway. She held the door open while they passed through it and then led them up the stairway. On the landing a dead tropical plant of considerable height and stature had been removed from its pot and leaned against the tiled wall, exposing the naked dirty ball of its roots. Beside it a large metal bucket of sudsy water hosted some kind of mop. They followed the nurse up the second flight of stairs, where she once again opened a heavy metal door and motioned for them to pass through.

This floor was identical to the one below it, but the rooms were empty. Even the chalkboards had been removed, leaving their ghosts behind on the painted cinder-block walls. Halfway down the hall, outside a door whose glass window was covered with newspaper, the nurse stopped. She turned to the man and the woman and said, You will see your child now. But I remind you that you cannot take him away until three days pass. You understand?

Yes, the man said. But we may visit him, right?

Yes, said the nurse. For an interval of an hour two times a day, once morning and once afternoon. Are you ready now?

Yes, the man said. He reached out and offered his hand to the woman, as if she needed help to enter the room, but she pretended not to notice. She seemed to have removed herself from the situation, acting like a queen visiting a hospital who must not betray any emotion. His hand, reaching out, empty in the air between them, appeared odd, or injured. Because the nurse was watching, he shook it as if it had fallen asleep.

What are you doing? asked the woman, suddenly observant.

My hand fell asleep, the man said.

The nurse opened the door and motioned for the man and the woman to enter the room. The lights were off and the curtains were drawn so it was very dark. The nurse switched on the overhead lights. The fluorescent tubes buzzed angrily for a moment and then flickered alight. There were ten cribs in the large room, placed around its perimeter; three on each side and two at either end. The air in the room was close and slightly fetid. From several cribs crying babies could be heard.

The nurse closed the door and said, Come. Now we will meet your child. She walked across the room and the man and woman followed her. She stopped beside the middle crib along the far wall and said, Here lives your baby.

The sides of the crib were covered with bunting so the man and woman drew close to look down into it. A small child sat upright in the middle of the crib. He was wearing a white ruffled pinafore over a mustard-colored hand-knit sweater and red corduroy pants. On his feet plastic bags covered thick knitted booties. A leather harness that strapped round his waist and over his shoulders was attached by a leash to one of the slats of the crib. Although he was sitting up, he appeared to be in a somewhat somnolent state, staring down at the plastic-covered mattress, which was patterned with a cartoon version of baby lambs frolicking in all directions. A shaggy green alligator whose widely opened mouth exposed many fabric teeth rested upside down at the far end of the crib.

The nurse leaned down into the crib and unsnapped the leash from the harness. She grabbed the child under his arms and hauled him up and out of the crib. She held him for a moment in the crook of her arm so that he faced the man and the woman.

He is good and fat, she said, jouncing the child in her arms. Let me see if he has done bad. She carried the baby over to a table in the center of the room. It appeared to be made of stainless steel and its surface was shining. She sat the baby atop the table and then gently pushed him down so that he was lying on his back.

Come, the nurse commanded them. Come and see.

The man and the woman approached the table and watched as the nurse lifted up the pinafore and pulled off the corduroy pants, beneath which the child wore a cloth diaper, which was very obviously soiled. The nurse uttered a single word in her own language and undid the safety pins that held the diaper in place. She peeled the diaper off the child and briefly examined its contents before folding it and placing it on the far end of the table. One moment while I wash, she said.

She left the couple standing by the table, looking down at the baby. His uncircumcised penis seemed disproportionately large and flushed a deep pink, while the rest of his skin was milky white. It looked like something that had been added to him rather than something that was integrally his. He wore a cap of beautiful blond hair and his eyes were as large and as soft as a dog's, and he appeared to be merrily smiling at them. He had a large purple birthmark on the inside of his right thigh, which seemed to be the price he paid for otherwise being so beautiful.

The nurse had gone over to a sink in the corner of the room and moistened a washcloth beneath the tap. She returned to the table with the cloth and briskly wiped the baby's loins clean, and then patted him dry with another cloth. Then she stood looking down at him, beaming proudly. A nice baby, you think?

Yes, the man said, he is a beautiful baby.

The woman said nothing.

You would like to carry him? the nurse asked. She cradled her arms and rocked an invisible baby by way of example.

The man, who could not imagine picking the baby up so soon, reached down and tenderly touched his cheek, and then gently nuzzled it with the backs of his fingers. The baby tried to grab at his finger and slapped at his hand. The man laughed and took his hand away. He looked at his wife. She stood a step or two away from the table and was looking down at the baby dispassionately, her arms crossed against the front of her parka. She had neglected to remove her hat, a fur-lined leather aviator's cap that had earflaps that could be pulled down and tied beneath her chin but which now somewhat comically stuck straight out on either side of her head.

Take off your hat, he told her.

What? she answered. She seemed submerged inside

herself, which was an affect she often had. He knew it was a way she had of dealing with her pain or her depression, as if to be completely alive and fully engaged with the world only exacerbated her condition. He reached out and pulled the hat from her head. She seemed not to notice the removal of her hat and continued to stare down at the baby on the table.

Touch him, the man said. He reached out and touched the baby as he had done before, and this time the baby seemed surprised by the touch and stopped fidgeting and closed his eyes and lay perfectly still, as if he were an opossum playing dead.

He's quite chubby, isn't he? the man asked. How much does he weigh?

Four, maybe five, said the nurse. Six perhaps.

Pounds?

Pounds? No. Kilos.

The man turned to his wife. How many pounds is that?

I have no idea. She seemed to have roused herself from her stupor, for she stepped forward and leaned down toward the baby. For a moment she only observed him, closely, as if she were nearsighted, and then she picked up his arm and held it for a moment. Then she let it go, so that it dropped down upon the table.

She made an odd sound that might have expressed surprise or disgust and said, His muscle tone seems . . . poor.

Muscle! exclaimed the nurse. We have a baby. Later, the muscles grow. Pick him up! Don't be scared! Hold your little baby!

But the woman had stepped back and once again crossed her arms before her, as if stopping them from somehow independently reaching out to pick up the baby.

To compensate for his wife's behavior, the man reached down and scooped the child up into his arms and held him tightly against his chest. Even through his clothes he could feel the warm weight of the baby. His naked legs were soft and delightfully warm. The man wished that he were naked too, wished he could hold the baby against his naked chest, his beating heart pressed softly against the child's. He closed his eyes. He bent forward and kissed the baby's blond head and inhaled the clean scent of his hair. Then he slightly increased the pressure of his grasp, because he wanted to make sure the baby knew that he was being held.

✦

When the taxi had left the parking lot of the orphanage and driven some distance back toward the town, the man turned to his wife, who was looking out the window.

Why were you like that? the man said. Why didn't you pick him up?

She shrugged, but the motion was almost lost inside her cocoon of clothes.

It seemed perverse, he surprised himself by saying.

That made her turn and look at him—perhaps that's why he had said it.

Perverse! What are you talking about?

To come so far, to come all this way, and then not pick him up. To drop his arm like that.

I'm sorry I didn't respond the way you wanted.

No, said the man. Don't be sorry. Just tell me why. Why did you respond like that?

I don't know. It just seemed so . . . odd.

Odd? How odd?

So random. I didn't feel connected to him.

Well, of course you didn't! We were seeing him for the first time. How could you feel connected?

But you did. I could tell. When you held him—you felt connected.

Yes, because I was holding him. That's why you should have held him. It was amazing—what it felt like, holding him.

That's why I didn't pick him up, the woman said. Because I knew even if I was holding him, I wouldn't feel anything. I'd just be holding him and feeling nothing. And I couldn't bear that.

But you don't know. How can you know that?

I know, said the woman. Part of what's happening to me—the change I'm feeling—is that I know things like that. Everything is very clear. Apparent. I feel like I know everything.

◆

They found the lobby of the Borgarfjaroasysla Grand Imperial Hotel uncharacteristically populated when they entered it. A large group of about twenty people occupied several of the archipelagoes of chairs and tables at the far end of the lobby just outside the closed restaurant. They ranged in age from very young to very old, but all were dressed in colorful and shiny finery. While the children raced round and round the chairs and screamed, the adults were occupied with bottles of champagne that lounged in silver buckets on several of the tables. It was obviously a celebration of some sort.

All hail the conquering heroes! cried Livia Pinheiro-Rima, striding toward them from the opposite direction. That's what you are—rushing all over this dismal town in this freezing weather! You deserve medals, really you do! Come and sit down and get warm. I'll ask Lárus to make us a nice pot of tea. Or would you rather some schnapps?

Tea is fine, said the woman. Tea would be lovely.

Then tea it is, said Livia Pinheiro-Rima. No, don't sit there—it's draughty by the door. Come over to my cozy little corner by the bar. It's ever so much warmer over there. *Sans parler d'intime.*

The man and the woman followed Livia Pinheiro-Rima to the corner outside the entrance to the bar. She helped them out of their coats and got them settled into two of the club chairs.

I'll be back in a minute, she said. With a nice hot pot of tea. She parted the red beads and disappeared into the bar.

We don't have to have tea with her, the man said. Do you want to go back up to the room? Are you tired?

No, said the woman. I'm tired but I'd love some tea. And I find her interesting. She was very good to me last night. And besides, we can't leave now, while she's getting the tea.

The man sighed but said nothing. He was beginning to find Livia Pinheiro-Rima's attention a little exhausting, not to mention suspect. He looked around the lobby. The large celebratory party was entering the grand dining room.

His wife appeared to be sleeping, slumped back in the deep chair, her head lolling to one side. Her face, bathed in the dim light glowing softly out of the golden sconces on the wall behind them, looked fuller and softer than he had seen it in a very long while. Her cheeks, which had been sunken and gaunt for so long, were actually convex, and he resisted an urge to reach out and touch her for fear of waking or disturbing her.

Was it possible that she had really been cured? Or changed in some way?

He must have fallen into a daze for a moment, and then suddenly Livia Pinheiro-Rima was there, gently lowering a large silver tray onto the table. On it was a small brass samovar and three brass cups.

This is a lovely white Darjeeling, she said. It's similar to white peony tea from China, but it's from India. She sat down and filled the cups from the samovar's spout and placed one before each of them. You can't tell from these cups, but it's the most unusual color—a sort of clear chartreuse. She picked up her cup of tea, held it beneath her nose for a moment and closed her eyes, and then took a sip. She opened her eyes and returned the cup to the table. It's heaven, she said. Not heavenly—no. Actual heaven. Try it, she said to the man. You must sip it, like a bird. She nodded at the woman. Is she sleeping? she whispered.

Yes, said the man. She's exhausted.

Poor dear, said Livia Pinheiro-Rima. I was really worried, the night you arrived. There seemed to be hardly anything left to her! But you know, she looks better than she did. Of course, women's lib and all that nonsense notwithstanding, any woman feels inordinately better wearing a dress. Especially a Balenciaga.

She likes the dress, the man said. She won't take it off.

Of course she won't, said Livia Pinheiro-Rima. It will keep her alive, that dress: She'll gain some weight and fill it out and look like Romy Schneider.

She thinks she's been cured, the man said.

I'm not asleep, the woman said. She opened her eyes and then leaned forward and picked up the little cup of tea. So it's heaven, is it?

It is, said Livia Pinheiro-Rima. But taste it. I doubt you'll agree.

Why do you say that?

Because I think your spectrum is rather narrow.

My spectrum? What do you mean?

Your capacity to enjoy and appreciate life.

And I suppose your spectrum is wide?

In fact it is, said Livia Pinheiro-Rima. Despite my great age. Or perhaps because of it.

The woman lifted the cup of tea to her lips and sipped.

It's odd, she said, but I like it. She took another sip and then returned the cup to the table.

No one said anything for a moment and then Livia Pinheiro-Rima softly clapped her hands together and said, So! It was quite a day for you, I imagine. I want to hear all about it.

Really? said the woman. That's odd.

But of course I do, said Livia Pinheiro-Rima. Why would it be odd?

Because it's really none of your business, is it? The woman said this kindly, without a trace of malice, and for a moment neither the man nor Livia Pinheiro-Rima responded. Then Livia Pinheiro-Rima smiled. She leaned forward and took one of the woman's hands into her own, and then rested her other hand on top of it, as if she were making a hand sandwich. The man was surprised to see that his wife did not withdraw her hand but allowed it rest between Livia Pinheiro-Rima's hands.

Oh, my dear, she said. I wasn't attacking you. Quite the opposite, in fact. Your soul has spilled into mine. Of course it concerns me. She held the woman's hand between her own and stared intently at her.

Perhaps she is the healer, the man thought. She has some power. Even he felt it.

After a moment, the woman withdrew her hand from between Livia Pinheiro-Rima's hands and stood up.

I'm tired, she said. I'm going up to the room to take a nap. It's been a tiring day. Exhausting, in fact. I'm sure my husband will tell you all about it.

Do you want me to come up with you? the man asked his wife.

No, she said. Stay here with your friend. She walked, a bit unsteadily, through the crowded field of tables and chairs and up the steps to the elevator, where she could no longer be seen.

After a moment Livia Pinheiro-Rima said, She's overwrought, poor thing.

Should I go up to her? asked the man.

No. Drink your tea. Sit quietly. Talk, or don't, as you please.

The man picked up his cup and took several sips of the tea and then replaced the cup on the table.

The man closed his eyes. He could sense Livia Pinheiro-Rima sitting across from him, waiting.

Do you know the Norwegian? he asked. The businessman who's always lurking about here in his suit?

Yes, of course, said Livia Pinheiro-Rima. I know everyone. But he's Dutch. What about him?

I slept in his bed last night, said the man.

Did you?

Yes, said the man. I did. I got mugged last night. Mugged and robbed.

What an exciting night you had: violence and romance. Tell me all about it.

It wasn't romance, said the man.

I'll be the judge of that. Tell me. Start at the beginning. With Adam and Eve in the garden.

The man told her what happened the night before. How he had been mugged in the toilet of the restaurant. How the businessman had rescued him and brought him back to the hotel.

Wasn't that nice of him? said Livia Pinheiro-Rima. To clean you up and put you to bed. I'd give anything to be cleaned up and put to bed. So you slept with him?

Yes, said the man.

I meant did you fuck with him, said Livia Pinheiro-Rima. Pardon my French.

No! said the man. I'm not gay.

Oh, come, said Livia Pinheiro-Rima. I wouldn't be too sure about that. Everyone's at least a little homosexual. And I'd say you're more than a little. I've thought that from the moment I first saw you.

How?

The timid way you entered the bar and the way you looked around, as if you were lost, or didn't belong.

I didn't feel either of those things, said the man. And I believe straight men can feel lost or timid.

They can, but they exhibit it differently. And being lost and not belonging are two very different things. Except perhaps for gay men. And women, too, of course.

You're crazy, the man said. He picked up his cup and saw that it was empty. He held it out toward Livia Pinheiro-Rima, who took it and filled it from the samovar. The samovar was old-fashioned; it had an ornate silver spigot with a flower-shaped handle that twisted open and closed. She returned the cup to him and watched him sip from it.

After a moment the man said, She thinks she's cured.

Yes, said Livia Pinheiro-Rima. So you've told me. And so has she. She told me that last night when I brought her her supper. It was quite beautiful.

Beautiful?

Yes, beautiful. The terrorful kind of beauty.

But she can't be cured. It's impossible.

Of course it's possible. Why wouldn't it be possible?

Well, medical science, for one thing, said the man.

Medical science has failed her. So it doesn't really figure in anymore, does it?

I suppose not. For her. But for me—

But this isn't about you.

So you think I should encourage her? Pretend I believe it?

Yes, of course. What would be the point in contradicting her?

I don't know, said the man. We've always been honest with each other.

That sounds rather dreary, said Livia Pinheiro-Rima.

You think honesty is dreary?

No. Honesty itself is fine—but my God! Not all the time! Honesty can be very unkind. And damaging. And that's at

148

the best of times. You have got to do everything possible to smooth the way for your wife. Whatever that way is. And that is for her to decide, not you. That is your job now.

Then why did you taunt her?

Because I'm not you. You have your job and I have mine.

What's your job?

Don't you worry about my job, said Livia Pinheiro-Rima.

I'm not worried, said the man. I just wondered.

Wondering, worrying—call it whatever you like. You should return to your wife. Enough time has passed so it will not seem you are running after her.

We saw the child today, the man said.

What do you mean by the child?

The baby that we have come here to adopt.

Well, then, isn't it your baby? Your son, your daughter?

It's a boy, said the man. A son.

The child, a boy, a son—how vague you are. Don't you have a name for him?

Maybe. We were thinking Simon. But we wanted to wait, to see him first, before we decided.

And now you have seen him. Is he Simon?

Yes, said the man. I think he is.

Is it a family name?

Simon? No.

Then why Simon?

Because it's unadorned. So simple. You know—Simple Simon.

Met a pie man going to the fair. But I hope you know that Simon wasn't simple in the way that means uncomplicated. He was simple in the dim-witted way.

Are you sure?

I'm very sure.

Well, you've ruined that name for us. The man stood up. Thank you for the tea.

You're welcome. And don't listen to me. Name him Simon if you like. It's a lovely name. It *is* unadorned. And it's very good to have names that alternate vowels and consonants. They have a solidness, an equilibrium that other names lack. Like Livia.

Well, said the man. We'll keep all this in mind.

Go up to your wife. But don't pretend I have driven you away. I know I amuse you. And comfort you, perhaps.

The man found that he was too tired to formulate a response to this claim. So he merely leaned down and kissed Livia Pinheiro-Rima's cheek, and then left her sitting there alone with the samovar and the tea that was heaven.

✦

The room was dark and his wife lay asleep on the bed, on top of the coverlet. She had not closed the drapes and so the dark winter light from outside made it possible to see. He stood for a while in the center of the room, watching his wife. Why did he always think she was feigning sleep? Because it was a way of displacing him, keeping him out.

Once, not long after they had been married, he dreamed that he was pregnant, and could feel the baby growing inside him, oddly enough not in his belly, but higher up, near his chest, in his lungs. And the next day she had told him that she was pregnant, and he felt certain that that knowledge had passed between them while they were sleeping. So at one point sleep had connected, rather than separated, them.

That was the first, and most heartbreaking, of their several failed pregnancies, and the only one that he had mysteriously intuited.

He drew the curtains and undressed in the dark and lay down beside his wife on the bed. He lay as close as he could to her without actually touching her.

◆

The woman awoke in utter darkness. For a moment she did not know where she was, and then she remembered. Her husband was holding her, pressed tightly against her. They were both lying on top of the coverlet. It was cold in the room except for the sliver of warmth spread between them; perhaps it was the chill that had drawn them together.

She lay very still and felt her husband holding her. Obviously in sleep her body had tolerated or perhaps enjoyed his intimate proximity, but now that she was awake it chafed her. She tried to lie still and fall back into the comfort and warmth of his embrace, but something had changed, and she unclasped his hands from the girdle they had formed around her waist and shifted slightly away from him. He woke, and quickly sat up, as if there were some sort of emergency—a fire, a sick child, a call to arms. He sat there for a moment and then reached out and found the lamp switch in the darkness and turned it on. He looked back over his shoulder at her and said, I was holding you.

What?

Just now—while we were sleeping—I was holding you.

She looked at him curiously and stood up. She went into the bathroom and shut the door.

He heard the pipes squeal as she opened the faucets and then the water crashing into the bathtub. She must have filled the tub completely, because the sound of the water went on for quite some time. Then it stopped. He waited a moment, until he was sure she had lowered herself into the tub, and then knocked on the bathroom door.

Yes? she called.

May I come in?

Of course, she said.

He pushed open the door and entered the steamy bathroom. She was lying in the huge tub, the water covering everything but her head, which she chin-lifted out of the water, like a child in a swimming class.

He sat down on the closed toilet. Sitting there, behind her, he felt like a shrink. Some of his best time—his most intensely alive moments—had been spent lying on his analyst's couch, revealing to the unseen presence behind him the secret truths about himself. This was a good setup for analysis, he thought, for surely lying naked in a tub of warm water could only foster a greater feeling of safety, and a subsequent ability to uncover and speak the truth. For a moment he wished, or wanted, his wife to start talking, putting words to all the things that were either misunderstood or unsaid. But she said nothing. The only sound was the water gently moving to accommodate her slight body.

Neither of them said anything for a few minutes and then she slightly raised herself out of the water and turned her head around to see him. She looked at him for a moment and then turned away as her body sank back into the tub.

You don't need to use the toilet?

No, he said.

Oh, she said. Then why . . .

Why what?

Why did you come in?

To be with you, he said. To talk to you.

Oh, she said. About something in particular?

Yes, he said. About the baby. About Simon.

Simon? You've decided?

Yes, he said.

Oh, she said. And then, after a moment, I don't think he's a Simon.

Then who is he?

An abandoned, unwanted baby.

I want him. You don't want him?

No. To be honest. That's why I was how I was—I realized right away I didn't want him.

But you did want him. And he's ours. So why don't you want him now?

I've changed. When I thought I was going to die I wanted him for you. But something . . . amazing has happened.

You're still going to die, he thought. He had his eyes closed but he heard the disturbance of the water and knew that she must have moved her body or touched it.

My whole body feels different, she said. It is at peace with itself. And if this miracle happened, why can't another?

What do you mean?

I mean perhaps I can get pregnant. Perhaps we don't have to adopt a baby. Perhaps we can have our own baby.

Simon is our own baby.

He may be your own baby, but he is not my own baby.

You know that you cannot have a baby. You've had a hysterectomy.

I said a miracle. I said it would be a miracle.

Oh, so you want two miracles now? We're getting greedy.

But don't you see? Every time a miracle happens, the chances for another miracle to happen increase exponentially.

The man said nothing. He watched as she took a bar of soap from the grotto in the tiled wall, dunked it into the bathwater, and began to vigorously suds her arms and legs. This was unusual, for since her illness she always handled her body with extreme tenderness, often wincing when she touched herself.

Do you really think you've been cured?

I do.

It just seems unlikely.

Well, of course it's unlikely! She turned to face him and flung a lacy trail of suds across the pink bathroom floor. But unlikely things happen, don't they? Why are you so resistant to the idea?

I don't know, he said. I'm sorry.

It's because you don't want a distraction. You want to focus on that baby. That's all you think about now. Not me. You want me gone.

That's not true, he said. You know it's not true. I think of you all the time. I was holding you, just before, in bed.

You already told me that. Why do you keep mentioning it?

Because it means something.

What?

It means our bodies still want each other. Belong together.

Holding me while we're asleep doesn't mean anything. Dogs—those dogs that pull sleds in the snow—they hold each other. They burrow into the snow and hold each other tight.

I don't think that's true, the man said. They sleep in the snow, yes, but not together. Each dog sleeps alone. I remember that from *The Call of the Wild*.

He stood up and for a moment he felt horribly dizzy, as

if he might faint, so he reached out and held on to the sink, steadying himself.

The woman turned and looked at him. Are you all right?

After a moment he said, Yes. Just dizzy. And hungry. I'm going down to the bar to get something to eat. Do you want to join me?

No.

Should I bring you something back?

I'd like some yoghurt, she said. I don't suppose you could find some?

I'll try, he said. There's a market around the corner. Anything else?

Oh, there's lots I want.

Anything that I might be able to get you?

No, she said. There is nothing that I want that you could get me. Besides the yoghurt.

Are you sure? he asked. I might surprise you.

Well, I'd like a perfectly ripe peach and an orchid and some balsam incense and a kitten. I think I might be truly happy if I had those things. With me in the bathtub. Well, maybe not the kitten.

So you're sending me on a treasure hunt. Shall I also bring you a goose that lays golden eggs?

I'd like that very much, she said. Can you imagine how lovely they would be? Golden goose eggs? So warm. I wouldn't sell them. No. I'd put them up, inside myself, where it's empty now. Golden eggs. I'm sure I'd have a baby then. A beautiful, golden baby.

Lárus was not tending the bar. His absence surprised the man, who, although he knew it was impossible, believed that Lárus never left the bar.

The present bartender was an alarmingly blond woman who wore a tuxedo that fit her with a punishing tightness. She appeared to be unhappy about this, or something else.

A very attractive older couple—seventies, the man thought—sat at the far end of the bar. They were both elegantly and impeccably dressed—the man in a tuxedo and the woman in a long, fitted dress of midnight-blue silk covered by a little jewel-encrusted bolero jacket. She wore a small velvet hat the same color as her dress; a black veil lifted away from her face and perched atop the hat. She held an unlit cigarette in her gloved hand; the man leaned close and whispered avidly into her ear.

The man sat down near the door and when the bartender approached him, brandishing a cocktail napkin, he proudly told her which three small plates he would like to have. And schnapps.

The elegant couple left the bar while the man ate his motley supper. They spoke French, and seemed to be in very high spirits, and the man had the feeling they were going out to some glamorous and splendid event—a first night at the opera, a banquet in honor of a visiting dignitary. But could such an event be happening anywhere in this dreary and frozen little city? As far as the man knew there was no opera house or art museum, no cathedral, no palace, no casino, and he had a wild urge to get up and follow the couple.

After they had left he asked the bartender if there was an opera house in the city, for he felt sure that was the glamorous couple's destination. But the bartender seemed not to understand him, or at least the words *opera house*, so he asked about a theater and she said yes, and then, *Amour?* and the man, supposing that she was alluding to the romance of opera, nodded enthusiastically, and the bartender smiled and hastened behind the upholstered door and returned a moment later with a small piece of pink paper which featured a black-and-white photograph of a woman with enormous breasts above the following words:

XXX Cine Paris Eros XXX
19 Kujanpääntie

50% réduction
avec ce billet

toujours ouvert
"cum anytime"

When the man had finished his meal he left the hotel and ventured around the corner to the little market. The large window that looked out onto the street was completely fogged over, and a long leather strip encrusted with silver bells jangled as he opened the door. Inside it was very bare and bright, and he was disappointed to find the market was the type where everything is stored on shelves behind the counter, and one must ask the shopkeeper to fetch the desired items. What an absurd arrangement, the man thought. He remembered that in the drugstore of the puritanical New England town he grew up in, the pornographic magazines were kept behind the counter, in a rack with their covers obscured, and just the names visible, so that one was forced to ask the druggist or his matronly wife for *Playboy* or *Penthouse* or *Oui*. In his boyhood he could not imagine anyone ever being brazen enough to do that, and so felt his first inkling of the amazing power of sex.

Another reason he was remembering the drugstore of his youth: the shopkeeper was wearing a white jacket with a Nehru collar, identical to the one that Mr. Pasternak, his hometown pharmacist, had worn. This costume, and the brilliant fluorescent lighting that antiseptically illuminated the white linoleum floor and counter, made the market feel more like a clinic, a place where things more delicate and dangerous than the purchase of groceries occurred. The man wished he could turn around and leave the store to avoid the inevitable humiliation of trying to purchase any of the things his wife wanted in this intimate way, but he decided to embolden himself.

Good evening, he said, as he approached the counter, which was unnervingly bare, except for a very old-fashioned cash register, as if a medical operation might possibly be performed upon it.

The shopkeeper nodded in acknowledgment of the man's greeting.

Do you have yoghurt? the man asked. And then, deciding that an imperative would be more effective than a question, he said, I would like some yoghurt.

Plain or fruit? Big or small?

Big, said the man. Fruit.

With Gummi?

Gummi?

Candy bear, said the shopkeeper.

Oh, said the man. No. No Gummi.

The shopkeeper nodded and disappeared back into the aisles of shelves behind the counter. He returned after a moment and placed a large glass bottle of deep purple yoghurt on the counter, equidistant between himself and the man, and said, You want many things?

No, said the man. Just a few. Do you have a peach?

In tin, said the shopkeeper. You want?

No, said the man. The kitten and the orchid, of course, were out of the question, but the man wondered if he might venture to ask about the balsam incense. What a triumph it would be to return with that! It would be almost as precious as the golden-egg-laying goose.

Do you have any incense? Balsam, if you have it.

Balsam?

Fir, said the man. Pine. Christmas tree. *Tannenbaum.* He raised his index fingers in the air and outlined the kind of Christmas tree a child first learns to draw.

No, said the shopkeeper. We have no tree.

No, no, said the man. Not a tree. The smell of the tree. Incense. Or a candle. But with a smell. He sniffed vehemently several times.

Ah, yes. I know now. The shopkeeper once again disappeared into the shelves and returned with a small packet of tissues, which he balanced carefully atop the jar of yoghurt. *Paperinenäliina*, yoghurt. More?

No, said the man. Nothing more.

✦

When he returned to the hotel room his wife was sleeping. He decided not to wake her. He drew back the thick drape and placed the jar of yoghurt on the windowsill, close to the frozen windowpane, and then pulled the drapes together again. He thought about getting in bed beside his wife and trying to fall asleep, but he knew he was not ready to sleep. He felt unusually awake and wondered if the drug the businessman had given him the night before had been tranquilizing him all day and had finally worn off.

✦

The man sat in the lobby for most of the evening, drinking schnapps. A woman dressed like a prostitute came and sat beside him for a while, saying nothing, just smoking a cigarette and suggestively crossing and uncrossing her stout legs.

Twice she asked him for the time—*Do you have the time?*—and twice he told her he did not. After his second disavowal she got up and went into the bar, but she reemerged moments later. Would you like a man? she asked. With me or alone. It is the same price. He told her he did not want a man. She acknowledged his lack of desire with a sigh and sad nod, but remained standing there in front of him, as if trying to think of something else that might entice him. But after a moment, apparently stumped, she shrugged and returned to the bar.

Soon after that encounter, feeling pleasantly smoothed by the several glasses of schnapps, he returned to the hotel room. His wife was sitting up in bed reading *The Dark Forest*. She looked up from her book and watched him as he undressed.

Tomorrow morning I want to go see Brother Emmanuel, she said. I want to go alone. I think it's better that way. I know you're skeptical and so I think it's better you're not there. I'm sorry.

No, he said. I understand. It's fine.

I'll go to the orphanage with you, she said. In the afternoon. But in the morning I'd like to see Brother Emmanuel.

That's fine, he said. Do whatever you'd like. I'm tired.

You've been drinking?

Yes, he said.

With your friend?

No. I've been drinking alone. Well, a prostitute joined me for a while.

Was she pretty? Were you tempted?

No, the man said.

No she wasn't pretty or no you weren't tempted?

No to each, he said.

Because I wouldn't mind, you know. In fact I'd be happy for you.

You'd be happy for me if I slept with an ugly prostitute?

Well, no—not happy. I'd be relieved. You know how bad I feel about our sexual life. That's why I'd be relieved if you slept with a prostitute. I realize it's selfish of me. I feel bad about that too.

Well, don't worry. I won't sleep with an ugly prostitute just to please you. He went into the bathroom and looked at his face in the mirror. He had never slept with a prostitute—not so much from lack of desire; it was the negotiations and transactions that stopped him. He couldn't imagine successfully navigating them. For a moment he thought perhaps he should go back down to the lobby and sleep with the prostitute as a sort of learning, confidence-building exercise, and if it made his wife happy so much the better. And it might be his last chance—he wouldn't feel right doing it when he was a father.

The woman had turned out the lights. He thought about mentioning the yoghurt hiding behind the drapes but decided it was best left till morning. He felt his way around to the far side of the bed and slid in beneath the coverlet. His wife did not acknowledge his arrival in the bed. He lay there for a moment and then said, Are you awake?

Yes.

I'm sorry you think I'm skeptical. I do support you.

But equivocally, she said.

I'm sorry. I wish I could support you in the way you need, but it seems wrong to pretend what I don't feel. Would it be better if I did?

Of course it would, said the woman. It means nothing to me, it doesn't help me, your honesty. It hurts me.

Honesty again—the man did not understand it. I want to help you, he said. But I want to be honest with you too. Otherwise I don't think I can be any help to you.

I suppose that's the really sad thing, the woman said. The thing that really does separate us.

What?

That you want to be honest with me.

I don't understand, said the man. If you don't want me to be honest, tell me. And I won't be.

No, said the woman. That's what's sad. I don't want to have to tell you how to be, because then you aren't being yourself, you're being who I tell you to be, and that's meaningless. I'd rather you be yourself and hurt me than pretend to be someone else.

The man said nothing. What could he say? He felt angry and tired and condemned. Her tenacity, which he had once admired, for he felt it made up for a strength he lacked, now overwhelmed him. She had sued the law firm where she worked when she was not made a partner, claiming discrimination based upon her health status, for her illness and its treatment had prevented her from working very much in the last year or two. The case was settled out of court and she had won a very large settlement, and now she seemed to battle everything in the same way.

He realized he wished she were dead.

He turned away from her and faced the wall. After a moment he heard and felt his wife shift in the bed and turn toward him. And then he felt her hand on his shoulder, pressing against it as if she were supporting herself.

I'm sorry, she said. I know I'm making things impossible for you. I would stop myself if I could. But I can't. Something—some kind of self-control—has left me. Of course everything is leaving me, but that has gone first. She turned away from him and began to weep.

His meanness stopped him from turning toward her, holding her. And every second he did not do it made it more difficult to do. And then, suddenly overcome with tenderness and shame, he turned and reached out and pulled her back against his body and held her tightly. After a while she stopped crying and pushed herself back against him. Her body had lost all of its voluptuousness and weight, and so it felt almost like nothing. To make it more real he slid his hand inside her silk underwear and cupped it gently between her legs, feeling the soft warmth there. They both felt him growing hard.

She reached down and moved his hand away.

Sorry, he said.

No, she said. I meant . . . She reached behind her and

held his penis in her hand and felt it swelling, like an animal that was alive, and shifted herself closer to him, and fitted herself onto him. She heard him gasp, or sigh, and he held her tighter and fucked in the gentlest way, rocking against her, and moved both his hands onto her breasts, and she felt the somewhat rough skin of his palms encasing them, and he turned his head sideways and laid it against the back of her head so that his mouth was near her ear, and she heard him say, I love you, I love you, I love you, in time to his timid thrusts, and she reached behind and grasped his buttock and pulled him more tightly into her, and rocked back against him, thinking of the golden eggs, the beautiful golden eggs he was planting inside her.

FOUR

The woman left immediately after breakfast to see Brother Emmanuel.

The taxi driver, a woman, wore a man's fur-collared overcoat atop a flannel nightgown. Her head was studded with metal curlers over which she wore a net beaded with bejeweled butterflies.

Could we make two stops? the woman asked. Could you take me two different places?

Not at once, the driver said.

No! Of course not. I meant take me one place and then wait and then take me to another. I'll pay you for the time I wait.

The time I wait! All life is waiting.

I want to go to the orphanage. And then to Brother Emmanuel's. Do you know these places?

Of course, said the driver. I know all places.

Good, said the woman. Then please take me. The orphanage first.

The driver put the car into gear and slowly accelerated. She gripped the steering wheel tightly with both of her hands and leaned her whole body forward, so that her bosom pressed itself against the wheel, and peered intently out at the snow-covered road that tunneled before them. She maintained the same exact slow speed, as if there were a bomb in the car and any acceleration or deceleration would cause it to detonate.

The woman remembered driving with her parents as a child and passing a long line of cars moving very slowly, with their headlights on. She asked why they were driving like that and her father told her it was a funeral cortege and that all the cars were driving to a cemetery to bury a dead body. Wait, he said, and in front of all the cars, the first car in the line will be big and black and look different from any car you've ever seen. And he had been right, and for the longest time after that the woman thought her father had called the procession of cars a corsage, and she always thought it was odd that a word could mean two very different things. But she knew that flowers figured in both death and burial and in dances and galas so perhaps there was a link after all.

When the taxi had stopped in front of the orphanage the woman leaned forward and said, You will wait?

Yes. For one hour, not more.

Oh, I'll be much quicker than that, said the woman.

Go, said the driver. I wait.

So the woman got out of the taxi and entered the orphanage. The vestibule was empty. She waited for a moment and was about to push the bell beside the inner doors when one of them opened. The nurse they had seen the previous day was now wearing knit slacks and a ski jacket. Good morning, she said.

Hello, said the woman. I'm—

I know who you are. You are here to see your baby? Does your husband come too?

No, said the woman. This morning I come alone.

Men! They are always like that. Come, and we will go see your baby.

✦

Several babies were wailing when they entered the room upstairs. The woman asked the nurse—or whatever she was—if she could take the baby into another room, so she might be alone with him, in a quiet place.

Yes, said the nurse. We have a room for such a visit. We take your baby there. She reached down and unhitched the leash from the harness the baby wore and hoisted him out of the crib. He is fat one, she said. Full of health. Let us give him new cloth, and he will be clean for you.

May I do it? the woman asked.

You want?

Yes, said the woman. I would like to change him.

If you want, good. We go here. The nurse carried the child over to the changing table and laid him down. Then she stepped away and indicated with one arm that she had relinquished control. The woman stepped closer and leaned over the child and lowered her head so that her face almost touched the baby's face. She closed her eyes and inhaled the complex smell, which was layered, like those perfumes that are made of musk or civet, and had a dark, fungal base. She breathed it in deeply.

She wished she had a memory for scents.

It wasn't until she had removed the pinafore and overalls that she remembered he wore old-fashioned cloth diapers. She was less sure about how to handle these and worried she might prick his skin with the safety pins. But she did not. The new diaper she put on him was not as tightly or elegantly affixed as the one she had replaced, but the nurse, after adjusting one of the pins, nodded her approval.

Is it time for him to be fed? the woman asked.

Oh no, said the nurse. He had his bottle before.

Oh, said the woman.

You would like to feed him?

Yes, said the woman. If it won't be bad for him.

It doesn't hurt. He is always hungry. Fat boy. Let me get bottle. Pick him up, she said. Hold him.

The woman picked up the baby and held him against her, one arm on his back and the other holding his head. She began to jounce him gently but apparently he did not like this for he began to cry. She stopped the jouncing. He continued to cry. The woman held him a little more tightly and murmured to him. Baby, baby, baby, good baby, good baby, baby, baby, baby . . .

He was still crying, but less determinedly, when the nurse returned with the bottle. Come, she said. I take you now to place for visit.

The woman followed the nurse out of the room and down the hall. The nurse opened a door and turned a light on. This room was much smaller than the other rooms the woman had seen. It contained a cluttered desk and metal bookshelves crowded with cardboard and plastic boxes. Also, a wooden rocking chair on gliders with gold-and-brown-plaid tweed cushions.

The woman sat down in the gliding chair and the nurse handed her the bottle.

The woman held it but did not offer it to the baby. It was made of glass and was warm.

Feed him!

May I be alone? the woman asked. I would like to be alone with him.

Alone with your little one, said the nurse. I understand.

Thank you, said the woman.

He is good baby, said the nurse. Already he love his mama. She turned and left the room, closing the door behind her.

When the woman was sure the nurse had moved away from the door, she put the bottle on the desk, stood up, and turned off the fluorescent overhead light. It was dark in the little room, but some light shone through the window in the door. The woman retrieved the bottle and sat back down in the chair. She slowly lowered it toward the baby's mouth and gently pressed the amber nipple against his lips. He stopped crying, and his lips parted. He began sucking.

As he nursed he stared directly at her, as if the flow of milk were dependent upon maintaining constant eye contact. Every few moments he would lift one of his fists toward her face.

He drank about two thirds of the bottle and then stopped abruptly and pushed it away from his mouth with one of his hands.

No more? the woman asked. She put the bottle on the desk and lifted the baby and held him against her and patted his back. She wondered, Was it a mistake for me to come and see the baby? Not for him, but for me? I wish I still had my old body, my complete body. I understood that body. I fit perfectly inside it. Even if it is a mistake, I was right to come. Whatever happens, it will matter that I have held him like this.

She felt him fall asleep while she held him. She stopped patting his back. She lowered her mouth so that she could speak directly into his ear.

I'm sorry, she said, but you can't be mine. But you will be his. All his. You must love him and take care of him. Many things he will do wrong but the important things he will do right. So try not to judge him, or blame him. As I have. If we are doing the wrong thing, a bad thing, a selfish thing, forgive us. It was my idea, so forgive me. I know how alone he is. He needs you.

Baby, baby, baby. Good baby.

♦

An hour later, the woman arrived at Brother Emmanuel's. She paid the driver and walked up the front steps as the taxi rolled slowly away. She pressed the bell.

After a moment the door swung open and Brother Emmanuel's helpmate stood inside the open door.

Ah, she said. You've come back.

I have, said the woman. May I come in?

All are welcome here. She opened the door wider and stood aside.

The woman entered the house of Brother Emmanuel. The helpmate shut the door and helped her take off her parka.

What is your name? the woman asked. You know my name and you have been so kind to me. I would like to know your name.

My name is Darlene.

She held the woman's coat folded over her arm, and held her arms close to her body, and by embracing her coat, the woman felt that Darlene was symbolically embracing her.

Well, said Darlene. So you have come again.

Yes, said the woman. I have come again. I have come

to see Brother Emmanuel, but if he cannot see me, I would like to stay here a little while. I feel safe here.

Safe? Safe from what?

Safe from my body, the woman said. Safe from the world.

Then please come and sit down. Would you like some tea?

Oh, I would, said the woman. I would. Thank you!

Go and sit near the fire. I will get the tea. She indicated the opened doors into the sitting room and disappeared through one of the doors beneath the stairs.

The woman stood in the hall for a moment, forgoing and anticipating the relief and pleasure she would feel upon entering the sitting room, for she realized it was there, in that bright and warm and fragrant room, that she had felt at peace with the world, and not been made to suffer it.

✦

After the man helped his wife into the taxi and watched it drive away, he returned to the lobby and sat in one of the club chairs. Someone had left an in-flight magazine on the table before him with a photograph of Peggy Fleming on the cover. Peggy Fleming? Out of curiosity he picked up the magazine and leafed through it, but he could find no mention or photographs of Peggy Fleming, or any other figure skater, in its pages.

He tossed the magazine back onto the table. It skittered

across the polished surface and disappeared over the far edge. I need to get out of here, he thought.

✦

The man walked in the opposite direction from the restaurant and orphanage, deciding he would turn corners at random until he was lost.

The wind was cruelly blowing the snow directly into his face, and turning corners did nothing to alleviate the problem. So he ducked his head and buried his chin in the folds of the scarf that was swaddled around his throat.

When he had lost all sense of direction and felt well and truly lost, he slowed his pace and began to pay attention to the shops he passed by. A warm golden light shone out of one, and he peered in though the foggy windows: a café, or bar, with a counter and several small tables lined along the walls. The lights were brightly lit and some sort of balalaika-ish folk music leaked into the cold outside air. And then he noticed a huge, fur-shrouded figure sitting at one of the tables, with its back to the windows, and he recognized Livia Pinheiro-Rima's Russian black bear coat. He pushed open the door. The small room was empty except for the single figure hunched over a bowl of what appeared to be steaming soup. Livia Pinheiro-Rima was swaddled in the great coat and wearing a large, complicated fur hat. The man watched as she carefully lifted the soup to her lips, blowing gently upon each spoonful before hurriedly devouring it.

Something about her aloneness and the almost devout attention she paid to her soup made the man feel as if he were intruding upon a private scene. He was about to turn and try to slip back out the door when a woman emerged from the back part of the café through a pair of little swinging doors.

She said something in the native language that the man assumed was a greeting, but there was a harshness to her tone, as if she had been expecting him and he was late.

Livia Pinheiro-Rima laid down her spoon and turned toward the door. Look what the cat drug in, she said. You're a sight for sore eyes. The more the merrier! Then she turned and said something to the woman in the same hectoring tone she used with Lárus. The woman bowed and scuttled back through the swinging doors.

Don't just stand there with your mouth agape, said Livia Pinheiro-Rima. Come sit down. I've told the serving wench to bring you some soup. I'm afraid that's all there is, and we're lucky there's that. You know, don't you, about the trains? The Vaalankurkku Bridge collapsed the other day under the weight of the snow, so no food's been delivered. I suppose we shall all starve before the winter's out.

The man sat down across the table from Livia Pinheiro-Rima. What about the roads? he asked.

Roads? There are no roads. At least not in the winter. The only way to get into or out of this godforsaken place is the train.

So we're all stuck here?

Until the bridge is repaired. Unless you have a sleigh and a team of reindeer.

How long will it take? For them to repair the bridge?

Oh, a few days. Or a few years. One never knows about these things. But in my experience it is always best to take the long view.

But we have to leave, said the man. My wife and I. And the baby. There must be some way to leave. What if there's an emergency? Surely there's a helicopter or something.

I'm sure there is a helicopter or something, said Livia Pinheiro-Rima, but as I have nowhere to go I don't concern myself with the question of leaving. My questions all have to do with staying. Excuse me but I am going to continue to eat my soup while it is hot.

Yes, yes, said the man. Please—go ahead.

Livia Pinheiro-Rima dragged the large silver spoon through the soup. Please, she said. Look away. No one likes to be watched while they are eating soup.

The man looked past her, out through the steamy window. A dog with only three legs hopped down the middle of the street, bucking in and out of the deep snow.

The dog disappeared and the serving wench approached with a bowl of steaming soup, which she carefully placed before the man. She laid a spoon swaddled in a white linen napkin beside the bowl. For a moment the man allowed the fragrant steam to rise up and warm his face. It was a dull khaki color and had an odd pungent odor he tried to find aromatic.

177

What kind of soup is it? he asked.

It's a kind of soup that doesn't have a name, said Livia Pinheiro-Rima. It's soup made from whatever is at hand—drippings and dregs and peelings. Actually, it does have a name. It's called garbage soup.

Garbage? The man put his spoon down.

Oh, don't be so American! Garbage isn't considered dirty here. We throw hardly anything away—it's impossible to get rid of anything with the land frozen solid most of the year. So garbage is thought of differently here. It's what remains, what waits to be reused. Literally. Isn't it delicious?

It's good, said the man. But it has a strange flavor.

And how could it not?

The man put down his spoon. Despite his attempt to convince himself otherwise, it was not a very nice soup at all.

You don't like your soup, do you? asked Livia Pinheiro-Rima.

No, said the man. The only good thing about it is that it's warm.

So eat it up. You've got a long chilly walk back to the hotel.

Is it true about the bridge? I can't believe we're stuck here.

As far as I know it is true, said Livia Pinheiro-Rima.

Everything has gone wrong, the man said.

Everything?

Yes, said the man. Everything. Or everything that matters. Matters to me.

Well, that's not everything. It's not even close to everything.

The man said nothing.

What's gone wrong? Tell me. I mean beyond the ordinary things I already know.

My wife has lost her mind.

How so?

She thinks she's been cured.

Oh—that. Why are you so opposed to the idea? Don't you want her cured?

Of course I do. How can you ask that?

Because I don't understand. If your wife thinks that she has been cured, and you want her to be cured, then what's gone wrong?

But she hasn't been cured. She cannot be cured.

You seem very certain.

I am.

And what, other than ignorance, makes you so sure?

Ignorance of what?

Oh, it's not that you don't know something. It's that you know nothing.

And you do? You think that quack has cured my wife of stage-four uterine cancer?

We're all quacks, you know. Hardly what we pretend to be.

Okay, but do you really think this particular quack has cured my wife?

It's possible. I've witnessed occurrences more miraculous

than that. But what's the point of all this? You wife is either cured or not cured. It all remains to be seen. So what's the point of debating it now?

You're observing from a great distance. It's different for me.

Of course it's different for you. But you asked me what I thought so I told you. Usually when one person asks another person a question it's because they want to know what that person thinks. They are seeking a vantage point different from their own.

I'm sorry, said the man. I do value your opinion. It's just—I don't know. I'm feeling very discouraged. And tired. And defeated.

All the more reason for you to eat your soup. It's a very healthful soup, because it combines so many different ingredients.

I don't like the soup, said the man. I don't want the soup. He tried to push it away from him but the plastic placemat it rested upon prevented him from doing this, and he only succeeded in causing the soup to throw a bit of itself up over the rim of the bowl.

It's all become too much for you, I expect, said Livia Pinheiro-Rima. The baby, and your wife, and the soup.

You're right. It has. Last night I wished she were dead.

Who? You wife or the baby?

My wife. The baby's a boy.

If everyone I wanted to be dead was dead, it would be a very lonely planet, said Livia Pinheiro-Rima. Wanting people dead is one thing. Killing them is something else entirely. And now, if you really aren't going to finish your soup, pass it over here. It's considered sinful to not eat every drop of this soup.

Why?

Because leftover garbage soup *is* garbage. There's nothing to do with it except throw it away. And so it must be eaten.

Can't it be reheated?

No. Don't be ridiculous. Would you like to eat day-old reheated garbage soup?

No, said the man. But then I didn't care for it when it was fresh.

It's a very American thing, isn't it—this thinking one should only eat what one likes?

And it's a very European thing, isn't it—this constant disparagement of Americans?

Touché, said Livia Pinheiro-Rima. And now that I, at least, am warm and fortified, shall we venture out into the snow? I assume you're headed back to the hotel?

Yes, said the man. And then to the orphanage. I'm meeting my wife there at three o'clock.

To pick up your baby?

No. We don't get to do that until tomorrow. And then we have to stay here for another day, in the hotel. And then we can leave.

If the bridge is fixed, said Livia Pinheiro-Rima. But I suppose you will cross that bridge when you come to it.

This time no one answered when the man knocked upon the front doors of the orphanage and so he opened them and stepped into the foyer. He could hear some kind of motor running and a baby's heartrending shrieks. He hoped it was not his—their—baby.

He sat on one of the pews beside the front door. Where was his wife? Had she gone up already, to see their baby? Or was she even later to arrive than he? He decided he would wait there for five minutes and then decide how best to proceed. He leaned his head back against the wall and closed his eyes. A duct just above the front doors blew hot air down upon him, and he found the baked fragrant warmth of it comforting.

A nurse was shaking him. It was a different nurse: her blond hair as artificially colored as the other nurse's had been red, and the man wondered at this. Was there perhaps a need, in this dark, cold place, to illuminate one's life by dyeing one's hair?

You sleep so good, the blond nurse said. Like a piece of wood.

I'm sorry, said the man. He had fallen so deeply asleep so quickly!

You come to see your little lamb? the nurse asked.

Lamb?

Yes, said the nurse. Your baby lamb. Your little lamb cake.

Yes, said the man. I am here to see my baby lamb cake. Is my wife here? I was supposed to meet her here, at three o'clock.

Ah, she a true mama! Come back again! Now mama and papa!

Can I wait for her before we go to see the baby?

You can wait, yes. But only until sixteen hours. No one sees a baby after sixteen hours. It is forbidden.

She left the man sitting alone in the vestibule, and the man knew that if he continued to sit there, in the warm draft, he would fall asleep again, so he stood up and opened the doors and stood on the front steps, hoping that this might hasten the arrival of his wife. But after five minutes of waiting outside in the freezing cold he went back inside the vestibule, thinking, She will get here when she gets here; where I wait has nothing to do with it.

At seven minutes before four o'clock he pressed the button and heard a deep reverberating faraway buzz. After a moment the nurse reappeared. Your wife has come?

She has not, said the man. I don't know what's wrong. But may I go now to see the baby?

Alone? asked the nurse.

Yes. Just to see him.

The nurse looked at her watch, which was pinned to the white cloth covering her bosom. It will only be for minutes, she said.

I know, said the man. I would just like to see him. To hold him.

Then we go, said the nurse. Follow me.

He followed her through the doors, down the hallway, and up the stairs to the second floor. The bucket of water and the mop had been removed but the dead tropical plant remained leaning forlornly against the ceramic tile wall.

He followed the nurse down the hallway and they entered the room with the ten cribs. It was dark inside and the nurse did not turn on the brutalizing overhead lights.

They sleep now, she announced. The little lambs.

The man followed her to his son's crib. He was once again sitting up. With one hand he held the stuffed alligator against the plastic mattress and with the other hand he was tearing the white fabric teeth out of its mouth.

Oh, you bad boy, the nurse said. She reached down and jerked the alligator away from the boy and then bopped him on his head with it, a bit harder than the man would have liked. But the child did not seem to be bothered by it. He lifted up his hands, grabbing for the alligator, which the nurse held cruelly just beyond his reach. Then she tossed it into the neighboring crib, which the man could see contained two very small sleeping infants.

The boy began to cry and continue to grab for the stuffed toy, although it had disappeared. The nurse reached down again and swiftly unbuckled his harness from its leather leash. She picked him up and held him high above the crib and tossed him a few inches into the air and caught him as he fell. The shock of all this stopped, or at least interrupted, his crying. She held him for a moment and then said, Here is your devil lamb.

The man took the baby from her and held him gently against his chest, the baby's heart beating against his own. He felt himself shaking a little—he did not know why— and held the baby tighter so he would not drop him. How terrible that would be, if he dropped the baby! They would probably take the baby away from him. Of course they would. You don't give babies to a man who drops them.

The baby must have felt he was being clutched too tightly for he began to cry, and then to shriek. It was a horrible sound, and the man held the baby out toward the nurse, hoping she would take him and comfort him, but she stepped away and said, Move him. Bum bum bum. She made an up-and-down gesture with her arms.

The man tried to jounce the baby in his arm, but he could not get the motion right and he felt as if he were shaking the baby, who wailed louder. But then the proper motion came to him, and he loosened his grip and jounced the baby gently in his arms. Bum, bum, bum, he said, following the nurse's instructions. After a moment the baby abruptly stopped crying and reached up one of his little hands toward the man's face. The man lowered his face so that the baby could touch his cheek, his nose, and he could suddenly smell his son, a potent odor of damp wool, spring leaves, and shit. He raised the baby upward and kissed him.

It is sixteen hours, said the nurse. I am sorry but you must go.

The man looked at her. One more minute? he asked. Please?

She looked at her watch again and frowned. Two minutes, she said. And then you must go.

Yes, said the man. Thank you. He held the baby close against his face and kissed the baby's warm blond hair. He remained like that, his lips pressed softly against the baby's warm head, trying in some fantastic way to connect them; he wanted his breath to permeate the baby's skin and skull and inhabit his brain like a warm breeze enters a room.

Eventually the nurse held out her arms and said, Give him.

The man handed her the baby, and she replaced him in the crib. Do not be sad, she said. Tomorrow you come and take him with you. You and your wife. Where is your wife?

I don't know, said the man.

But tomorrow she comes?

Yes, said the man. Tomorrow she comes.

Good, said the nurse. Because you cannot take the baby alone.

I can't? asked the man.

No. A baby must have mama and papa. We must see mama; we must see papa.

She was here yesterday, said the man.

Yesterday, today, it does not matter. Tomorrow is the time that matters. Of course she comes. How could she not come to receive her child, her baby lamb?

◆

The woman awoke in what first seemed to be complete silence and darkness, but after a moment she heard the soft pinging of the snow against an unseen window, and slowly the room she was in became less dark.

She was lying on her back in a bed in a small room.

She tried to sit up but found that she couldn't move. I've been put in a straightjacket, she thought, but then realized that the bedclothes had just been tucked with immobilizing tightness around her. She wriggled her arms out from beneath them and then pulled them away.

She sat up. The room seemed less dark now, the few objects revealed like timid animals who had hid themselves at her awakening and were now timidly emerging from their lairs. She got out of the bed and stood in the room, looking around for a lamp or a light switch, but saw neither. It was very cold and her feet were bare on the linoleum floor. She was wearing a long shift-like nightgown that tied with a ribbon around the neck, but the strings were not tied, so the gown slipped off one of her shoulders. She pulled it up and tied a tight, almost-choking bow just below her throat. She stepped toward the window and felt for the split in the curtains and pulled one panel aside. It was completely dark outside and all she could see were kamikaze bits of snow hurling themselves against the glass.

She was not sure where she was—she seemed somehow untethered from herself and her past, and the strange dark room did not offer an anchor. Was she dead? Except for the chill, it felt quite serene. She stood in the center of the room for a period of time she could not measure, and then she heard a noise somewhere outside the door to the room, and footsteps approaching it. She heard the door open behind her and found herself suddenly standing in a rectangle of dim light that appeared on the linoleum floor. She could feel the person who had opened the door standing a few feet behind her, in the doorway, and was aware of the shadow falling onto her back, and beneath her, onto the floor, a dark unfelt embrace.

Was it God?

She turned around to see a man standing in the doorway. Because the light was behind him, at first she could only make out his tall thin silhouette. But then, as if he knew she could not see him, he turned slightly, and the light from the hallway fell so that it revealed his face.

She realized then that it was Brother Emmanuel, but she had not recognized him because he had removed his ecclesiastical costume and was dressed very simply in trousers and a turtleneck sweater.

Please, get back into your bed, Brother Emmanuel said. It's cold. He gestured toward the bed and stepped forward, as if he might help her get back into it, but then stepped back again, afraid, it seemed, of getting too close to her, or the bed.

Only because she was so cold, the woman sat on the bed and carefully drew her legs up from the floor and slid them beneath the bedclothes. Then she lay back and pulled the blankets up around her neck and waited, gazing up at the ceiling, like a child at bedtime. Would Nanny visit her again with supper on a tray?

She heard a noise and turned to see that Brother Emmanuel was dragging a small wooden chair away from the wall. He placed it in the center of the room, a distance from her bed, and sat down on it. She did not understand why he had not drawn the chair closer to her bed. She waited, thinking that he might sense the inappropriateness of his distance from her and move closer, but he did not, so she surprised herself by saying, Will you come closer?

Closer? he asked.

Yes, she said. You're so far away. I can barely see you. This was true: the only light in the room was the light that fell in from the hallway through the open door, and Brother Emmanuel sat on the far side of that light, in shadow.

He waited a moment, and then moved the chair nearer to the bed, placing it exactly in the center of the pool of light.

She looked at Brother Emmanuel carefully for a moment, emboldened by the fact that he was now visible while she was obscured by darkness. She remembered she had come to see him that morning—unless it was longer ago than that; she had no sense of how much time had passed.

What time is it? she asked.

About five o'clock, Brother Emmanuel said.

In the morning?

No. The evening.

Why am I here? she asked. What happened?

You don't remember?

No, she said. I remember coming here, and asking to see you, and waiting—

And nothing else?

No, she said. I remember the fire, the fire in the fireplace.

Yes, said Brother Emmanuel. I'm not surprised. Fire is elemental. We always remember fire.

But what happened?

You became upset, said Brother Emmanuel. We thought you might harm yourself, so we gave you a sedative. You've slept all afternoon. How do you feel?

Cold, she said. I was upset?

Yes, said Brother Emmanuel. Very. You don't remember?

The woman tried to think, tried to remember, but the fire in the fireplace was all she could recall: the heat and sound and energy of it, like something alive, something that belonged outdoors, trapped inside the room.

My husband, she said. I was supposed to meet him at the orphanage this afternoon. Has he come here?

No, said Brother Emmanuel.

What must he think? Where can he be?

Darlene left word for him at the hotel. He knows you are here.

Then why didn't he come?

I don't know, said Brother Emmanuel. Perhaps there are no taxis. The snow is overpowering today.

The snow, the woman said. How can you stand it? Why do you stay here?

In the summer it is beautiful, said Brother Emmanuel. The days are green and golden, and very long.

Yes, said the woman. But still—why don't you go away in the winter?

I like the weather here. In the summer and in the winter. For me it is all beautiful.

Are you from here? asked the woman. Or did you come here?

I came here, said Brother Emmanuel. But what does it matter? There is no need for you to understand me. But we must discuss something.

What?

Brother Emmanuel looked down at his hands, which were folded in his lap. Along with his face they were the only part of him that was exposed, and there was something odd about the way he looked at them, as if they were not his hands but merely a pair of hands he held on his lap.

When he did not speak the woman repeated her question: What?

There has been a misunderstanding, said Brother Emmanuel. You have experienced a delusion.

A delusion?

Yes. If I understand correctly. Did you tell Darlene that you thought I had cured you?

For a moment the woman said nothing. She, too, looked

at the hands folded in his lap. They appeared, for a moment, to be lit from within, but perhaps it was just their opalescent paleness.

She thought: Here is the church, here is the steeple, open the doors, and see all the people . . .

They're like a church, she said. Your hands.

You are wrong to think that I may have cured you, he said. It is impossible. We have not even begun.

You cannot know, she said.

It has not happened, said Brother Emmanuel. People often think that something has happened when nothing has happened. Their desire for it is so great. The body fools itself.

But what is that—for the body to fool itself? Isn't that something happening? How can you say that is nothing? How can you know that is not itself a cure?

You must listen to me, said Brother Emmanuel. You must hear me. I know it is difficult, but you must understand. Otherwise nothing can happen.

But something has already happened! You cannot tell me it hasn't. I feel it! Here, inside me! I know it!

It is only your wanting something to happen that has happened. What I do is not science, but neither is it magic. You must not devalue me. I cannot help you if you have this delusion. And you must not upset yourself again. Please, try to stay calm.

The woman looked back up at the ceiling. She lay quietly for a moment. She thought, If I say nothing, and he says nothing, if we are both silent, nothing can happen.

Nothing will change. I will forever be lying in the bed and Brother Emmanuel will forever be sitting in the chair. And the snow will forever be blowing against the window, at least until summer, when the days become very long. And green and golden.

So I am going to die, she said.

We are all going to die. There is no cure for that.

I know that. I don't want a cure for that. I want a cure for my body. I had a cure for my body, but before it could even begin to work you took it away from me.

What you felt was not a cure.

How do you know? How can you possibly know?

I'm sorry, said Brother Emmanuel. I misspoke. I do not believe that what you felt—or feel—was a cure. At least I do not think it was a cure I had anything to do with.

But why would you say that—even if you don't think I'm cured by you or anyone else, why would you tell me that? Why wouldn't you let me believe it?

Because you came here for my help. And I cannot help you if there is a misconception, a misunderstanding between us. It is not something I do alone. We must do it together. So you see, I had to tell you.

The woman looked at Brother Emmanuel for a moment and then turned her face away, toward the wall. She said nothing.

I'm sorry, said Brother Emmanuel. I'm not saying it is hopeless. I'm only saying that to continue, we must be in accordance with each other.

The woman reached out and touched the wallpapered wall. In the darkness she could not make out the pattern, but she could feel it, repeating itself over and over again all around the room.

Brother Emmanuel rose from his chair and stepped near the bed. He reached out and gently put his hand on hers and pulled it away from the wall. He placed his own palm against the woman's. He held their palms together for a moment, and then placed her hand tenderly upon the counterpane.

May I stay here tonight? the woman asked.

Of course you may. You may stay here as long as you would like.

No, said the woman. I'll leave in the morning. I promise you. But if I could just stay tonight, I'd be grateful. The cold, and the snow outside—I don't think I could bear it.

Stay in bed, said Brother Emmanuel. Are you warm enough? Would you like another duvet? A hot water bottle?

I'm fine, said the woman. It's lovely and warm in this bed. Is it a feather bed?

Yes, said Brother Emmanuel.

It's like sleeping on air. Like floating. Like being dead.

Brother Emmanuel stepped away from the bed. You must be hungry, he said. I will have Darlene bring you some soup.

Brother Emmanuel left the door to the room open, so that the glow from the hallway continued to dimly light the room. The woman lay in bed, waiting for Darlene to bring her some soup. She thought: This is the part of my life when I lie in a strange bed in the middle of nowhere and wait for a woman to bring me soup. It is a part of my life. It may be one of the few remaining parts.

✦

When the man returned to the hotel the clerk at the front desk handed him a small envelope along with his key. The envelope was the size of business card, and inside it was a small piece of paper, folded in half. He unfolded it and read:

> Your wife is recovering from an incident of emotional and physical anguish. Because she must rest she will stay the night. If you wish you may come and see her tomorrow morning.
>
> Emmanuel de Mézarnou

Is everything happening fine for you? asked the clerk.

No, said the man. Everything is happening badly.

I'm so sorry. But it is often the way things happen, don't you agree?

Yes, said the man. I agree. Is there a phone I could use down here?

There is a public phone in the bar. Lárus protects it.

Thank you, said the man. He crossed the lobby and entered the bar. He found Lárus maintaining his stoic vigil.

The businessman sat at the far end of the bar with an alarmingly red cocktail placed before him.

Good evening, the man said.

Why, good evening, said the businessman.

May I use the telephone? the man asked Lárus.

Telephone?

Yes. The concierge told me there was a telephone here I might use.

Of course, said Lárus. He bent down and when he rose he was holding a large black Bakelite telephone, the kind the man remembered being in the front hall of the house he grew up in. It sat upon a perpetually gleaming Hitchcock console table. A Windsor chair stood beside the table, guaranteeing that telephone conversations were brief. Other families had white or green or brown telephones hanging on the wall in the kitchen and on tables and desks throughout the house—there were even sleek pink princess telephones in the bedrooms of some girls—but his mother insisted that a family needed but one telephone, and it must be black, and rotary dialed, and reside in the front hall, which was, for some reason the man never understood, unheated. His mother, like so many wealthy New Englanders, was extremely—frighteningly—frugal. What was the point in heating hallways? Hallways were for passing through, not for living. That was why rooms had doors!

The phone Lárus held trailed a very long cord. Lárus placed it on the bar in front of the man and said, You are my guest.

The man had never used a phone provided like this in a bar and all he could think of was scenes in old movies where people in nightclubs had phones on long cords brought to their table. For a brief moment he felt glamorous and consequential. He was aware that both Lárus and the businessman were watching him, but then he realized that he did not know Brother Emmanuel's number, and he stood for a moment, dumbly holding the receiver, as if it might come to him. But of course it did not. He looked again at the message, but of course the number had not been added to it in the interval since he had last looked. He replaced the receiver and stood there, exposed as the fool he was.

Do you know the phone number for Brother Emmanuel? he asked Lárus.

I have no brother, said Lárus. He is dead.

No, I mean Brother Emmanuel, the healer. He lives in a house not far from here. And I'm sorry about your brother.

He killed himself, said Lárus. How sad it was! He was far better than I.

I've got the number.

The man turned to see the businessman reaching into his breast pocket and withdrawing a slim leather-bound book. He flipped through its pages. You'd better let me dial, he said. It's a little tricky.

Thank you. The man held the receiver out, but the businessman did not get up.

Bring it here, he said. For God's sake!

The man picked up the phone and walked around to the far side of bar where the businessman sat. He set the phone before him and handed him the receiver. The businessman dialed what seemed to be a very long number on the rotary dial and then handed the receiver back to the man. While the phone rang, the man picked up the phone and walked back to the other end of the bar. He did not want to be beside the businessman while he spoke. After five rings the call was answered. A woman's voice chimed what was no doubt a greeting in the native language.

Good evening, said the man. This is— and here he said his name, and hearing it said like that, he panicked for a moment because he was suddenly not sure it was his name.

Yes, the voice said. This is Darlene.

I received your message. May I speak to my wife? Or to Brother Emmanuel?

Your wife is sleeping. But of course you may speak with Brother Emmanuel. One moment, please.

It seemed a long time—but he really had no idea how long—before he heard Brother Emmanuel's voice. Good evening, it said.

Good evening, said the man. I received your message. I'm concerned about my wife. May I come and get her now?

It is not right to move her tonight. Come in the morning.

What's wrong with her? What happened?

She became upset, upset emotionally, but the barrier between her emotional and physical self is so porous that she collapsed. We are taking good care of her. She is sleeping now, and that is good. She should not wake until the morning.

Why? asked the man. What have you done to her? Have you drugged her?

Don't be alarmed. We gave her a natural remedy to soothe her by allowing her sleep. Sleep is a great healer, perhaps the greatest. We repair our bodies every night while we sleep.

Is she all right? Was whatever happened bad for her?

I think it was good, said Brother Emmanuel. An advancement. A clarification.

An advancement?

You would not understand. Come in the morning, and you may see her.

Brother Emmanuel hung up, and after a moment, so did the man. He pushed the telephone across the bar toward Lárus. Thank you, he said.

Lárus nodded and replaced the telephone somewhere beneath the bar.

Two more, Lárus! said the businessman. You need a drink, I think. Come sit here. He indicated the adjacent barstool.

The man felt too defeated and exhausted to disobey. He sat beside the businessman and they both watched Lárus make their cocktails. It was a Negroni, the man realized. He liked Negronis, but he associated them with summer, with the beach at Misquamicut, Rhode Island, where his mother's family had what they called a "cottage."

Lárus approached with two Negronis and placed one in front of each of them. The businessman picked his up and held it out toward the man. May our cocks always be harder than our lives, he said, and touched his glass against the man's.

The man took a sip of his drink and felt it enter his body, like a magic elixir. He realized he had eaten nothing but the garbage soup all day. I want some food, he said. Do you want some food?

I always want food, said the businessman. He patted the belly that extended rotundly above his belt. He took the man's hand and held it against his belly, as if he were pregnant and wanted the man to feel his baby kicking.

The man quickly withdrew his hand, but not before he felt the comforting pillowed warmth beneath it. We'd like to order some food, he called to Lárus. Lots of food!

Lárus approached them and the man said, Bring us two of everything. And ham in the sandwiches! The man felt proud that he had not consulted the menu or the businessman regarding their order of food.

Lárus disappeared behind the upholstered door, which swung back and forth a few times after his exit, and when it was still the businessman said, So your wife's mixed herself up with the holy man.

I don't think he claims to be holy, said the man. He can just heal people. He says.

That sounds holy to me. Sounds fucking miraculous.

I don't want to talk about it, said the man. It is what it is.

Or perhaps it isn't what it is. It's something, and something is good. Something is better than nothing. I mean for her: something is better than nothing for her.

And for you? Is something better than nothing for you?

I don't know, said the man. It depends what the something is.

So you also have nothing?

I didn't mean that, said the man. But yes, maybe. Who knows? Do you know what you have?

Yes, said the businessman. I have shit. Shit. Nothing but shit.

Lárus returned and placed a plate of hard-boiled eggs on the bar between them.

We ordered two, said the man. Two orders of everything.

It is two, said Lárus. Count them. I don't cheat. He disappeared, abruptly, behind the upholstered door.

The man realized that there were many egg halves on the plate: more than he would ever want to eat. He counted them: eleven. An odd number. Something, somewhere, had gone wrong. Had Lárus, perhaps, eaten one? There could be no other explanation.

Have you really got nothing but shit? the man asked.

Yes. I never lie. Why do you think I'm here, in this fucking freezing godforsaken place?

I thought you were here on some sort of business. You don't live here, do you?

No, said the man, I don't live here. I'd rather die than live here. I'd rather die a horrible painful death than live here.

Lárus emerged from behind the door with a large tray upon which were several plates. He placed these before the two men and disappeared back behind the door.

Look at this, said the businessman. A feast. A feast of crap. He took two of the fish croquettes and made a sort of fish croquette sandwich with them, a sandwich with no filling, and hungrily bit into it. It took him a moment to chew and swallow all that he had bitten off, and when he had, he wiped his mouth with a napkin. Lárus! he called.

After a moment Lárus emerged from the land behind the upholstered door. Yes?

Two more drinks! said the businessman. He held up his empty glass. Come on, boy—do your job!

The man had not finished his drink, so he picked it up and drank all that was left. He placed it carefully back on the bar because he had a sudden fear that he might break it, that even so much as placing it back upon the surface of the bar might shatter it. But it did not shatter, or break, and the man felt relieved, and proud of himself, and thus emboldened he heard himself cry: Schnapps! I want schnapps! Not this sissy pink drink!

The businessman seemed surprised by this outburst. Yes, schnapps, he said to Lárus. But we'll have Negronis as well. Won't we? He turned to the man.

Yes, said the man. We will have schnapps *and* Negronis. And don't forget, two of everything on the menu!

Your food is there, said Lárus, nodding to the welter of plates and bowls he had placed on the bar before them.

Ah, said the man. Yes. Thank you, Lárus! Lots to eat and lots to drink!

We shall drink and be merry, said the businessman. We shall drink and eat and fuck.

Lárus placed a small glass of schnapps before each of them. The man picked his up and swallowed it in one gulp. He pounded his empty glass down upon the bar. Another! he cried.

Well, said the businessman. Look who's off and running.

I am, said the man. I am off and running!

Yes, but no more schnapps until you've had your Negroni. And you'd better eat something.

I want to get drunk, said the man.

You're well on your way. But the evening is young. Pace yourself.

For what? Pace myself for what? What is there to pace myself for? I have always paced myself and look where it has gotten me.

Here with me, said the businessman. Eating and drinking and fucking.

We aren't fucking!

Not yet, said the businessman. But we will.

You may be fucking. But not me. There will be no fucking tonight.

It remains to be seen.

Don't talk about fucking, said the man. Please. It makes me sad.

That's odd. Why?

I don't know, said the man.

But it was true: the talk of fucking had made him sad. The exuberance he had just felt was gone. He looked dejectedly at the unappetizing array of food before him.

You've ruined everything, he said to the businessman. He pushed the plate of hard-cooked eggs toward the edge of the bar.

The businessman reached out and stopped the plate from toppling to the floor. Easy now, he said to the man. What's gone wrong? A moment ago you were gay as a lark.

Stop this gay talk. I'm not gay.

I know. But you were. Gay as a lark.

Quickly, before the businessman could stop him, the man pushed the plate of eggs off the bar and onto the floor. The plate crashed. Lárus, who was standing sentinel in his spot, flinched. He quickly looked down at the mess on the floor but then looked away.

It was quiet for a moment and then the man said, Look what I've done. I'm sorry. He stood up and leaned over the bar so that he could see the mess he had made and then sat back on the barstool. I've made a mess.

It's not so bad, said the businessman. But perhaps we should put you to bed, before things get worse.

I'm not a child, said the man.

Lárus disappeared behind the door and reemerged a moment later with a dustpan and brush. He knelt down and swept up the shards of plate and slivers of egg and dumped them into the garbage. Would you like more egg? he asked the man.

No, the man answered. No more eggs. And I'm sorry, Lárus. I'm sorry I acted badly and made a mess. Thank you for cleaning it up.

It's my job, said Lárus. I only do my job.

You do it very well, said the man. Thank you.

Anyone can do this job.

The businessman stood up. He withdrew his billfold from his jacket, extracted several bills, and placed them upon the bar. I think we should allow Lárus to have an early night, he said. Do you agree? he asked the man.

Yes, said the man.

The businessman steadied the man as he climbed off his barstool. The man started walking toward the door but the businessman said, Wait. We need provisions. He studied the plates of food arranged on the bar top and then put two of the meat sandwiches atop the bowl of ham and potato salad. Follow me, he said to the man. He held the man's arm with the hand that wasn't holding the food, and half pushed, half pulled him toward the door. They both paused before the beaded curtain. A little help? the businessman said. I've got my hands full.

The man reached out and parted the strands of beads, and the businessman pushed him through the jangling screen into the lobby. The businessman did not release his hold on the man as they crossed the lobby, as if he was afraid the man might suddenly bolt. They climbed the steps to the landing and entered the elevator and stood close together as it ascended. When it stopped the businessman motioned to the man to open the door, and when it was open he pushed the man gently out of the elevator onto the fourth-floor landing.

I'm on five, the man said.

Come with me, the businessman said, and led the man down the hallway. He stopped outside a door, knelt down, and carefully placed the bowl of sandwiches and potato salad on the floor. Then he stood up and unlocked the door. He flung it open and gently pushed the man before him into the room and closed the door behind them. It was completely dark in the room. The two men stood in the darkness. Even though it was completely dark the man closed his eyes. Although there was no sound he wished he could stop up his ears as well, and remove himself as completely as he could from the world. Once, while he was on business in Frankfurt, a colleague had taken him, after a somewhat drunken dinner, to a place where they floated in sensory-deprivation tanks. The tanks were like coffins filled with salt water, each in its own closet-like room; the man was told to strip and lie down in the tank and pull the cover closed above him; in an hour lights would come on inside the tank and he would know it was time to get out. It was the best feeling the man had ever had, floating alone in the darkness. He forgot his body and his mind, which had been racing but gradually quieted itself into a sort of conscious unconsciousness, a waking sleep, where the man somehow had access to the true and free self that emerged only in his dreams. Remembering this experience, the man wanted to lie down on the floor of the businessman's hotel room, lie down in this perfect darkness and silence and let go. He began to sink to the floor but he felt the businessman reach around him, pull him up, and hold him against the wall. He could feel the businessman's large belly pressed against his own and smell and feel the businessman's warm breath touching his face. Although he could not see the businessman's face, he knew that it was very close, perhaps almost touching his own. And then he felt the businessman's mouth lightly touching his mouth, and he relaxed his lips slightly against the gentle pressure, and the businessman's tongue slid into his mouth, fat and warm, and the man opened his mouth wider and felt his own tongue come alive and then felt the businessman take both of his arms and raise them above his head and pin them there against the wall. The businessman pressed his body hard against the man, grinding him into the wall, and the man could feel the businessman's cock pushing against him, humping his leg, and then pressing hard against his own cock, and still the businessman held the man against the wall with his arms raised above his head, kissing him and bucking into him as if there might be some hole, there in the front of him, he could fill.

◆

When the man woke up he was in the businessman's bed and the businessman was sitting up against the headboard, smoking a cigarette. A lamp on the end table was turned on but was shrouded with a dark-colored handkerchief, so it glowed dully.

What time is it? he asked.

The businessman leaned over and picked up a little travel clock that sat beside the lamp. It was the kind that folds into its own little leather case. The businessman looked at it and then held it against his ear.

It's twenty past five, he said.

Why aren't you sleeping?

I can't sleep when somebody's in my bed. I want to fuck too much. Even if I've already fucked. And fucked.

The man felt there was something wrong and looked around the room. The bed was backward, he realized: it had been on the opposite wall.

Did you move your bed? he asked the businessman.

No, said the businessman. This is a different room. I change rooms every other day.

Why?

Because there's nothing more depressing than living in a fucking hotel room. So I change rooms. Although in this hotel every room is a nightmare.

Where do you live?

In hotels.

You have no home?

I have apartments. One in London, and one in Istanbul. You and wifey live in New York?

Yes, said the man.

I can just picture it: lots of family heirlooms. Uncomfortable chairs the pilgrims carted over on the *Mayflower*. Maybe a few Zuni pots thrown in to spice things up.

Our pots are Oaxacan.

Of course! said the businessman. That's the ugly black shit, right?

You must be very unhappy.

Why?

Because you have such disdain for everything. Or pretend to. It's more than a bit tiresome.

Oh, please. Don't get all faggy and psychological on me.

The man got out of bed. He looked around and saw his clothes on the floor and began putting them on. Where are my underpants?

I don't know where your fucking underpants are, said the businessman.

The man put on his pants without his underpants. He put on his undershirt and shirt and sweater, an Irish fisherman's knit sweater his wife's mother had made for him the year they got married. Eleven years ago. It had always been too big for him, and he realized that his mother-in-law had thought he was a larger man, or wished he were, but he liked the sweater even though it did not fit him well. It was warm. He looked around for his coat, but it, like his underpants, had disappeared. He must have left it down in the bar. But not his underpants. He would not have left his underpants in the bar. He turned around and looked at the businessman, who remained sitting up in the bed, smoking. He looked fat and unhappy.

◆

The man took the stairs down to the lobby and entered the bar. It seemed darker than usual in the bar and there was no sign of Lárus, or anyone else. But he saw his coat hanging from one of the pegs on the wall. He put it on because he suddenly felt cold, or eviscerated. He felt in need of an additional layer. He sat on a stool he had never sat on before, as if this might change his luck.

After a moment Lárus appeared. The man realized that of everyone, he loved Lárus the most. Perhaps because he was the one most impossible, most resistant, to love.

Lárus! Oh, Lárus, he said. May I have a schnapps?

Lárus nodded. He pulled the silver stag's head from the bottle of schnapps and poured some into a glass and placed it before the man.

Thank you, Lárus, the man said.

Lárus nodded and assumed his position against the wall. After a moment, he began to speak. He was looking, as always, through the beaded curtains, and the man assumed he was speaking to someone standing just outside them, in the vast murk of the lobby.

We always hoped the Olympics will come here, Lárus said. We build things so that they will come. This hotel is one thing. But they never come. Since I was a boy they never come. So we build more things. A mountain for ski. A large home for ice. Everyone says if they come we will be happy for a time. And rich, perhaps. But they will never come here. Even if we build everything they want they will not come here.

Lárus stopped speaking, and looked at the man, who nodded. Lárus looked away but continued speaking.

They kill all the dogs one year because they think dogs not good for Olympics. That ugly dog in street keep Olympics away. And the shit of the dogs. But of course it is not the fault of dogs. But still they kill. Anything to get Olympics. In the winter I allow the dogs to be gone. But in the summer, no. There should be dogs in the summer in field and wood and river. Swimming, perhaps, or running. Barking. What you kill like that does not come back. The dogs know, I think. Or else they would come back. Even in summer they would come, along the roads. But they know, I think. We have broken with them. You understand?

Yes, said the man.

Why do I stay? asked Lárus. Would you stay?

No, said the man. I would not stay.

Then you must leave, said Lárus. You must go back.

But I can't, said the man. No one can.

Because of why?

The Vaalankurkku Bridge, said the man. It has collapsed. Haven't you heard? Because of all the snow.

There is no bridge at Vaalankurkku.

For the railway. A railroad bridge. For the train.

No, said Lárus. There is no bridge at Vaalankurkku. And bridges do not collapse here. Not from snow. Snow is nothing here.

Livia Pinheiro-Rima told me, said the man. I had lunch with her today. She told me that bridge had collapsed and there was no other way to leave here.

Don't tell me that you believe in this woman.

Of course I do. Why would she lie about a bridge?

Because she lie about everything. I thought you knew.

Oh. I believed her.

She lie because she wants you to stay here. Everyone wants everyone to stay here. Especially in winter. But you can leave.

So can you, said the man. We can both leave. If we want. We could leave together.

You can leave, said Lárus. I cannot.

Of course you can, said the man. If you want.

Of course I want. But it is not a matter of want.

I don't understand, said the man. What prevents you from leaving here?

It is my home, said Lárus. My only home.

But lots of people leave their homes. And find new homes. Better homes.

Did you leave your home, and find a better home?

Yes, said the man. In America, almost everyone does that. Home is not where you were born. I mean, perhaps it is, for some people, yes, but not necessarily. Not always. You could find another home, Lárus. Anywhere in the world.

Only in this world? That is the only choice you give me?

✦

When the man got to his room he realized he did not have the key. He remembered it had been given to him, along with the message from Brother Emmanuel, when he returned from the orphanage, but he could not find it in any of his pockets. He realized the key must have fallen out of his pocket in the businessman's room—they had undressed very hurriedly in the darkness and flung their clothes all about them in an adolescent rush to be naked.

He was not about to go knocking on the businessman's door, so he went down to the lobby and rang the little bell on the altar of the front desk, but no one came. Everyone was asleep or gone. Or hiding.

He took the elevator up to the fifth floor and marched down the hallway to his room. He tried to open the door, but of course it was locked. He stood back and then jumped forward, lifting his right leg as high as he could and kicking it against the door, just beside the doorknob. The door was hollow and his kick dented it considerably, and the second time he kicked it his foot went through the door but got stuck on the withdrawal and he fell backward onto the hallway floor with his foot hooked through the broken door. The wind was knocked out of him and so he lay on the floor for a moment, his foot still stuck through the door, and then he managed to free it by kicking back and forth and widening the hole. He stood up and reached his hand through the hole and unlocked the deadbolt. He then kicked the door once again and felt a huge, almost transfiguring satisfaction when it obediently swung open. He had never kicked a door open before and the fact that he had done this improbable thing made him feel almost happy. It would have been perfect if he had not gotten his foot stuck and fallen backward in that shameful fashion, but as no one had witnessed it he decided to erase it from the narrative. He had kicked the door open! Or maybe he had even kicked it down! It would be a good story to tell his child someday.

He entered the room and closed the door behind him. He stuck his hand through the hole and then bent down and peered through it, enjoying this view across the hallway at the opposite door. He could also kick that one down if he wanted to. So what if the doors were hollow? That was another fact that could be expunged. It was an old hotel, built like a castle, and the door was thick and solid, the hinges made of iron, and he had kicked it down.

The excitement of kicking down the door had restored his flagging energy—he had planned to collapse on the bed immediately upon entering the room, but that no longer was an option. He wanted to perform another violent act—with his hands this time. Could he punch through the fake brick wall? It was probably as cheaply constructed as the hollow doors, and he imagined the satisfying and exciting sensation as his hand pushed through the fiberglass and particleboard, or whatever other shoddy materials comprised the wall. He looked closely at the wall and realized that it was just begging to be violated. He moved closer and ran his open palm across the faux brick surface, and then drew his hand away, made a fist, and punched it as hard as he could.

After a moment—or perhaps it was longer than a moment, he had no idea—he realized he was once again lying on the floor. The wall, like the door, had thrown him backward. And then he felt that a very large throbbingly painful cabbage had been attached to the end of his arm where his hand once had been. Some prehistoric innate wisdom told him it was best if he did not get up, perhaps ever again, that by lying still on the floor he could accomplish no further violence. He instinctively moved his cabbage hand beneath his body, and pressed down upon it with all his might, and although this was painful it was a more endurable pain than the other, for it stilled the throbbing, contained it somehow, like one of those heavy lead blankets that deflect X-rays.

FIVE

The man woke to find something disagreeably wet and furry invading his mouth. He was lying facedown upon the floor, with his face mashed into a puddle of drool on the shag carpet. He quickly lifted himself up onto his hands and knees and then rubbed at his mouth with one of his hands, pulling at the moist fibers stuck to his lips. He went into the bathroom and rinsed his mouth out and washed his face and felt much better.

He heard someone knocking on the door and left the bathroom. Halfway across the hotel room he noticed the large hole in the door and he remembered what he had done the night before. Through the hole he could see someone standing in the hallway, and for a moment he had the ridiculous urge to lean down and speak through the opening, but he more sensibly opened the door.

The elderly concierge with the walrus mustache stood in the hallway.

I understand there has been an accident, he said.

Good morning, said the man.

Good morning. There has been an accident?

Where?

The concierge nodded toward the door and then reached out and inserted his hand through the opening. He withdrew it and then reinserted it, moving it back and forth within the opening, as if to prove without a doubt that the hole was real and not a magical illusion.

Oh, the door, said the man. That was not an accident.

It was not?

No, said the man. I lost my key last night and there was no one at the front desk. What else could I have done?

There is always someone attending the front desk. If they are not there, they shall return within minutes. You had only to wait to get your key.

I did wait, said the man. But there was no one there and no sign that anyone might appear. Or reappear. And I needed immediate access to my room.

Immediate? You could not have waited a moment or two? Was your need so urgent?

Yes, said the man. My need was extremely urgent. I needed to sleep. It is, after all, primarily what one comes to a hotel for.

I am afraid we must add the cost of replacing the door to your tariff.

Fine, said the man. Do that. It's a very cheap door so it can't cost very much.

On the contrary, said the concierge. It is a very valuable door. In fact, one might call it irreplaceable.

Irreplaceable? You're kidding me. It's hollow.

Just because something is hollow does not mean it is without value.

I'm not saying it's without value. I'm just saying if it cost ten dollars I'd be surprised.

All the doors in the hotel were salvaged from the original Khedivial Opera House in Cairo. They are UNESCO-certified artifacts.

I don't believe you, said the man. Why would an opera house have all these doors? And the last thing they'd be is hollow.

For the first, said the concierge, the Khedivial Opera House was all boxes. Each box had two doors. For the second, every door in an opera house is hollow. It is what keeps the sound alive.

Thank you for elucidating me, said the man. But now I must go to Brother Emmanuel's and collect my wife. Can you arrange for a taxi to take me there?

Certainly. You wish to leave—

Now, said the man. Or as soon as possible. Will you call me when the taxi is here?

Yes, of course, said the concierge.

✦

Darlene opened the door at Brother Emmanuel's almost as soon as the man knocked on it. She told the man he was expected and showed him into the room with the fireplace and the parrot. This morning the fire had not been lit and it was cold in the room. The parrot's cage was shrouded with a black leather cover, which appeared to be snugly custom-fitted.

Darlene told the man that Brother Emmanuel would be with him shortly and left the room, sliding the two doors closed behind her.

The man stood near the cage and listened for the bird. He thought of the total darkness inside the cage and imagined the bird sitting inside, alive, like the beating heart in the dark cavity of his chest. He listened carefully but there was no sound from the bird. The man was disappointed. He wanted some proof that the bird was inside the cage, and alive. How did it breathe? The leather must be invisibly perforated. Tiny pinpricks through which air, but not light, could travel.

The man became aware of a presence behind him and turned to see Brother Emmanuel standing just inside the opened doors. He was once again dressed in the black cassock that buttoned diagonally across his chest. Its skirt fell all the way to the floor. He stood there, motionless, gazing at the man.

The sudden and silent appearance of Brother Emmanuel unnerved the man, and in an effort to regain his sense of control he asked if the bird was in the cage.

Yes, Brother Emmanuel said. He is sleeping.

How do you know? asked the man.

How do I know he is sleeping?

Yes, said the man. I hear nothing.

Of course. He makes no noise when he sleeps.

Shouldn't you take the cover off? It is daytime. Shouldn't he be awake?

On most days, yes, said Brother Emmanuel. But Artemis slept poorly last night. In fact, we all did. So we are letting him rest this morning. You see, he is an extraordinary creature. He always senses when there is distress in the house. It upsets him.

And last night there was distress in the house?

Yes, said Brother Emmanuel. I'm afraid there was. But this morning things are calm. Everything is fine. God has been good to us.

I'm glad to hear it, said the man. I have come to get my wife. We must go to the orphanage today and take possession of our baby.

Brother Emmanuel said nothing for a moment, and in the quiet the man thought that he did perhaps hear a faint rustling sound from within the cage.

It seems an odd way to express it, said Brother Emmanuel.

Express what?

To take possession of a baby. As if it was something you had purchased.

In a way we have, said the man. It was difficult for us to adopt a baby. Because of our age. And my wife's health.

So you bought one? That now you must take possession of?

Yes, said the man. Exactly. And I cannot do that alone. I need my wife. Would you get her?

Sit down, said Brother Emmanuel. He stepped farther into the room and indicated the long sofa that faced the fireplace.

Why? asked the man.

Please, sit down. I need to speak with you. It is necessary for us to speak before you see you wife.

Why? Has something happened?

Yes, said Brother Emmanuel. Something has happened. Please sit down. Once again he indicated the sofa.

The man sat at the end of the sofa nearest to him. Brother Emmanuel came close and knelt on the floor before the man.

You wife has made a decision, Brother Emmanuel began. It was a difficult decision for her to make, a decision that cost her much anguish. If you love her, it is a decision you must respect. You must know that she arrived at this decision herself. That is why you must respect it.

What did she decide?

Your wife has decided to stay here.

For how long? asked the man. We are expected at the orphanage this afternoon.

You don't understand, said Brother Emmanuel. She has decided not to leave here.

You're right, said the man. I don't understand.

She has decided this is where she wants to pass.

Pass? asked the man. You mean die?

I, myself, do not use that term.

I do, said the man. And it is impossible. She is my wife. She must come back with me. She must come home.

Home, yes, said Brother Emmanuel. Exactly. But she now feels that this is her home. It is very clear to her, very strong, this feeling. She is at peace. It is good.

It is not good, said the man. And you have no right to keep her here. If she thinks that this is her home it is because you have brainwashed her.

Brother Emmanuel abruptly stood up and stepped back, away from the man. It might be said that he recoiled.

You have insulted me, he said.

I don't care, said the man. He, too, stood. Where is my wife? I demand to see my wife. Now.

Your wife has decided it would be better—easier—if you do not see each other. She feels that her life with you has ended. I beg you to respect her wishes. You must let her go.

I will not let her go, said the man. I will not leave here until I have seen her. He grabbed the iron poker that stood along with a brush and little shovel in a tray beside the fireplace. He pointed it at Brother Emmanuel. It shook because his hand was shaking.

If I have to, I will kill you.

Brother Emmanuel reached out and held the end of the poker that was pointed at him. His hand was steady and the poker stopped shaking. The two men stood for a moment, thus connected, the poker unwavering between them. Then the man relaxed his shaking grasp on the poker and Brother Emmanuel gently pulled it away. He returned it to its home on the hearth. He wiped his hands together, because his end of the poker was the one that was used to maneuver the logs in the fire and was consequently dirty.

Put away the things of this world, he said to the man. Put away your sword. Put away your fear, and your anger.

I cannot, said the man. Could you?

I understand, said Brother Emmanuel. I am asking too much. Your wife is asking too much. There is a limit to what you can understand, and give.

Yes, said the man. There is a limit.

And you cannot leave her now? You cannot give her this?

No, said the man. What would anything mean if I left her now? And isn't there something she must give me?

What is it you want from her?

I want for her to not turn away from me. If you have told her that is what she must do, I don't blame you. I know you are trying to help her. But you must respect me as well as her.

But she is dying, said Brother Emmanuel.

I know that, said the man. That is why I must see her. Surely you can understand that.

Brother Emmanuel reached out and laid his hand upon the man's shoulder, and although he tried not to, the man felt in the sudden warmth a stilling gentleness. He remembered Livia Pinheiro-Rima patting his back in the bar of the hotel the night they arrived. Had he always been touched like this, or had something changed about him, had a need become apparent, that had elicited all this coddling? This contact happens all the time, he realized, but we've all become inured to it. That is why we long for sex and are excited by violence: because that is the only touch we can still feel, the only touch that penetrates our armor.

Come with me, said Brother Emmanuel. The man followed him out of the room. Darlene stood in the vestibule with a sense of permanence that made it seem as if she might never leave it. Brother Emmanuel climbed one of the staircases and opened a door on the second floor. The square room they entered had no windows, only two doors in each of its walls. All these doors were closed and so the room was dark. The only light came from an alabaster chandelier that hung on tasseled ropes from the ceiling, glowing dimly like a moon seen through a scrim of clouds. In the exact center of the room, directly beneath the alabaster chandelier, bathed by its lunar glow, stood an S-shaped tête-à-tête love seat upholstered in green silk. Brother Emmanuel opened one of the doors on the opposite wall, which revealed a narrow and steep staircase. He turned back to look at the man.

She is up here, he said. Follow me.

But the man did not move. He felt safe there. He wished Brother Emmanuel would shut the door he had opened so they could be alone in the closed box of the room. All he wanted was to fall to the floor and sleep.

Brother Emmanuel closed the door and stepped back into the room. He looked at the man. Are you frightened? he asked.

The man was frightened, but had not realized it until Brother Emmanuel asked his question.

Yes, he said.

Of course you are afraid, Brother Emmanuel said, but you must be strong now. You have strength and she does not.

But she is strong, said the man. She has always been stronger than me, and less afraid.

That is no longer true, said Brother Emmanuel. May I embrace you?

Yes, said the man. Please.

Brother Emmanuel pulled the man close and held him against his chest—one hand on the man's back, and one hand holding the man's head against his tunic, pressing his cheek into the gold buttons that crossed his chest.

The man could feel Brother Emmanuel's heart beat in his chest.

After a moment Brother Emmanuel gently pushed the man from him and stepped away. Come with me, he said. Do not think too much. In fact, do not think at all.

He turned and opened the door, and this time the man followed him up the dark narrow staircase to the third floor, emerging into a hallway lined with several doors, each of them open except for one. The open doors revealed small bedrooms, each one simply and identically furnished with a bed and dresser and chair. A duvet was coiled into a roll at the foot of every bed. A small circular rag rug lay in the center of every floor.

The room with the closed door was at the far end of the hall and Brother Emmanuel walked deliberately toward it, and the man followed behind him. Brother Emmanuel opened the door without knocking and entered the room. It was completely dark. Brother Emmanuel reached down and turned on a lamp that sat on a small table beside the bed. The man entered the room and saw that his wife was lying in the bed. Her face was turned toward the wall and the sudden light and men entering the room did not appear to disturb her, for she did not move or in any other way acknowledge these alterations to her environment.

Brother Emmanuel knelt beside the bed and placed both of his hands upon the duvet. He moved his hands several times, sliding them far apart and then drawing them back together, as if he were attempting to gather something up at the center of the woman's body. And then he lifted his hands and let them hover for a moment over her body, the way pianists lift their hands above the keyboard and let them hang there, momentarily, as the last notes fade away. But Brother Emmanuel's hands fell gently back upon the duvet that covered the woman's body and rested there for a moment. Then he lifted one of his hands and reached and touched the woman's face. He placed all five of his fingers softly upon her cheek.

Your husband is here, he said. He has come to see you.

For a moment the man thought his wife might be dead. She had not moved during Brother Emmanuel's interference and did not respond when he touched her face. Surely she must be dead to allow herself to be touched in this extraordinary way. But after a moment she shifted in the bed, turned her head, and looked directly at the man. He could not read her expression. She had none.

I will leave you, said Brother Emmanuel. He moved a chair away from the wall and positioned it beside the bed and then left the room, shutting the door behind him.

This all happened more quickly than the man had expected. He had not thought he would be left alone with his wife, not without some period of reacquaintance.

The man felt himself shiver. I'm cold, he said.

The woman said nothing and her face did not alter but she slid closer to the wall and lifted the far edge of the duvet.

Get in, she said.

It was odd that she offered such an invitation to intimacy as a command.

The man sat on the chair and took off his boots and then got into bed with his wife. For a moment he lay on his back beside her, not touching, but then he turned and gathered her in his arms and held her carefully against him.

What are you doing? he whispered. Why are you here? Why won't you come with me?

I'm tired, said the woman.

Yes, I know, said the man. But still—

I have decided to stay here, said the woman. Please accept that.

But why here? Why not with me?

Because, said the woman. This is where I want to be now.

Do you still think he has cured you?

The woman made a sound like laughter, but it was mirthless and brutal. Yes, she said. In fact, I do. But he says he hasn't. It's just my luck, isn't it? Finding a healer who says he hasn't healed me. Only I could do that.

But maybe—maybe what you sense, or feel, is a premonition.

Yes, she said. Perhaps.

It's possible, he said. It's your body after all. You could know better than him.

The woman said nothing. She reached out and touched the wallpaper, a nonsensical design of sheaves of wheat interspersed with bugles and roosters.

What does it mean? the man asked.

What?

The wallpaper, he said. He reached past her and touched it himself. The wheat, and roosters, and bugles. What does it mean?

It means life, she said. They are all symbols of life.

Roosters?

Yes, she said. Of course. Cock-a-doodle-doo. They alone start the world again every morning. Or so they think.

He held her a little bit closer to him.

And the bugles wake us up as well, he said.

Yes, she said.

And the wheat?

The staff of life.

Of course, he said. I forgot.

They were quiet for a moment, both regarding the wall-paper, as if there might be a flaw in the pattern: a rooster with two heads or a bugle facing left instead of right. The man liked the idea of patterns, that once something proportionately replicable was established it could go on and on repeating itself, spreading like kudzu or cancer.

I know you want to stay here, he said. But will you come with me?

Where?

To get the baby, he said. I need you to get the baby.

Why? They saw me. I was there.

I know, he said. But they won't give him to me unless you are there.

Of course they will. You just have to say—something. That I have a cold. That I have caught a chill. They can hardly doubt that, in this frozen place.

You need to be there with me, he said. They have made that very clear.

The woman sighed. She pulled away from the man and shifted closer to the wall.

The man let her go. He felt the cold space open between them.

I don't think you ever wanted a baby, he said.

The woman touched the wallpaper again, but this time she pressed her palm flatly against the wall. As the man watched, the pale skin on her hand blushed, and he realized that she was bracing herself.

Then, suddenly, the woman pushed against the wall, turned toward him, and sat up in a single contorted motion. She reached her hand out and hit him, several times, tried to beat his arms and his chest, but she had so little strength that the gesture had only symbolic effect. After a moment the man took her hand and held it, and then, when he felt her fury had abated, released it. She rubbed the hand with which she had beaten him with her other hand, as if it had been hurt, and looked at him as if the fault was his.

How could you say that! she cried. How dare you! There is nothing I wanted more than that. Nothing! My God! Don't you remember what I did for a child? All the injections, the pain, the relentless fucking. That's what killed me, I think, trying to have a baby! How dare you say that!

I'm sorry, he said. I didn't mean—I only meant—forget it. Please, lie down. I'm sorry. Lie down.

She stared at him for a moment and then lay down on the bed and pulled the duvet around her. She lay on her back, the duvet clutched with both hands beneath her throat, gazing up at the ceiling.

Would you go? she asked. Please go. Can't we just—

What?

Let go, she said.

Let go of what?

Of us, she said. Let go of us. I've let go of you. Won't you let go of me?

No, the man said. Why would I let go of you? I don't understand you anymore.

I know, said the woman. You don't. So let me go. Please.

I can't let you go. He reached out to touch her but then thought that he'd better not. He pulled the duvet up and tucked it more snugly around her. It was warm in the bed. If her body had lost vigor and strength, it had not lost heat. Perhaps that was the last thing to go.

Fine, said the woman. Don't let me go, then, but at least leave me alone.

I won't, said the man. I can't.

The woman said nothing. She sighed and turned back toward the wall.

The man got out of the bed. He once again fitted the duvet snugly around his wife. He knelt down beside the bed and rested his arms upon it with his hands clenched, as if he were praying.

Please come with me, he said. I beg you.

He reached out and touched her, tried to turn her gently away from the wall, but her body was tense and impossible to move.

Come with me to get the baby. I beg you. And then you can come back here, and stay here, or do whatever you like.

Go have a baby with another woman. That's what you should do. You always wanted your own baby. That's the only reason you fucked me.

Please don't say these things. We have . . . we have always been kind to each other. Can't we at least keep that?

She turned back toward him. Exactly! she exclaimed. Kindness! How I hate it! I never wanted kindness. Especially not from you.

What did you want from me?

What a question! How can you ask it?

The man said nothing.

Love! said the woman. I wanted love! She began to cry.

Of course I loved you. Love you. Kindness is a part of love.

It's got nothing to do with love, the woman said. Kindness—what a horrible word!—is what we give to those we don't love. Can't love. We're kind to those we don't love for that very reason. That's where kindness comes in—when there isn't love.

The man stood up, unbalanced. He reached out and steadied himself by holding on to the chair, which creaked a little from the pressure he placed upon it. For a moment he thought it might collapse, but it did not. It was an old chair, well made and strong. He pushed it over and kicked it, so that it skidded across the floor until it reached the circular rag rug in the center of the room.

The woman looked at the chair. It lay there on its side, as if it had fainted or collapsed.

I'm sorry, she said. I don't wish to blame you. You always did what you could. I know that.

But it wasn't enough, the man said.

It's not the amount. It's the thing itself. It wasn't what I wanted, or needed.

Why didn't you tell me? How was I to know?

She reached out her hand, and when he did not take it, she turned it over, palm up, and shook it. He reached out his own hand and held hers. She pulled it gently so he was forced to sit down beside her on the bed. She turned toward him, curling around him, and let their joined hands fall into his lap. Her head was slightly behind him, so he could not see her face when she began to speak.

Everything feels different when you're dying. Words mean different things, or nothing at all. It's why I shouldn't talk to you. I wish I could make you understand. It's got nothing to do with how I feel about you. Or felt about you. So please don't ask me these questions.

She stopped talking. After a moment she squeezed his hand. Do you understand? she asked. Even a little?

Yes, he said.

Thank you. Thank you for understanding.

A little, he said.

Yes, she said. A little. Go and get the baby. I know you want it and I think it is yours. Please go now. I'm tired.

It's not it, said the man. It's him. He's Simon. He waited, but the woman said nothing. He stood up. I will come back tomorrow.

Please don't, she said. Please. I beg you.

I will leave now only if I can come back tomorrow.

She sighed. She turned away from him and faced the wall, faced the roosters and bugles and sheaves of wheat.

✦

It was early evening when he returned to the hotel but it felt like the middle of the night. It had been dark for hours. He stood on the sidewalk and watched the taxi slowly drive away.

The night was very still and quiet. The cruel wind that usually blew through the streets had momentarily subsided. In fact, nothing moved; there were no cars or people anywhere in sight. The street looked like an opera set just as the curtain is going up and no one has entered. Perhaps he thought of opera because he could hear, faintly, the barcarole from *The Tales of Hoffmann* being played on the piano inside the lobby.

It was so cold standing there that he felt the skin on his face might crack, so he turned away from the street and pushed himself through the revolving door. Once he was inside the lobby he took off his gloves and held both his hands against his face, covering his eyes, like someone crying.

In fact he was crying, but that was not why he had covered his eyes. He stood like that, clasping his face, listening to the music. He and his wife had seen a production of *Hoffmann* at the Met on one of their very first dates.

After the second intermission, the curtain rose on the scene set in Venice, and in the golden gloom a gondola floated miraculously from the wings to the center of the stage and the man had felt so exhilarated by the sublimity of the moment he had reached out involuntarily for the woman's hand and held it, thrillingly, during the entire act. It was the first time he could remember touching her.

When the barcarole ended, he took his hands away from his face. He looked across the lobby, which seemed to be filled with a fine smoky mist, which may have been caused by the pressure his hands had placed upon his eyes, for as he looked it disappeared. Livia Pinheiro-Rima was seated at the piano, wearing a black toga-like gown that revealed her white bony shoulders. Something glittered on her head—a little sequined fascinator. She looked around the room—only a few people sat in the lobby: two men, each sitting alone, and a party of two men and a woman seated together—and saw the man standing by the door. She looked at him curiously, as if she did not recognize him, and then she leaned down and opened a little spangled bag and extracted a matchbox and a cigarette. She flicked the cigarette into the air and caught it neatly in her mouth, and then struck a match, lit the cigarette, inhaled, and ex-haled a plume of smoke toward the dark distant ceiling.

She put the cigarette down and struck a few chords and then picked it up and took another drag, which she simi-larly exhaled.

It's very lonely, you know, performing solo like this. It's

like a tree that falls in a forest when there's no one there. I know there are a few of you here, but I hope you'll forgive me if I tell you that you don't form a critical mass. I'm supposed to be singing Brecht tonight but really, haven't we all had enough Brecht? I mean there's nothing like him, no one else touches him, but nevertheless, it's a bit exhausting after a while, isn't it? All that flaying and flensing of the soul. But if anyone here does want to hear Brecht, stand up and set yourself on fire. Good. This next song I'm going to sing, since we're renouncing Brecht, is from Noël Coward's musical *Ace of Clubs*. I understudied the role of Pinkie Leroy, officially played by Pat Kirkwood, who was a real darling but having a terrible time. She had just returned from a treacherous year in Hollywood, starring in a wartime picture with Van Johnson. The film studio wanted to slim her down and gave her some pills that affected her thyroid and pituitary and lots of other glands as well, and she ended up spending several months in a sanatorium somewhere in the Rocky Mountains. Well, when Pat finally got back to London, more dead than alive, Noël took pity on the poor thing and wrote the role of Pinkie for her, but her glands were still vacillating and so I went on for her almost every night. Enough: "Why Does Love Get in the Way?"

When Livia Pinheiro-Rima had finished singing the song she stood up and said that she'd be taking a short break. She walked over to where the man was still standing just inside the revolving door.

What's the matter? she said.

I'm fine, said the man. I'm just tired.

Well, come with me to the bar and we'll have a drink. You obviously need one. Come. She took his arm and led him across the lobby, through the beaded curtain, and into the bar. A person of indeterminate gender sat at the far end of the bar in the seat usually occupied by Livia Pinheiro-Rima, so she pushed the man onto a stool near the door and sat down beside him.

Of course he's never here when you need him, she said. Lárus! she called, and a moment later the padded door swung open and Lárus appeared.

We'll each have a double, said Livia Pinheiro-Rima.

Good evening, said Lárus.

Good evening, said the man.

Good evening, Lárus said again, this time directly to Livia Pinheiro-Rima.

Oh, you great big fool, don't play that game with me! Good evening. *Hyvää iltaa. Buona sera, bonsoir.* Happy now? Two doubles, if you please.

Lárus placed a small paper napkin on the bar top in front of each of them and then reached down below the bar for glasses, which he placed carefully upon the napkins. Then he turned and took the schnapps bottle and carefully poured an equal amount into each glass. He twisted the silver antlered stopper back into the bottle, returned it to its spot, and then assumed his usual place, leaning against the wall in front of them.

Livia Pinheiro-Rima picked up her glass and said, To

your health and happiness. The man raised his glass and touched it to hers. He said, To yours. They each took a sip of the schnapps and then put down their glasses.

Have you had a day anything like the kind of day you look as if you had? Livia Pinheiro-Rima asked the man.

Yes, he said. I have.

Well, I'm sorry to hear it.

Oh, and by the way, the man said. Lárus told me that the railroad bridge you told me had collapsed hasn't collapsed.

Well, we all can't agree about everything.

He said there isn't even a bridge there. And that in any case bridges never collapse here.

It sounds as if you and Lárus had quite the conversation. I didn't know he was capable of anything like that.

I like Lárus, the man said. We have an understanding.

An understanding of what?

Of life, I suppose. So am I really stranded here? Or did you just make that up?

Whether you are stranded here is not a question I would presume to answer.

Did you lie about the bridge?

I don't like that word: *lie.*

Yes, but a bridge is either up or down.

I assume you're speaking of London Bridge. And it proves my point perfectly: London Bridge *is* falling down, falling down, falling down. It isn't up or down. It's falling. But I find all this talk of bridges boring. Tell me about your difficult day. Where did you go? Who did you see?

Isn't that Elizabeth Bishop?

Yes. How did you know?

I read poetry, said the man. Or did. In college.

Well, Lota de Macedo Soares was my second cousin.

Are you Brazilian?

My mother was Brazilian. My father was English. But we digress. You were about to tell me about your day. How is your wife? Where is your wife? Where is your baby? For a man with a family you seem remarkably alone.

I am alone, said the man. My wife is at Brother Emmanuel's. The baby is at the orphanage. I may never see either of them again.

I'm sure you exaggerate. Why do you say that?

My wife forbids me to see her again. And they won't give me the baby unless my wife is with me.

Listen, I thought the baby had a name. Didn't we establish that?

Yes. Simon. But it's not going to be my baby so it isn't Simon.

Of course it's Simon. He's your baby and he's Simon. They can't keep him from you just because your wife is indisposed. That's absurd. It's criminal. People here make a great show of following rules and regulations but they could really not care less. You've just got to speak to them very plainly and show them that you mean business.

The nurse I spoke with made of point of saying they wouldn't release the baby if my wife wasn't there.

Of course she did. But that doesn't mean she won't give

him to you without your wife. If your wife won't go with you, I will. I know how to handle these people. We'll tell them I'm your mother. Little Simon's grandmother. And they'll hand him right over, mark my words.

I suppose it's worth trying.

Of course it is! Unless you don't really want the baby. Is that why you're prevaricating?

I'm not prevaricating! I want the baby. Simon. I've done everything I could possibly do to get him.

Then you shall have him. Of course that's a horrible way to put it—no one ever *has* a child. Most of the misery in the world comes from people thinking that they do, that they own their children when all they're doing is taking care of them until they can take ownership of themselves. And some children do it very early on—I've known six-year-olds that are completely self-possessed and autonomous. But I'm sure Simon needs some looking after. So we will go and get him tomorrow.

Thank you, said the man.

There's no need to thank me. It's an adventure. I love adventures and they don't come along very often. I can't remember the last time I had an adventure . . . oh, wait: I can, but I shan't tell you about it because it ended somewhat disastrously through no fault of my own, but nevertheless it wasn't a particularly happy adventure. And I'm sure our adventure tomorrow will be very happy.

Maybe this isn't a good idea, the man said.

You'll never manage to get poor little Simon out of there by yourself.

Perhaps you're right, said the man.

Of course I'm right! There can be no doubt about it. Now you must go to bed. You look exhausted. Have you had your supper?

No, said the man.

Well, you must eat something. Lárus, bring our friend here some of your delicious scrambled eggs. And fry some of those little potatoes along with them. I must return to the piano. Some of us must sing for our suppers.

Livia Pinheiro-Rima drank the schnapps that was left in her glass and slid off her stool. She reached out and touched the man's cheek, cupped it with her hand for a moment, and looked into his eyes. Then she bent down and kissed him, tenderly, on his lips.

Don't worry, she told him. Everything will be fine.

✦

Someone had taped a piece of cardboard over the hole in the door, which of course didn't protect him at all—anyone could easily rip it off and reach inside and open the door, as he had done. He supposed he should ask for another room with a properly locking door, but he realized he did not care very much about this.

He unlocked the door and entered the room. He decided

not to turn any of the lights on, for he did not want to see the room. He did not mind being in the room, but he did not want to see it. He entered the dark bathroom and felt his way to the toilet. Then he went to the sink and felt for the taps. Even though he had a pretty good idea of where his toothbrush and toothpaste were, he decided to forgo brushing his teeth. He splashed cold water on his face—the cold water here was, unsurprisingly, very cold—and then he felt for the towel on the rack and patted his face dry.

He returned to the bedroom and stood for a moment in the darkness, trying to think if there was anything he should do, or anything he had forgotten. There was such a lot to remember. He wanted to remember something he should do so he could do it and subsequently feel that he was in control of his life, or at least that he was not forgetting to do all the things he should do, but he could think of nothing. Of course he had not brushed his teeth and that was something he should do but it was fine not to do that as long as he was aware of not doing it.

He took off his clothes but left on his long silk underwear and lay down on the bed, on top of the coverlet. He reached inside his underpants and held his penis in his hand. He did not stroke it but simply held it, gently squeezing it now and then. Holding his penis like this made him feel safe, and self-contained, like an electrical extension cord that is coiled up and then plugged back into itself.

✦

The woman could not sleep. A deep restlessness had come over her. It was as if her body were pumped full of some ricocheting current. It hurt not to move her arms and legs. And something was shaking in the air. Or the air itself was shaking. She sat up and saw that a woman was sitting on the chair the man had kicked over. The shaking air made it difficult to see her, but the woman knew it was not Darlene. This woman sat on the chair sideways and had turned and rested her arms along its back. She was positioned to look at the woman but her gaze had no direction. And then the woman recognized her—she was the woman who had appeared in her hotel room the night they arrived.

Hello, she said.

The woman in the chair said nothing. She leaned toward the woman in the bed as if she wanted the woman to see her more clearly, and then she pushed herself off the chair and rose backward through the window. The drapes had been opened.

The woman fell back upon the bed. The wind that had pulled the woman out the window had somehow pushed her as well. She tried to lie still but the coursing energy had returned to her body. She quickly got out of bed and went to the window. The moon had appeared and was casting a phosphorescent light over the fields of snow. She realized that she was sweating, so she opened the window wide and leaned out as far as she was able into the chilling air. Suddenly something within the woman folded open, succumbing to a constant pressure, and, feeling freed, she turned away from the window and crossed the room. She opened the door and walked down the hallway, down the stairs and through the room with the alabaster lamp and the tête-à-tête, down through the dark house and into the vestibule, where she paused for a moment, trying to pull the warmth and color of the house into her, and then she opened the door and stepped out onto the dirt-covered steps. The row of sentinel fir trees shook themselves in the wind and beckoned, but she stepped down onto the drive and walked around the side of the house, moving through the snow like a ship, out into the vast field she had seen from her window. As she walked she could feel the restlessness leave her body, and she grew tired and finally had to lie down in the snow. It was only then that she felt the cold, painfully biting at her, and she tried to stand up, but she could not, the snow held her to it, and once she gave up her struggle she felt herself growing warm, deliciously warm, and she realized that someone had kindly swaddled her in Nanny's Russian black bear coat.

SIX

The sound of water filling the bathtub awoke the man. He sat up in bed and looked at the bathroom door, which was closed. Was his wife inside? Could they now go and get their child and leave this place and go home? For the first time since he had left it, he thought of New York City: it might be snowing there but the snow would turn to rain as soon as the sun rose. The clouds would part and the sun would emerge and the clean wet sidewalks would shine. There would be ten hours of daylight and your face would not freeze the moment you stepped outside. And soon it would be spring and robins would be pecking the tender green lawn in Madison Square Park. And he would be walking through the park with the baby in a stroller, in the soft warm spring sunlight, pointing to and naming the birds, the budding flowers, the leafing trees . . .

The taps were turned off with an angry squeal. He got out of bed and knocked softly on the closed bathroom door.

Oh, are you awake? a voice asked. It's me.

He tried to make the voice sound like his wife's but he could not. It was too strong and bright, and he knew it was the voice of Livia Pinheiro-Rima.

Livia?

Yes, it's me. It's shocking, I know, commandeering your bathtub. You see, I've only got a horrible little sit tub in my room; it's like bathing in a teacup and getting in and out of the damn thing requires the flexibility of a contortionist. So when I saw your lovely large tub—really, it's almost the size of a swimming pool—I couldn't resist. Do you mind awfully? If you do I'll get out.

No, no. Of course not.

Do you need to use the toilet? If you do, come on in. We can both shut our eyes.

No, I'm fine, said the man, although he did need to use the toilet. But what are you doing here?

I thought I just explained that.

No, I mean here in my room.

Oh! Well, I came up to check on you. It's almost noon, you know.

Is it? My God, I have got to go and see my wife.

What about the baby? Simon. Aren't we going to collect him together?

Yes, said the man. But first I need to see my wife.

Yes, yes, I suppose you must. So go, and I'll enjoy a nice long bath, and when you've returned we'll go and adopt Simon. This bath is delicious. The basic human need for ablution is primal. We all used to be fish you know, I mean not you and me personally, but our ancestors, if you go back far enough, which isn't very far, there we are, or were, swimming in the briny depths, and now we all long to submerge ourselves, like a pickle, like a coin in a fountain, like a stone tossed into the sea. I'm going to stop talking now and immerse myself.

✦

Darlene opened the door and told the man to wait in the room with the fire. She would tell Brother Emmanuel he was here. The man had barely sat down when Brother Emmanuel entered the room, with an uncharacteristic haste. In fact he was panting, as if he had run from a great distance.

The man stood up. Good morning, he said.

Oh, my friend, Brother Emmanuel said. Sit down.

The man sat and Brother Emmanuel knelt before him and told him that his wife's soul was free.

What do you mean? the man asked. Is she dead?

Yes, said Brother Emmanuel. If you think in those terms.

I do, said the man. How? he asked. What happened?

Brother Emmanuel told him how, early in the morning, they had found her missing and had followed her footsteps through the snow. They had carried her inside and tried to revive her but could not. She was dead. Her soul had left her body.

The man asked if he could be alone.

Of course you may be alone, said Brother Emmanuel. For as long as you need. But I must tell you one more thing, and then I will leave you alone. I want to say this now so you have it all at once. Your wife told me that she wanted her body to stay here. She did not want it taken away. She wanted to be cremated, and she wanted her ashes to remain here. She wanted them placed in the bowl of narcissi so they might nurture new life.

I don't care about her body, the man said. Or the narcissi. Please leave me alone.

Yes, said Brother Emmanuel. I am sorry if I have failed you. I was trying to help your wife. I was trying to ease her path.

Yes, said the man. Fuck you.

The man sat on the sofa for a long time after Brother Emmanuel left. He could not comprehend what he had been told and after a while he stopped trying, stopped thinking anything at all, just sat and let the stillness gather around him. And then he heard a voice and looked up to see that Artemis was watching him from within his cage. He repeated the same word several times, but it was in a language the man did not understand.

✦

That afternoon the man and Livia Pinheiro-Rima left the hotel together and took a taxi to the orphanage. The man wore a three-piece suit beneath his parka and carried the little suitcase they had prepared for the baby. Both he and his wife had packed special clothes to wear on the day that they finally received the baby. His wife had bought a simple yet elegant moss-green woolen dress from Brooks Brothers and had had it altered to fit her dwindling body. The man thought of the dress, hanging in its protective plastic sheath, in the closet of their hotel room. It was the only thing that she had hung in the closet; the rest of her clothes were jumbled in her suitcase or thrown over a chair.

His suit was too big for him and in truth made him look a little ridiculous, like a child wearing grown-up clothes. It had belonged to his grandfather, his father's father, who had died when the man was three in a hunting accident that the man's father later told him was certainly a suicide. Fortunately he had shot himself with a rifle in a forest, making possible the fictitious hunting trip.

The man had no memory of his grandfather, but he did have a photograph of his grandfather holding him upon his lap, and in this photo his grandfather wore the suit the man was now wearing. It was taken at Christmastime, in Lüchow's restaurant in New York City, a few days before his grandfather shot himself. An elderly waiter in a white jacket stood just behind his grandfather, looking into the camera as if he were meant to be included in the photograph, but of course he was only passing by the table.

Livia Pinheiro-Rima sat against the door and gazed out the window. She was wearing her Russian black bear coat and the kind of perfectly round dark glasses people in movies who are blind wear. She acted as though she were alone in the taxi. But then she suddenly turned toward him and said, For some reason I'm terribly nervous. Would you mind if I smoke?

It's fine, said the man.

Not really, she said, but I'll go ahead. Would you like one?

No, said the man.

She held a velvet bag upon her lap that had two gold bars across the top, which latched together with a little hands-holding clasp. Livia Pinheiro-Rima unsnapped the clasp and withdrew her cigarette case. She pressed a button and it sprung itself open. She fetched a lighter from her bag and lit her cigarette. She closed her eyes and took a few long, deep drags.

For a moment the man watched her smoke.

You have beautiful hands, he said.

Why, thank you, she said. They're rather large. And one, alas, is larger than the other. Look at this. She gave him her cigarette and held her hands before her, palm pressed to palm, finger to finger, as if she were praying. You see, she said, they don't match. Most people are symmetrical, but I'm not. It's why I couldn't act in films. The camera is so unforgiving; I look like some freakish Picasso damsel on film.

She reclaimed her cigarette and continued smoking. Do you know, when I went to acting school, way back in the dark ages, they taught you how to smoke onstage? We had an entire class on smoking and eating onstage. Drinking too. It was called Acting and Imbibing. For instance, you always keep your hand in profile when you smoke, so the audience can see the cigarette, so if you're facing downstage you've got to smoke out of the corner of your mouth. If you have beautiful hands you use the cigarette to display them. There's nothing better for a hand than a cigarette. And you never exhale downward; always send the smoke up, above the heads of your fellow actors. Of course, that is, if you have fellow actors. The only nice thing about being alone onstage is that you can send the smoke anywhere you want. Yet I always send it up, out of habit, I suppose.

She paused for a moment and tapped some ash off her cigarette into the pocket of her bearskin coat.

Don't look at me, she said. Look out the window.

Why? asked the man.

Because I can't say this next bit if you're looking at me.

The man turned away and looked out the window. The fields stretched all the way to the horizon, where they blurred into the gray sky.

He heard Livia Pinheiro-Rima say: Acting with someone is very intimate, you know. It isn't so very different from sleeping with someone. In a way it's more intimate, because it's easy to fake intimacy in bed, but if you act well, if you do it right, you're raw, you're completely vulnerable, it's like you're porous, your body ceases to have boundaries. Your mind too, and your heart. She paused for a moment and then said, I've felt that with you, some of these moments.

She paused, but he said nothing, so she continued: When I was young, she said, when I was just beginning—my circus days, I suppose—and even after that, when I was a not very young, for most of my life, in fact, I have wanted to make love with just about everyone I met. I mean, not everyone of course, but with so very many. Men and women. In some way it seemed a crime to me to be alive, to be on this earth, and *not* make love to everyone. It wasn't nymphomania. No. It was that I could see too clearly, too devastatingly, the thing, things, about people that were hurt and therefore loveable, the beautiful sacred space in them that needed touching. And once you've seen that in someone, it's difficult not to love him. Or her. At least it was for me.

She paused for a moment, but still he said nothing, and so she continued: You see, I'm afraid of going dead inside. Of course I can't make love with you, I know that, I mean intellectually I do, but there's something wrong with me. This should count. This should be valid enough.

What? the man asked.

This, said Livia Pinheiro-Rima. Just sitting here together in this car. It *should* matter. It *should* count.

And it doesn't? asked the man.

Perhaps it does. That's the joke of my life: that it all does matter, all these quiet moments, this moment, but we just want to get fucked and applauded, so we think that's what matters, what counts, and in the end we realize it's just the opposite.

She was silent for a moment and the man was about to turn away from the window when he heard her speak again.

It's important for me that you know that, she said. That you know how I feel about you.

He turned then and looked at her. She sat very erect, facing forward, staring through the front windshield. The man saw for the first time her frailty. It seemed to him that it was only her clothes, the girth and weight of her monstrous fur coat, that contained and protected her.

He reached out and touched the arm of her coat, and then leaned forward and kissed her on her cheek. Thank you for doing this, he said. Thank you for coming with me to get the baby.

◆

They entered the lobby of the orphanage to find that it was empty and unattended. We must push this button to summon someone, the man said. Otherwise we may languish here forever.

Then by all means push it, said Livia Pinheiro-Rima. Push it with all your might!

The man pushed the button and they heard its shrill clang momentarily alarm the entire building.

Well done, said Livia Pinheiro-Rima. I'm sure we will be attended to momentarily. Meanwhile, I will sit upon this monstrosity and reacclimate myself. One is perpetually shedding or donning garments in this country. It's fatiguing.

The man had removed his parka immediately upon entering the anteroom and laid it upon one of the pews that flanked the entryway, for he felt it seriously compromised the effect of his grandfather's suit. If he had brought a topcoat, he might have left it on, for it was cold in the anteroom, but he had not—he had only brought the parka, in which he always felt slightly ridiculous, as if he were acting as a penguin in some elementary school winter pageant.

Now, listen, said Livia Pinheiro-Rima. Relax. Just be yourself. Pretend you adopt a baby every day of the week. Can you do that?

I'll try, said the man.

You've got to do more than try. If they sense you're nervous they'll throw the baby out with the bathwater.

The man said nothing.

I was making a joke, said Livia Pinheiro-Rima. The baby with the bathwater. It didn't amuse you?

No, said the man.

I was trying to get you relaxed. If you don't know what to say, say nothing. Just look at me and I'll take over. You've got to relax. I'll tell you what to do—it's an old theater trick: jump up and down and flap your arms. Do it. It works wonderfully.

I don't think that's a good idea, said the man.

I tell you, if they sense you're nervous they'll smell a rat. They'll smell a rat abandoning a sinking ship.

The man laughed. That one was good, he said.

Jump, said Livia Pinheiro-Rima. Flap!

The man began to jump up and down and flap his arms. It felt very good. He closed his eyes. And then he felt a hand pressing down upon his shoulder, stilling him. He stopped jumping and opened his eyes. Livia Pinheiro-Rima stood beside him, her hand on his shoulder, pressing him down with a force that was peculiarly strong and adamant. And beside her stood a man. He sported a pince-nez and wore a white lab coat over a three-piece suit that was remarkably like the man's own suit, and for a moment the man thought it was his suit, or his grandfather's suit, and he did not know how it had gotten off him and onto this other man. But then he realized he was still wearing his suit. And the other man's suit was better tailored and fit him very neatly.

It's all my fault, said Livia Pinheiro-Rima. I told him to jump. She kept her hand pressed upon the man's shoulder as if he might start jumping again if she took it away.

He was terribly nervous about everything, she said to the man in the white coat. I'm sure that by now you are well acquainted with the hysteria of adoptive parents. They must process in a few minutes the most fundamental change known to man. Natural parents have nine months to process the transfiguration of their lives, but the adoptive parent has but minutes. He was beside himself, and so I told him to jump, because nothing restores equanimity like jumping. It

255

is a well-known physiological fact. Those brave beautiful soldiers who stormed the shores of Normandy—they were ordered to jump as they crossed the channel.

Yes, of course, said the man in the white coat. I am Doctor Oswalt Ludjekins. I am the director of St. Barnabas. Allow me to welcome you.

He held out his hand and both Livia Pinheiro-Rima and the man shook it. You are both most welcome here. But tell me, please, Miss Pinheiro-Rima, what brings you to St. Barnabas?

Oh, do you know me?

Of course I do! I am, perhaps, your greatest devotee. Unless there is an emergency here at St. Barnabas, Friday evenings will invariably find me in the lobby of the Borgar-fjaroasysla Grand Imperial Hotel drinking whiskey, smoking a cigar, and listening to you sing.

Oh, so you're the gentleman with the cigar!

I'm afraid I am. Does the smoke bother you?

Oh, no. It comes with the territory, as they say.

I'm relieved because I would hate to think I am in any way compromising your artistry.

Well, I shall blame all future gaffes on you.

Please do, said Doctor Ludjekins. Yet none of this explains why I have the great pleasure of welcoming you to St. Barnabas. I believe that this gentleman and his wife are adopting one of our foundlings, but you, my dear Miss Pinheiro-Rima, what brings you to St. Barnabas? Are you also in want of an orphan?

Is there not, my dear Doctor Ludjekins, someplace where we might speak more comfortably? I'm afraid that anterooms like this, being neither here nor there, set my nerves on edge. And I fear I am standing in a draught.

But of course, said Doctor Ludjekins. I'm afraid the excitement of meeting you, Miss Pinheiro-Rima, has caused me to lose my manners. Shall we make a bee's line for my office?

Perhaps, said Livia Pinheiro-Rima, we may venture upstairs. I know my son is very eager to see his son.

Doctor Ludjekins turned to the man. Your son?

Yes, said the man. Today is the day he becomes mine. We have been here for six days now.

But where is your wife? asked the doctor.

His wife has had a most unfortunate accident, said Livia Pinheiro-Rima. Last night she slipped on some ice and injured her ankle. We fear it is broken. She wanted so badly to come with us, of course, but the doctor forbade it.

Ah, the ice is treacherous at this time of year! It is a miracle we are not all hobbling about on sticks! But I am sure she will be perfectly well again quite soon. Tomorrow, perhaps. And then you can come and gather your new child together.

Ah, but they are leaving here tomorrow, said Livia Pinheiro-Rima. And bringing their child out of this cursed darkness and off to the land of milk and honey.

But we cannot give a little baby to only a man. A baby must have mother and father.

And so shall this baby have, said Livia Pinheiro-Rima. He will meet his mother as soon as we return to the hotel. She is waiting there with open arms. Open arms and a broken foot! She opened her arms wide by way of illustration, but Doctor Ludjekins seemed to think she was about to embrace (or attack) him, for he raised his hand and took a step backward.

That is all well and good, he said. But we can only transact a baby to two parents.

I understand, said Livia Pinheiro-Rima. But surely you can make an exception in this case? It would be a shame for the little dear to lose his chance at a happy home on account of a broken foot.

Where babies are concerned I am afraid there can be no exceptions, said Doctor Ludjekins. My hands are tied.

Oh goodness, said Livia Pinheiro-Rima. Tied hands *and* broken feet! This is a muddle, isn't it?

You must change your plans of departure, Doctor Ludjekins said to the man. And your woman must regain her feet. And then all shall be happy.

Listen, said Livia Pinheiro-Rima. My dear doctor, please listen. I'm going to tell you something about myself I very rarely reveal. It may shock you. I am older than I appear to be. Old enough to be a grandmother, in fact. This man you see before you, this dear sweet man, is my son. And his wife is my daughter-in-law. I know it seems impossible, but it's true. I am old enough to be a mother once-removed from that poor darling baby above us, I shall be his Nana, his Nona, his Bubbie, his Granny, his Mimi; I shall be his very special and devoted Momsy, and I am here, here right now, here with two working hands and two operating feet, and I think if you do not release that baby into the care of his loving Papa and his doting Momsy, you will rue this day forevermore.

The doctor seemed somewhat overwhelmed by this speech, for he took another step backward, as if Livia Pinheiro-Rima were a fire whose heat was becoming too intense. He turned once again to the man.

She is your mother? he asked.

The man looked at Livia Pinheiro-Rima and was about to declare she was his mother, but then it occurred to him that if he was given this child on the basis of lies, he would never feel that the child was truly his.

No, the man said. She is not my mother. But please, give me my son. What more can I do? Do you want more money? Tell me, just tell me, and I'll do it. But give me my son!

He stopped talking when Livia Pinheiro-Rima reached out and touched him on the small bare part of his neck that rose above his white shirt collar.

Relax, my darling, she said. My dear, dear boy. Everything will be fine. You are overwhelmed. She gently patted his cheek and then withdrew her hand. She turned to the doctor.

Don't you see? He is overwhelmed. My poor boy. The impossible journey here, and these days of waiting, and the cold, and then his wife's accident; can't you understand it has all been too much for him? Of course, I'm his mother. Do you think he would be here if I wasn't? Do you think he would come to this godforsaken place to adopt a baby if he weren't my son? He came here because I begged him to. Because he is a good son. A son who loves his mother, and who will love his son. It is all connected, the love we feel for our parents and children.

I don't understand you, said Doctor Ludjekins. What has this to do with the baby?

Everything! It has everything to do with the baby! I told you, it's all connected, the love of parents and children. You can't be so heartless as to not acknowledge that.

Of course I acknowledge it. Who would not? I simply fail to see what bearing it has on the matter in hand. I think perhaps you decide I am a dunce. I have a medical degree from Johns Hopkins University in the city of Baltimore, the state of Maryland. Do you know of it?

Of course I do, said the man. It is a very fine school.

So you see I am not some *dummkopf*.

Oh, my dear doctor! exclaimed Livia Pinheiro-Rima. Of course you are not! My son and I have the utmost respect for you, and for this marvelous institution you direct. I myself plan to leave a large part of my small fortune to St. Bartholomew's.

It is St. Barnabas, said the doctor.

Of course it is! St. Barnabas. One of the finest institutions of its kind.

We follow all international protocols, said Doctor

Ludjekins. We do not sell babies. Procedures may have been like rubber under my predecessor, Mrs. Tarja Uosukainen, but I assure you that St. Barnabas is no longer the hodge-podge it once may have been. Everything is now clean and above the boards.

Of course, doctor—that is exactly why I suggested St. Barnabas to my son. I knew that since you have taken over it is an institution beyond reproach. That is precisely why we are here, and why my son is so eager to claim his son.

We do not contribute our babies to lonesome parents, said Doctor Ludjekins. They must all be here to welcome the baby.

Yes, of course, said the man. And my wife would be here, if it were not for her broken leg. If it's really so important, I will go back to the hotel and drag her here, limping all the way. She would do it happily. She would crawl here on her hands and knees. He did not realize he was aggressively ges-ticulating until Livia Pinheiro-Rima reached out, grabbed one of his pinwheeling arms, and lowered it to his side.

Hush, she said. Poor boy. You're upset. She turned to the doctor. He's upset, she said. It's only natural. Excuse us for just a moment, if you would be so kind.

She took the man's hand and pulled him into a corner of the anteroom and positioned them so that she was facing him with her back to the doctor. She mouthed a word with her lips, which were painted a bright deep red, but the man did not understand what she said and so he shook his head. She winked at him.

You're upset, my dear, she said in a voice that could easily be overhead by the doctor, who was standing just a few feet away. Why don't you go outside and smoke a cigarette? It will calm you. And I will have a chat with Doctor Ludjekins.

But I don't—

Of course you do. Here. Livia Pinheiro-Rima opened her little bag and reached into it and withdrew her cigarette case.

Hold this, she said to the man, and handed him her bag, which he clutched rather awkwardly with both hands, as he did not like the doctor seeing him holding a woman's handbag. Livia Pinheiro-Rima flicked open the case and pulled one cigarette out from beneath its silver clasp. Give me my lighter, she said. It's in the bag.

He reached into the bag and found her lighter, which he withdrew.

Take it, Livia Pinheiro-Rima said. She handed him the cigarette she had extracted from the case and took the bag from him. Now go outside and smoke. I know it's cold but the cold will do you good. I will come and get you when I am finished with the doctor. Do you understand?

Yes, said the man. I understand.

Good, said Livia Pinheiro-Rima. Go. She pushed him toward to door. Don't come back until I fetch you.

✦

The man had not smoked in several years. But he felt foolish standing idly on the steps of the orphanage, and so he
lit the cigarette and smoked. It was very cold outside and
he wished he could fill his entire body with the warm,
poisonous smoke. He smoked it down to the filter and then
threw it in the snow. It was too cold to stand still and so
he descended the steps and walked across the small parking
lot to the road. Across from the orphanage was a building
that looked as if it might once have been a gas station but
was now clearly abandoned. There was no other building
in sight, only fields of snow. Even though it was early afternoon the sun was setting in the west. It leached a pale
yellowish light along the horizon. Nothing moved or made
a sound.

The man felt very capable of making noise, and he
wished he had a gun so he could fire it and hear the violent
disturbance. Instead he shouted the word *cabbage* as loud as
he could into the cold air. Cabbage had been the name of
his childhood dog, a fat dachshund that when curled up
was said to resemble a cabbage. The dog often ran away—
apparently it did not like living where it lived—and the
man, when he was a boy, spent many hours out in the fields
surrounding his family's house shouting the dog's name.
Cabbage! Cabbage!

He had loved the dog but had also hated him, because
he was always running away. Usually he would reappear,
but once he did not and the man saw him the next day from

the window of the school bus, lying by the side of the road, crushed. He had wanted to tell the bus driver to stop but could not, for the school bus was a ruthless place where any sort of emotional behavior was violently ridiculed. When he got home from school that afternoon he rode his bike to the place where the dog lay and brought him home, holding the dog against his chest with one hand and the handlebar with the other. The crushed dog leaked blood and guts onto his school shirt and he was punished by his mother because he had not changed into his play clothes before going to fetch the dog.

Cabbage! Cabbage! Come!

He turned away from the field and walked across the parking lot to the steps of the orphanage. He wished he had another cigarette to smoke. Perhaps he would start smoking again. It was for his wife he had stopped, and now she was dead. But if he had a child he should not smoke. It was one of the many things he would give up for the child. Well, he had already given up smoking, so he could not give that up for the child, but he could at least not start smoking again. He wished he could sit down, but the icy steps were heavily dusted with ashes. Someone had shoveled a narrow path to a bench that stood in the field beside the parking lot but the bench was covered in snow. Odd that someone would shovel the path to the bench but not the bench itself.

His wife was dead. The part of his life that had been his marriage was over. It had been a good part of his life, except for the past year. In the next part of his life he might have a child, be a father. Or he might not. Doctor Ludjekins had seemed adamant, but then Livia Pinheiro-Rima was a formidable opponent. He would miss her when he left this place. Perhaps she would come to visit him and the child, as if she really were his grandmother. Otherwise the boy would have no grandparents, for both his and his wife's parents were dead. If everything went well, he could be home in three days. With a son. Even if everything did not go well, he could be home in three days.

A sweet wee bairn inside is crying for his Dada.

The man turned to see Livia Pinheiro-Rima standing on the top step.

You're a father, she said. Now come inside and collect your son.

What happened? the man asked.

Why do you care what happened? Everything's fine. The wee bairn is yours. They're inside now putting all the papers in order. You've just got to sign on the dotted line.

He's mine? Really?

I wouldn't joke about something like this. Now come inside before you freeze to death.

✦

In the taxi on the way back to the hotel the man held the child on his lap. Livia Pinheiro-Rima smoked and looked out the window, even though it was dark and the only thing she could see was her smoking reflection.

The child was sleeping soundly. He wore the puffy silver snowsuit the man's wife had picked out after an hour of neurotic deliberation in Babies "R" Us. It was designed to resemble a space suit and even had a patch proclaiming JUNIOR SPACE RANGER on its sleeve. Some of the child's straight blond hair protruded from beneath the hood and his cheeks were flushed. It was as if he, too, had been through an ordeal like the man and was similarly exhausted. He was heavier and more substantial than the man had imagined he would be. And he would only get bigger. Is he too much for me? the man wondered. Am I big enough for him?

Look at him, he said to Livia Pinheiro-Rima. Isn't he beautiful?

Livia Pinheiro-Rima rolled down the window and threw her cigarette out into the night. Then she turned and looked at the man and at the child.

He will break hearts, she said. Yours among them, I've no doubt. Children do that.

Do you have children?

Yes, she said. Two. One I've lost touch with—I suppose he might still be alive. But I know the other is dead.

And did they break your heart?

Yes.

Both of them?

Each in his own cunning way.

The man looked down at the child he held. I don't think Simon will break my heart, he said.

Of course you don't. No parent does. Here—give him

to me. Let me hold him. Now, while he's all rosy-cheeked and sleeping. Before you take him away forever and I never see him again, the thought of which I cannot bear.

The man carefully handed the child to Livia Pinheiro-Rima, who held him against her bear-fur coat. She gently stroked one of his flushed cheeks with the backs of her fingers. The man saw that she was crying.

After a moment of watching her, he said, Will you tell me what you did?

What do you mean? She did not look up at him. She continued to caress the child's cheek.

I mean back there, at the orphanage. What did you do?

The baby is yours, she said. You don't want to know what I did. It shouldn't be a part of his story, or yours.

But you've got to tell me!

Have I? She stopped caressing the baby and looked at the man.

Yes. Otherwise I'll always worry.

Why would you worry?

I just want to feel safe. That he is mine.

You are safe. He is yours. I assure you.

Did you give him money?

Here, she said. Have him back. He's yours. That should be all that matters.

The man took the baby back from Livia Pinheiro-Rima. She turned away from him and once again lit a cigarette and regarded her face in the dark window.

They rode in silence until the taxi entered the narrow

winding streets of the old town. Livia Pinheiro-Rima reached into the pockets of her coat and extracted two black leather gloves that she carefully slid over her large slender hands, pushing down the V between each of her fingers so that they fit her snugly. Then she folded her gloved hands in her lap and looked back out the window.

I'm sorry, said the man. I can't tell you how grateful I am to you. For everything you've done. For my wife, and for me, and for the baby. None of this would have happened if it weren't for you. What you said before, on our way out, about how you felt. I have felt the same. Feel the same. I'm sorry I didn't say that then.

Livia Pinheiro-Rima turned away from the window and looked at the man. Well, thank you, she said. It's nice to know. Although what good it will do either of us, I know not.

✦

The man held the baby and Livia Pinheiro-Rima pushed them all through the revolving door and into the lobby of the Borgarfjaroasysla Grand Imperial Hotel.

Come, she said. We must celebrate this occasion with a drink.

The man followed her into the bar. Livia Pinheiro-Rima walked around the bar to her seat in the corner. She un-hooked the horn toggles on her coat and shrugged it off, allowing it to fall onto the floor. She was wearing the black sequined evening gown she had worn the night the man had first met her, and the man thought, She must have known we would succeed at the orphanage, otherwise she would not have worn that dress. He followed her around the bar, sat down beside her, and looked around as if there might be someplace to stow the baby but of course there was not so he held the baby on his lap.

It was a bit awkward, he realized, carrying a child around with you.

When they had settled themselves, Lárus detached himself from his wall and came and stood before them. He took no notice of the baby. Schnapps? he asked.

Livia Pinheiro-Rima turned to the man. Schnapps?

No, said the man. Champagne! We're celebrating. Champagne for us all. Bring us a bottle of your finest champagne.

Our finest champagne is very fine, said Lárus. It is perhaps too fine for you.

I expect it is, said Livia Pinheiro-Rima. Bring us a bottle of the Billecart-Salmon.

The blanc de blancs or the rosé?

Don't be a fool. The blanc de blancs. We'll have a toast. Our dear friend has just become a father. He has a child, you see.

Yes, I see, said Lárus. Children under sixteen years of age are not allowed in the bar.

He's seventeen, said Livia Pinheiro-Rima. Go.

Lárus turned about and exited through the upholstered door.

Livia Pinheiro-Rima sighed and placed her bag upon the bar. She opened it and fished out her cigarette case. One supposes one should smoke at a time like this, she said. Or are you afraid it will harm the little one?

I think he'll be fine, said the man. I'd like one too.

Mais oui, bien sûr. She extracted two cigarettes from her case, put them in her mouth, and lit them both. She handed one to the man and inhaled upon the other.

I realize now, she said, that a glass of Billecart-Salmon is exactly what I have been craving. I'm so sick of that damn schnapps, you've no idea.

Do you think I should take his snowsuit off? asked the man. Do you think it's too warm for him in here?

Oh, I doubt it, said Livia Pinheiro-Rima. Plus better too warm than too cold. If you start catering to every little whim of his now there'll be no end to it. It's good for children to suffer a little. It builds character.

No wonder your children broke your heart, the man said.

I admit I wasn't the best mother in the world. Or even a particularly good one. I wanted my children to be independent, self-sufficient. To go off on their own and make their own lives as soon as they possibly could. In the old days children were sent out into the fields or down into the mines as soon as they could handle a hoe or a pick. Now they're all mollycoddled and live at home until they're middle-aged.

If this is advice you are giving me I shall follow none of

it, said the man. I expect I shall be the type of parent you hate.

I've no doubt you will be. You'll ruin this poor lovely child faster than you can say Cornelia Otis Skinner. But don't abandon your own life. Don't conflate it with his. Don't conflate it with anyone's. That's my real advice.

Is it really? asked the man. It sounds lonely.

Oh, I don't mean that you should be lonely. Or necessarily alone. I mean you shouldn't do anything out of a fear of being alone. That's when the trouble starts.

Lárus backed through the door. He held a large silver tray upon which sat a bottle of champagne and four flutes. He lowered it carefully onto the bar beside the man. He unbelted and removed the foil wrap that shrouded the head of the bottle and then untwisted the wire cage. He then pulled the cork out of the bottle and held it at arm's length as it calmed itself. He poured a small amount of champagne into each of the flutes; it raced up the walls of the glasses and stopped just before overflowing. The hissing foam loitered at the rim of the glasses for a moment and then began collapsing back into itself, and as it settled Lárus slowly poured more champagne onto the retreating foam and this time the champagne mounted inside the glass with less drama. He equally filled all four glasses and placed one before Livia Pinheiro-Rima and one before the man. Then he picked up one of the two remaining glasses of champagne.

Who is the fourth glass for? asked Livia Pinheiro-Rima.

Lárus nodded at the child the man was holding in his arms. For the seventeen-year-old, he said.

Livia Pinheiro-Rima laughed. That's fine, she said. That's just right. She slunk off the stool and stood, holding her glass of champagne before her, like a lighted sparkler. It was still effervescing.

He must come back when he is seventeen, she said. We must all come back. We must hold this child safely in our dreams until we meet again, in seventeen years. And what a fine and handsome youth he shall be, and what a happy childhood will he have had! We ask for God's blessing upon this boy, ask that he be healthy and happy and wise and full of art and magic. And love. All this we wish for Simon! Godspeed! Mazel tov! *Kippaikija!*

✦

After a short while the child began to fret and cry, so the man took him out into the lobby. He laid him down on one of the low round tables and peeled the snowsuit off. Beneath it he wore a pair of red corduroy OshKosh B'gosh overalls and a pink turtleneck shirt patterned with yellow smiley faces. He wore thick black socks on his feet and no shoes. Although the man did not expect the child to be dressed quaintly in some ethnic or national costume, he was a little disappointed by the familiarity of his clothes. The nurse had explained to him that all the clothes the children at the orphanage wore were donated by a Lutheran church in Selinsgrove, Pennsylvania.

He assumed the child needed his diaper changed, but the diaper bag, which contained a dozen eco-friendly diapers and assorted organic emollients and powders and wipes, was up in his room, and the man wanted to attend to his child privately, not in the hotel lobby, as he felt both sentimental about this first intimate interaction with his son and also unsure of his diapering prowess. If it went badly he did not want witnesses.

The child, though freed from his snowsuit, continued to cry, so the man picked him up and held him gently against his chest, one of his hands palming the child's small head. He gently rocked himself and the child and to his amazement the child stopped crying and burped quite loudly. Instinctively, the man patted and rubbed his child's back, and he burped again.

The man thought this was a very good start and hoped that it boded well. Perhaps it was all instinctive and he would be a natural parent. He sat down in one of the club chairs and held his child. He began to speak quietly to him. He told him who he was and the circumstances of their both being there, in that place, together. How his wife had wanted to be there so that she could love him too. How he would love him double to compensate for his mother's absence, as if such an absence could ever be compensated for. He held the child close to him and gently circled his hand upon his back, feeling his warmth and softness beneath the layer of OshKosh. He said all he could think of to say to the child, even though he knew the child did not understand him, but nevertheless he wanted it said; he wanted it to have been there, between them, at the very beginning.

He moved his face close to the child's head and smelled his scalp and softly pressed his lips against the warm skin covering his fontanel, where he thought he could feel the baby's brain murmuring. He was glad the child had become his before that portal was irrevocably closed.

✦

The businessman man knocked on the door of the man's hotel room. Through the hole in the door—the cardboard had been removed—he could see the soft pink glow of one of the bedside lamps. He knocked again, but there was still no response. He tested the doorknob and, finding it was unlocked, opened it and stepped into the room. He stood just inside the battered door and observed the man and the child sleeping on the bed, which had been pushed against the wall. The pillows had been arranged around the bed's perimeter in a low soft wall. The man lay beside the child; one of his arms was extended and his hand rested upon the child's stomach, as if the child were buoyant and the man was keeping him from floating away.

After a moment the businessman crossed the room and sat down on the edge of the bed that was not pushed against the wall. His arrival woke neither the man nor the child, so he reached out his arm and gently shook the man's shoulder.

The man sat up abruptly, sliding toward the foot of the bed and knocking one of the pillows onto the floor. He stood up and looked toward the door, as if whatever had awakened him might be trying to escape. He did not see the businessman sitting on the bed until he sat back down.

I'm sorry if I startled you, said the businessman. I didn't mean to.

You scared me, said the man. What are you doing in here? He looked down to see that the child was still sleeping. He reached out to touch the baby but then, thinking perhaps it was best not to disturb him, withdrew his hand.

I assume that's the kiddie you came here to adopt, said the businessman.

Yes, said the man. That's my son. Simon.

Sleeping like a baby, said the businessman.

He's been very good, said the man. He *is* very good.

Enjoy it while it lasts. My kiddies were sweet enough until they turned about eight. Then, practically overnight, despicable little shits.

I'm surprised, with you as their father, it wasn't much sooner, said the man. He reached out again, and this time he did touch his child.

Listen to you, said the businessman. Fatherhood is making a man out of you. You picked up a set of balls along with the kiddo.

What are you doing here? asked the man.

Dragon Lady told me you were leaving tomorrow morning. She also told me about your wife. I'm sorry. I'm glad things worked out with the kiddie, but I'm sorry about your wife.

The man said nothing. He had somehow put the death of his wife aside, like a parcel whose delivery had been unsuccessfully attempted and was waiting to be collected with a little pink slip at the post office.

Are you really leaving in the morning?

Yes, said the man. What time is it now?

The businessman pushed back his cuffs and looked at his watch. It's eleven forty-five, he said. I'm sorry I woke you. But I wanted to say goodbye. And also to say—

What? asked he man.

I'm sorry, said the businessman. I wanted to apologize. For all my violence and rudeness. In case you haven't figured it out, I'm a very fucked-up and miserable man. I know it's no excuse, but—

Forget it, said the man. Everything was strange and awful here. You were no worse than anything else. In fact, perhaps you were a distraction.

Oh, don't get all sentimental. I did rape you, after all.

You didn't rape me, said the man.

Well, I wasn't very nice to you, was I?

You weren't so bad.

I did take good care of you after you were mugged. I was tender then, wasn't I?

Yes, said the man.

Most of the time I was a prick, though. A mean drunken prick.

Forget it, said the man. It doesn't matter. It's what happens at night.

The businessman stood up and stared for a moment at the man and the baby on the bed. There's something calm and soft about you that I like, he said. That you have and I don't.

The man said nothing.

Well, said the businessman, I've said what I came to say. I'll leave you and your son alone now. He's a handsome little fellow. I'm sure you'll be one of those pansy dads that children love.

Fuck you, said the man. Go away.

You need to get a sense of humor, said the businessman. Along with the balls and the kiddo.

The businessman stood still for a moment. What happens at night, he said, I like that. He reached down and patted the man's shoulder, and then he left the room.

SEVEN

The man's alarm seemed to ring moments after the businessman had left the room. Only the fact that he woke up convinced him that he had been asleep. He sat up and quickly looked around to see that his child was lying peacefully on the bed. Breathing, so he was still alive. He could not believe how good the child had been so far; with the exception of his crying and fretting in the bar he had behaved perfectly. Although he didn't seem to want to look at the man and several times when the man tried to touch the baby's face he had flinched and turned away.

But of course he was a stranger and had taken the child out of the only environment he had ever known. Anyone would flinch in such a situation.

The man woke the baby and fed him a bottle and then changed his diaper. Then he laid him back on the bed and gave him a small stuffed monkey. The child shook it back and forth and flung it off the bed. The man was amazed at how far his son could throw a stuffed monkey. Perhaps he would grow up to be a baseball player. He retrieved the monkey from the floor and gave him back to Simon—he was trying to think of the baby as *Simon* and not *the child* or *the baby*, but referring to him in this familiar way seemed almost presumptuous, like using *tu* instead of *vous* when speaking French.

The game of throwing the monkey continued while the man dressed and packed up the luggage. He looked around the room to see if anything remained, for he had a bad habit of leaving things behind in hotel rooms. There was nothing beneath the bed, but behind one of the drapes, sitting on the windowsill, he found the jar of yoghurt he had bought for his wife. Its proximity to the window had kept it chilled. He thought about taking it with him, but decided to leave it there, well hidden behind the drape.

In the lobby he saw Livia Pinheiro-Rima sitting on one of the club chairs, wrapped in her bearskin coat. A silver pot of tea or coffee, two cups and saucers, two plates, and a silver platter of pastries sat on the table before her.

She stood up and waved, as if she were not the only person sitting in the lobby. Come and sit down, she called. Give my grandson to me and sit down and have some coffee and franzbrötchen! You've got plenty of time before the train. Come and sit!

The man joined Livia Pinheiro-Rima and watched

while she poured coffee into one of the cups. She added milk and sugar without asking him if he wanted them, and even stirred it briskly with a little golden demitasse spoon before placing it on the table before the man.

Give me the little angel, she said, and reached out her hands. You've got him in that contraption backwards, you know.

I do?

Yes. He should be facing forwards so he can see where he's going.

That seems very odd, said the man. Don't I want him facing me?

No. He'll have plenty of time to look at you. Let him see the world.

Well, there's plenty of time for that too, said the man. God willing. My main object now is to get him safely home. Are you sure?

Of course I'm sure. Hand him over.

The man extracted the baby from the papoose and handed him to Livia Pinheiro-Rima, who cradled him against the thick glossy fur of her coat.

The man helped himself to one of the pastries on the plate and drank his coffee. He had stopped taking milk or sugar in his coffee many years ago, when he graduated from college and felt it necessary to adopt some new customs and habits that seemed more adult, and had forgotten how appealing it was served in this fashion. When he had finished his coffee and the pastry he took two more of the strudels off the plate and put one in each of his coat pockets. They were delicious.

Then he stood. We should go, he announced. I don't want to miss the train. Will you hold him while I settle my account? I asked them to call for a taxi last night, but I don't suppose it's here. And I don't know how I'll get the luggage out to the street.

Oh, don't start fretting now, said Livia Pinheiro-Rima. You've a very long journey in front of you. Everything will be fine and if it isn't fine it will be bearable.

◆

In the taxi the child sat on Livia Pinheiro-Rima's lap and reached up to touch her face, which she bent over and dangled above him. The man was beginning to worry that the child preferred Livia Pinheiro-Rima to him and was eager to separate them before she could establish a maternal bond. Secretly he hoped it was the bearskin coat and not Livia Pinheiro-Rima herself that the child liked.

He doesn't do that with me, he said.

What? Livia Pinheiro-Rima looked away from the child and over at him.

He doesn't respond to me like that. He doesn't really seem to notice me. And he flinches a bit when I try to touch his face.

Then don't try to touch his face. Give the little lad a chance. Can you imagine how lost and disrupted he must feel? Perhaps I remind Simon of one of the nurses. And perhaps you remind him of the doctor, who gave him shots and stuck thermometers in his bum.

So you think he'll like me eventually? asked the man.

I think he will love you, said Livia Pinheiro-Rima. If you relax. Don't smother him. Just take care of him, and let it evolve slowly. That's my advice.

I thought you were a terrible mother, the man said.

I never said that, said Livia Pinheiro-Rima. I was a wonderful mother. I just had recalcitrant children.

Ha, said the man. And then: Can I ask you a favor?

Of course.

I left all my wife's things at the hotel. I packed everything into her suitcase, which I left in the room. Can you get it and—well, do whatever you want. You can throw it all away or donate it or sell it or keep it. I don't care.

Of course, said Livia Pinheiro-Rima. There's a shelter for battered women in Kronskatjen. They can always use women's clothes.

Thank you, said the man.

What are you doing about her?

What do you mean?

What are you doing with her body? You didn't just leave that in the hotel too, did you?

No, said the man. I left it with Brother Emmanuel.

You're just leaving her behind? With her suitcase and her clothes?

She's dead, said the man. There is no her to leave. And

besides, she wanted to stay there. She felt good there, safe. She will be cremated.

But what about a funeral?

Neither of us really cared about things like that.

Oh, but you should. You must. Even though you don't care about it now. It isn't about now. It's about then. After.

After doesn't matter, said the man.

Oh, but it does, said Livia Pinheiro-Rima. Of course it matters! I've got my funeral all planned. And paid for. I've heard too many hair-raising stories of agnostics encountering God on their deathbeds, so I'm not taking any chances. I've got a plot with my name on it in the graveyard at Saint Innocent of Irkutsk. And I've arranged for a High Mass with all the trimmings: incense, altar boys, a castrati choir, six elephants, and one hundred blind white doves.

You're kidding me, said the man.

I am, said Livia Pinheiro-Rima. Except about the incense. Sometimes I think you're not really listening to me. I know that's the price one pays for talking too much—people stop listening. But I'd rather talk and not be listened to than not talk at all. At least then you've gotten it out there.

What do you mean?

I mean your words, your thoughts, your ideas. If you don't utter them, what's the point? They die with you. But when you utter something, it's in the world. Who knows what happens to sounds? We think they disappear but it's just as likely they continue vibrating and float out into the universe and perhaps someone or something will feel that vibration a hundred million years from now. Perhaps they'll hear exactly what I'm saying to you now.

That's a horrible thought, said the man. Imagine the din!

I think it would be a lovely sound. Like an orchestra, tuning up. I so enjoy that part of a concert. It's so hopeful. Music itself can be so predictable.

The man looked out the window. They were passing through the narrow, winding streets of the old town.

Where are we going? he asked.

What do you mean, where are we going? We're going to the train station.

Are you sure it's this way? We didn't come through this part of town when we arrived.

Of course you did. You just weren't paying attention. You were exhausted from your journey.

Yes, said the man. We were. It seems a very long time ago. The taxi slid off the road into a ditch. We had to push it out.

At this time of year the roads are very much in flux. It's hard to keep track of them with all this snow. Each day the plow veers a little off course, and by spring we realize the roads have been shifted across someone's front garden or into a ditch. We call them *haamu tie*, a phantom road, a ghost road. It's very nice in the spring, when the snow finally melts. All the things that have been hidden for so long are revealed. The earth is, quite literally, given back to us. I'm sure it's why we revere it. People who don't live in polar regions take the earth for granted. The soil, I mean.

We don't. In fact it's customary for everyone here to eat a spoonful of dirt on May Day.

They had by this time passed through the old town and were traveling through a newer part of the city the man had never seen. Before long they pulled up in front of a boxlike building made of steel and glass.

What's this? asked the man.

The train station, said Livia Pinheiro-Rima. What do you think?

This isn't where we got off the train, said the man. It wasn't anything like this.

Of course it was. There's only one train station. Everything looks different when you first arrive in a strange place.

But the station we got off at was out in the countryside. It was a tiny little building that was all boarded up. It was nothing like this.

Oh, said Livia Pinheiro-Rima, you fool! You must have gotten off at the way station. The train always pauses there because of some old law. Don't tell me you got out there!

Of course we did, said the man. We saw a sign that said Borgarfjaroasysla.

You didn't! You fool! How did you manage to get into town from there? It's miles away. It's nearer to Kronskatjen than it is to here.

It wasn't easy, said the man. But finally, we found a taxi.

A taxi? At the way station? That's impossible. You must have dreamt it.

The man paid the driver and they all got out of the taxi and entered the station, a glass shed with a concrete floor and two tracks divided by a single platform. Apparently it was a terminus because both tracks ended at a concrete embankment.

It's very modern, said the man.

Yes, said Livia Pinheiro-Rima. It was built when we were trying to get the Olympics here. That was a pipe dream! Or a boondoggle, depending upon who you were. Some made a very tidy profit off others' dreams. But of course that's just the way of the world, isn't it? That's capitalism.

I suppose, said the man. He looked around the station. One track was empty; on the other track a train of about six carriages stood spewing clouds of steam from its engine. There appeared to be a ticket office, a newsstand, and a café, but they were all presently closed, and closed in a way that suggested it had been a long time since they had been open.

Livia Pinheiro-Rima saw him looking around and said, You have your ticket, don't you? Because you can't get one here.

Yes, said the man. He reached inside his parka and extracted two tickets and his passport from the inner pocket.

I have two tickets, he said, holding them for Livia Pinheiro-Rima to see.

Ah, yes, she said. One for her.

Yes, said the man. One for her.

Give that one to me, said Livia Pinheiro-Rima. She

shifted the child so that she held him with one arm and held out the other. Give it here, she said. I may have to escape from here someday and it will come in handy.

The man wondered if he should keep the ticket. He had saved, in a silver Asprey humidor his grandmother had given to him as a wedding present (she was hopelessly behind the times), a number of tickets and other sentimental ephemera that chronicled his courtship and marriage, and he thought that this return ticket might be the perfect item to conclude the collection. To rest on top of all the other sourvenirs, beginning with the *Tales of Hoffmann* ticket stubs, which were covered with the place cards from benefit dinners with their names written calligraphically, the matchbooks from restaurants where they had celebrated birthdays and anniversaries, their dog Lally's license tag, the first sonogram of fetuses lost . . .

But before he could make a decision Livia Pinheiro-Rima had snatched one of the tickets out of his hand.

Do I need a ticket for him? the man asked, nodding at the child in her arms.

No, she said. Children travel for free in this country. Come—it's freezing in here. Let's get you settled in your carriage.

She looked at the ticket she was holding and began to walk down the platform, carrying the baby. The man followed her, rolling the suitcase behind him. He had slung the other bags around his shoulders and felt rather like a Sherpa.

Livia Pinheiro-Rima stopped at the second carriage, opened the door, and climbed inside. The man climbed in behind her, leaving the suitcase on the platform. He hoisted the bags from his shoulders and put them down on one of the seats. The carriage was exactly the same as the one in which he and his wife had arrived in: a door on either side and two cushioned banquettes divided into four seats facing each other, separated by a narrow aisle. This one had speckled yellow linoleum on the floor; the man was fairly certain the carriage they had arrived in had a wooden floor. He stepped back down onto the platform and lifted his suitcase up into the carriage. It seemed heavier than he remembered it being on the journey out. Or perhaps he had grown weaker. He certainly had exercised very little in the time since he had left New York City. When he reentered the carriage he saw that Livia Pinheiro-Rima sat in a seat in the far corner of the carriage, jouncing the baby upon her lap and making some sort of animal sound. He hoisted the bags up onto the rack but left the suitcase on the floor. Then he sat down across from Livia Pinheiro-Rima and held out his arms.

Oh, let me keep him, she said. We're having a very jolly time. It appears as though he and I have an especial rapport.

The man heard a whistle blow and looked out the window and saw a conductor standing on the platform, waving his arms above his head.

Is it time? Are we leaving already? The man stood up quickly and banged his head upon the luggage rack above the seat. For a moment he felt he might lose consciousness and so he sat back down. Everything was happening too quickly; it was all being played at the wrong frenetic speed and he could not keep up. But he had to—he had to stay in control and make sure nothing terrible happened. He reached up and touched the back of his head because he felt it was bleeding, but it wasn't.

Calm down, said Livia Pinheiro-Rima. We've plenty of time still. Take a deep breath.

I don't think I can do this, said the man.

Do what? Calm down or breathe deep?

All of it, said the man. Anything. He touched the back of his head again but it still wasn't bleeding. He wanted the emergency, the excuse, of blood. Surely he would be forgiven if he were bleeding.

Am I wrong to take him? he asked.

Wrong? Whatever do you mean?

Perhaps he should stay here, with you. Who am I to take him so far away?

His father, said Livia Pinheiro-Rima.

But I'm not. I can only pretend, imagine, and that's not good enough.

Good enough for what? For whom? You or him?

Both.

You're wrong about that. Perhaps not for you, but for him it's enough. It's more than enough. You're being selfish now. He needs you more than you need him.

But I don't want to fail him.

So you'll leave him here? Isn't that failing him?

Yes, said the man. But at least I won't have harmed him.

Oh, yes, said Livia Pinheiro-Rima. You would. Simon's been harmed enough. Of course we all have, but we can bear it. He can't. He needs you.

Livia Pinheiro-Rima hoisted the baby from her lap and held him out to the man. He dangled in the air between them, kicking his snowsuited legs.

Take him, she said. He's yours.

The man reached out and took the child from her. He lowered him onto his lap. He bent down and kissed the top of the child's head, but since his hood was still up it meant nothing. So he bent lower and kissed the boy's cheek.

The child began to cry, and wriggled, and reached out his arms toward Livia Pinheiro-Rima.

How I wish I had my Kodak with me, she said. I was a dunce not to bring it. I'd take a photo of you holding him like that, so I could remember my two bonny boys.

She had begun to cry and wiped at her eyes with her hand, which was still holding the extra ticket.

Come with us, the man said. Please. Please come with us.

Come with you?

Yes, said the man. He was talking quickly but surely. It had suddenly all become clear to him, what needed to happen, he was absolutely certain, and he had so little time. Don't you think you're meant to? I need you. And so does Simon. And maybe, perhaps, you need us? And you have the ticket. He nodded at the ticket in her hand.

Please don't leave us. I know I shall make a terrible mess of it alone. I'm not—I'm not big enough, or strong enough, to do it alone.

What do you mean? Come with you as far as the ferry? Or Schiphol? Heathrow?

No, said the man. Come home with us. To New York.

Ah, said Livia Pinheiro-Rima. Come home with you.

The conductor's whistle blew again from farther down the platform. The train jerked backward, as if it were bracing itself for departure. Livia Pinheiro-Rima stood up and looked out the window at the dirty snow-covered glass dome of the railway station. A few birds flew back and forth between the steel girders that supported the glass ceiling, swooping down toward the platform and then arcing back up into the air. The man realized he had not seen any birds at all in this place, and wondered if the railroad station was where the few who did not migrate spent the winter.

Livia Pinheiro-Rima turned away from the window and looked at the man. It's dear of you, she said, very dear indeed, to invite me to come along with you. But I know that you know that I can't.

I don't, said the man. Why can't you?

Oh, there isn't anything as consequential as a reason. It's just something we know, don't we? I can't leave here. I've learned this the hard way. I barely make any sense here, and anywhere else, especially New York—well, I'd be a gorgon, wouldn't I? A freak. People would run screaming down the streets.

You're wrong! People would love you in New York. You could act, and you could sing. You could perform. And not just for somnambulistic businessmen and oil riggers.

Oh, it isn't as bad as all that. They wake up from time to time. And besides, sleeping people hear things more profoundly than the woken.

Then just come for a little while, just to help me get settled. Until I learn everything I need to know.

Everything you need to know! You'll never learn that. Especially from me.

The platform began to slowly slide past outside the window, and the man realized that the train was moving.

Livia Pinheiro-Rima opened the carriage door. Let's not say goodbye, she said. It's why I've waited till this last moment. I couldn't bear to say goodbye to you. Say nothing. Nothing! Nothing!

She stepped out of the carriage but lost her balance on the step, stumbled to the platform, and fell forward onto her hands and knees. When she stood up and turned around the carriage with the man and his child had passed by. The carriage she looked into was empty, and so were all the ones that followed. Both of her gloves had ripped neatly across the palm.

◆

The man tried to get out of the carriage along with Livia Pinheiro-Rima, but he was unable to open the carriage door that the forward motion of the train had swung shut, and then the train was moving too quickly. He opened the window and stuck his head out into the rushing air to see her and call out, but the train had curved out of the station and she was gone.

He closed the window. Beyond the glass dome it was snowing. The child in his arms seemed transfixed by the sound and motion of the train and stared hypnotically out the window at the falling snow. The man felt similarly stunned and also watched the snow, which fell thickly and slowly.

Perhaps she will realize that she is meant to come with us, he thought. She will take a taxi and meet us at the way station.

They passed through an ugly, modern part of the city that the man had never seen before. It seemed a different place entirely. What else had he missed; what else had he failed to see?

After a moment the man returned to his seat and held the child up to the window so he could watch the falling snow. There was very little else to see, for they had passed through the city and were now traversing the wide-open spaces of the countryside. The man thought about everything that was buried beneath the snow and realized that a year is like a day here—half of it in darkness and half of it in light, and so the winter is really nothing more than a single night. A long night followed by a long day. Perhaps that was a better pace for life, and his own ceaseless and inescapable revolution of days and nights, being yanked from the depths of sleep and slammed into a new day every twenty-four hours, was all wrong. It was certainly brutal and exhausting.

The train ran faster as it traveled from the city, as if liberated and eager to get as far as it could from the constraints of communal life. The child seemed to delight in the speed, and beat his muffled fists against the window in time with the clacking of the wheels beneath them. He had an excellent sense of rhythm, the man thought, and maybe even an instinctual knowledge of syncopation, for now and then he would tap the window with two quickly successive beats instead of the one steady beat, as if to vary the rhythm. But gradually, as the train's speed plateaued and remained steady, the clacking sound monotonously disappeared. The child stopped tapping the window and closed his eyes. The man felt the child waver on his lap as he lost consciousness, and he gently pulled the child against him, and the child let himself fall against the man and sleep.

The man leaned back against the seat. He closed his eyes and was surprised to feel himself sinking quickly into sleep and he realized, suddenly, how exhausted he was. But he did not trust himself to sleep while holding the baby in his arms and so he picked him up and reinserted him into the contraption he still wore atop his parka. He placed the baby so that he was facing inward, the front of him pressed against the front of the man, and held him close and tight against his belly and chest, as if to staunch a wound.

The slowing of the train woke the man. Its speed gradually diminished until it was moving very slowly, almost as if it were trying to advance without exhibiting any forward motion.

And then it stopped, with that familiar backward recoil. The stillness caused the child to stir, but he did not wake; he only fitted himself more snugly against the man, mashing his face into the padding of the man's parka and mouthing the satiny material. Was he teething already?

Could they already have arrived at the way station? He had hoped it would take longer, so that Livia Pinheiro-Rima would have time to travel there. He knew it was foolish to hope for this but that did not prevent him from hoping it.

Nothing could be seen outside the window, except that it was snowing harder now, the snow crowding the sky and rising as much as falling.

The man shifted across the cushioned banquette so that he was sitting beside the opposite window of the carriage. His breath fogged the glass and so he carefully lifted one of his hands away from his son and rubbed a clearing on the window. He saw once again the small wooden building and the lamppost on the platform, which was covered with snow. And, much to his amazement, he saw a figure sitting on the bench beneath the painted letters BORGARFJAROASYSLA. It was a woman wearing a black bear coat. She sat perfectly upright upon the bench, but her head was bowed and so he could not see her face. She made no acknowledgment of the arriving train. But it had to be Livia Pinheiro-Rima; no one else had a coat like that. Had she fallen asleep?

He opened the door and called her name, but she did not look up. He stepped down onto the platform, leaving the door open behind him, thinking irrationally that if the door was open the train would not depart.

And then the woman slowly raised her head and gazed at him, and he saw that the woman sitting on the bench wearing the black bear coat was his wife. She sat on the bench, staring forward, but she did not seem to see the man. Her arms were braced, one hand upon each of her fur-covered knees, and he saw that she was not wearing gloves; the hands on her knees were bare, and this, more than anything else, made him rush forward.

He knelt and put his own warm hands on top his wife's hands, which were, as he had expected, freezing. He tried to pick one up and warm it between his hands, but it seemed to be solidly attached to the coat.

What are you doing here? he asked.

She looked around for a moment, up and down the snow-covered platform, and then, once again, past him, as if to locate herself.

Waiting, she said.

Waiting? For what?

Oh, not for anything, she said. Just waiting.

Aren't you cold? Freezing?

Oh, no, she said. No.

But your hands are freezing, he said. Where are your gloves?

I've lost them, I think. Somewhere along the way.

Take mine, he said. He stood up and pulled his gloves out of his jacket pockets. By yanking them out he dislodged the pilfered franzbrötchen. They fell into the snow.

Are you hungry? Would you like some pastries?

No, no, she said.

He picked them up out of the snow and placed them on the bench beside her. They're here, he said. Eat them. They're delicious.

I don't want them, she said.

Should I stay here with you? he asked.

Oh no, she said. Go.

Can you come with us?

Where?

Home, he said.

No, she said. I'm staying here. You should go. Look—it's moving.

The man turned to see that the train had begun to crawl forward. He stood up.

Will you put on the gloves?

Yes, she said. Later. It will give me something to do.

And eat the pastries. They're there, right beside you.

Go, she said. Hurry.

He stood for a moment, wondering what he could or should do, but he could think of nothing. He got back on the train.

Soon the train had resumed its speed and the palely dark snow-world rushed by outside the window. Simon started crying. The man fished a glass jar of baby food out of one of the bags and fed it to him, and he ate it hungrily. Then he gave him one of the three bottles he had prepared for the day's journey, and the baby drank half of it before he fell asleep.

✦

A change in speed once again woke the man. The train was moving slowly through the dark forest, and the thick-trunked pine trees crowded close to the track on either side of the train.

The baby was still sleeping. Simon. A tiny bubble of snot delicately inflated and deflated itself in one of his nostrils, like the puffing throat of a tropical frog. His eyelids fluttered and the man wondered what he was dreaming.

The train began to accelerate and the trees lost their individuality and became a rushing mass. And then the train suddenly emerged from the woods and was racing across fields of snow.

The man realized that while he and the baby had been sleeping the train had traveled south, not so very far, but far enough so that the sun was visible here, a bright orange disk crammed against the horizon, spreading a warm golden light across the surface of the white fields, which re-flected it up into the windows of the train and illuminated the carriage like a torch.

The man woke Simon and held him up against the window. He wanted him to see the sun before it disappeared.

Acknowledgments

The author wishes to express his gratitude to Andrew Cameron, James Harms, Victoria Kohn, Craig Lucas, Leigh Newman, Anna Stein, Edward Swift, the Corporation of Yaddo, and the MacDowell Colony.

PETER CAMERON is the author of seven novels (including *Someday This Pain Will Be Useful to You* and *Coral Glynn*) and three collections of stories. His short fiction has appeared in *The New Yorker*, *The Paris Review*, *Rolling Stone*, and many other literary journals. He lives in New York City and Sandgate, Vermont.